MW00477531

How to Keep a Husband for 10 Days

BOOKS BY JESSICA HATCH

My Big Fake Wedding

JESSICA HATCH

How to Keep a Husband for 10 Days

bookouture

Published by Bookouture in 2023

An imprint of Storyfire Ltd.
Carmelite House
50 Victoria Embankment
London EC4Y 0DZ

www.bookouture.com

Copyright © Jessica Hatch, 2023

Jessica Hatch has asserted her right to be identified
as the author of this work.

All rights reserved. No part of this publication may be reproduced, stored in
any retrieval system, or transmitted, in any form or by any means, electronic,
mechanical, photocopying, recording or otherwise, without the prior written
permission of the publishers.

ISBN: 978-1-80314-904-2
eBook ISBN: 978-1-80314-903-5

This book is a work of fiction. Names, characters, businesses, organizations,
places and events other than those clearly in the public domain, are either the
product of the author's imagination or are used fictitiously. Any resemblance
to actual persons, living or dead, events or locales is entirely coincidental.

To my own PDP gang—L.E., P.C., H.F., S.F., M.W., C.D., S.D., and C.E.
And especially to Paul, who's stuck with me from here on out.

CHAPTER
ONE
AUGUST 7, 2020

Two years ago

"I can't believe this is your last PDP!"

Though her friend Sophie kept saying it—screeching it, really, over the Flaming Lips record Brown had put on when they entered the apartment—Lina Thompson-Mitchell refused to believe it was true. This was not her last Progressive Dinner Party. She and her husband, Brown, were only moving out of the building. It wasn't like they were leaving Jacksonville.

After all, they and their friends had been throwing Progressive Dinner Parties, monthly get-togethers where they hopped from one apartment to the next for each course, for several years now. It was a time-honored tradition. There was no way it would end just because they were moving.

Brown offered Lina one of his signature looks—a clipped smile and raised brow that seemed to say, *Hey, surrender; arguing with her is hopeless*—before he turned his attention to serving up dessert.

"Oh, don't call it the last one," Lina said, snuggling against Brown's sturdy height. "That sounds so final." He had finished dishing up the pie by now, and gently squeezed her waist to emphasize his support.

By way of counterargument, Sophie waved a perfectly manicured hand at the moving boxes all around them.

Lina was grateful for Brown's support. Otherwise, Sophie's insistence might have spoiled the party. PDP desserts typically provided a golden glow to the evening, like the pleasant sheen of grease left on an indulgent plate of food. Tonight, they'd had a tiki fountain and Spam musubi for cocktail hour at Freddie's, followed by incredibly poppable mushroom caps and an aged beef roast at Mara's. Sophie had surprised them with a game of Drunken Twister for the Wild Card round. (If your right foot landed on red, blue, or whatever and there was a shot glass on it, you had to take the shot. Some had allegedly had water in them, but, distracted by the way her husband's arms enticingly tangled around her legs, Lina had left-hand-greened her way into three half shots of vodka.) They were meant to be following it all up with pie and ice cream at Lina and Brown's, but the way Sophie kept claiming this was their very last dinner party was turning the golden grease of the evening rancid.

Lina frowned and focused on sticking her fork into the last bite of gooey apple crumble she'd baked in between packing up the apartment so they could move tomorrow morning. Brown had made his own vanilla-cinnamon ice cream—it tasted like the milk left behind after a bowl of cereal—and a homemade, Kahlua-based affogato. There were times being married to a bartender was more than worth it, and since Lina was a junior associate at a law firm, whose culinary talents extended to following the recipe on the box, this was one of those times.

"I'm sure we'll have PDPs after we move," she offered, walking a handful of coffee cups over to the sink. She brushed her long, dark hair off her shoulders and straightened her T-shirt's hem before she began soaping them.

"Of course we will!" Lina's best friend, Mara, cried. "Come on, Soph, don't be such a party pooper."

"Yeah, Soph, gosh." Brown snorted at Mara's rejoinder, though his blue-eyed smile was all for Lina.

Lina returned his grin. She and Brown, as Millennials in their late twenties, had beaten the odds and told all those avocado toast memes where to shove it. They had worked hard, pinching pennies here and pulling long hours there. Now, together, they were going to be *homeowners*. Brown's smile turned to a smarmy, silly eyebrow waggle, and Lina knew he was thinking of his vow that they'd be 'christening' every room in the house, starting the instant their movers left. She giggled at his expression, her tongue caught between her teeth, and turned back to the dishes.

"Fess up—you're moving out because I'm managing the building now," said Freddie. They had been hanging off to the side of the group, wearing their standard uniform of mix-and-match eighties vintage and inspecting Lina and Brown's vinyl collection, which Lina had encouraged them to go through. Brown, a true audiophile, had only agreed after setting aside the albums he couldn't live without.

"That's not true!" Lina walked over and affectionately chucked their shoulder, well-buttressed in a blue-and-black plaid Doncaster jacket. "Seriously, I wish we were sticking around to have you for a live-in building manager," she said. "You're so much more reliable than the last one, though I guess it helps that we're your friend. No more having to sweat through the night, waiting for the super to come at seven a.m., when your AC conks out."

"Or having to string a clothesline through your living room when the ten-year-old dryer goes on the fritz," Sophie added.

"I always thought having a washer and dryer in the unit was a nice touch," Mara said, crossing her tattooed arms over her plain, black tank top. "Especially given that our rent is cheaper than a lot of places downtown."

That was true. As much as they complained about the building, it was done in the way you'd complain about a long-term partner: affectionately, with a tendency toward fierce loyalty if anyone outside the relationship chimed in. The building was more than a hundred years old and sandwiched between a jeweler's and The Blind Pig, the speakeasy-style whiskey bar Brown tended. It had Old Florida charm, with hardwood floors and heaps of natural light streaming through the tall, sashed windows, illuminating the exposed prewar brick.

All these amenities had drawn Lina to the building. It was so charming compared to the modular, cookie-cutter designs of recent builds. The friendships she'd found here, not to mention the ease with which she'd paid down a good chunk of law school debt, made things like hurricane-force rain seeping through cracks in the brick, a mold problem that had eventually required new kitchen cabinets, and the occasional maintenance issue no big deal.

By contrast, Lina never complained about her *actual* long-term partner. She had found her opposites-attract match in Brown, and not just in his boyish grin, glowing beneath a head of long, blond curls, or in his six-foot-plus height, which offset her petite stature, a collection of sharp angles. She loved that he reminded her not to fixate on the little things that she as a perfectionist so often honed in on. Life was more vibrant, joyful, and relaxing with him around. The fact that they had gotten married in the building's courtyard a mere two months ago made this PDP even more bittersweet.

Not that it was her last one.

Because it wasn't.

Lina turned back to the conversation.

"I suppose we should end this night as we began it, with a toast," Mara said. She smoothed the mop of chestnut curls over her undercut and lifted her plastic cup, which had been filled impishly to the brim with a margarita. "Wow, Lina and Brown... getting married and buying a house? This pandemic has been pretty good to you."

Lina jutted her sharp jaw forward. "That makes me feel guilty. It's been horrible for a lot of people..."

"It has been, and we're not discounting that," Mara replied. "But you're allowed to be proud of your accomplishments. We are all really thrilled for you."

Mara's smile crumpled in on itself then, like she was trying not to cry. Lina knew how she felt. If she hadn't moved into this apartment four years ago, then she wouldn't have met any of these wonderful people. She wouldn't have rubbed Sophie's thin and shaking shoulders as she mourned her grandmother's passing. She wouldn't have high-fived Freddie when they quit a job they hated or when they got into the University of North Florida's business program. She wouldn't have met and romanced easy-going Brown or fallen in best-friend-love with the bossy but endearing Mara. This building had given her a life she hadn't known she was missing, and now, she would really miss the place itself.

In fact, she was so distracted by her thoughts that she nearly didn't catch the end of Mara's toast. "Oh! Cheers!" Lina clicked her plastic cup against the others. To herself she whispered, "To *not* the last PDP," so that she would believe it.

After they, on Mara's insistence, drew names for next month's courses, Brown seemed to be in a similar headspace to his wife.

"Anyone want to go downstairs for a nightcap?" he asked as he pocketed his and Lina's scrap of paper, which had *Main Course* printed on it in Freddie's precise, block handwriting. "I don't want this party to be over yet."

"You won't be saying that when you're shunting boxes

around at seven o'clock tomorrow," Sophie said, looking up from where she was busily tapping away on her phone.

"We'll see you then, though?" Lina said.

Sophie gave her a friendly wink at the door. "Wouldn't miss it for the world."

Two hours later, Brown was getting ready for bed, and Lina had told him she'd be in soon. The air conditioning kicked on as she sat, cross-legged in an old T-shirt and sleep shorts, surrounded by their moving boxes. It hit her then, with a thrill up her spine. She would never be in this same spot under these same circumstances again. With luck, this would be her last rented property, her last time moving out of an apartment.

She looked down at the pen and paper in front of her bright blue toenails, already labeled *The Wish and Will of Lina Thompson-Mitchell, Former Denizen of Apt. #305*, and started writing.

To those who inhabit this space after me, I bequeath:

The creaky noise the air conditioner makes when it first kicks on.

The dust motes that dazzle in the afternoon sun if you leave your northern exposure windows open.

The pink blossoms that burst into a flurry of yellow on the tree in the courtyard, right outside your bedroom window, during spring and fall, those most magical times of the year.

The aroma of roasting coffee beans, drifting on a westerly wind from the Maxwell House factory.

The best parking spot in town—within walking distance of the football stadium and the Saint John's River.

The old factory work bell that still blares ten blocks north of here; use it as a reminder to clock in and out and check on yourself.

The fact that Chamblin's has the best lox bagels, and they're right around the corner!

The ability, thanks to your fantastically low rent, to save for things you really want and need, like paying down student loans and buying a house, instead of renting an apartment in perpetuity.

She tapped the pen against her freckled cheek in thought. There was so much she wanted to convey to the new renter that could only come from experience in this building, and yet, she felt obligated to try.

To those who inhabit this space after me, I hope:

You make great friends out of the other tenants. They are a smart, funny bunch, so don't be a stranger. If you see someone at the mailboxes or in the elevator, which we call Otis, say hello.

You take full advantage of having the bar downstairs. You get a discount as a downtown resident, so be sure to introduce yourself there too!

You have the best hurricane parties, holidays, and thirsty Thursdays in this space. Friends are always impressed by the architecture, and food delivery folks seem to think they've stepped into a service entrance to Narnia.

You leave this space even better than you found it.

This building is a sanctuary and a creative space. It is a place filled with love, a haven from the rush of even a small city like Jacksonville. In my time here, I have met new friends, saved up to buy a house, met and married the love of my life. I've laughed and shared so many things. This place has been a gift for me, and I sincerely hope that, by the end of your time here, you can say the same.

"Lina?" Brown came around the corner from their bathroom, drying his hair with a towel. When he saw she was sitting on the floor near the coffee table, he came to crouch beside her. "You coming to bed soon?"

"In a sec. I was having a last, quiet moment with this old place," she admitted. "Part of me doesn't want to go, I'll miss it so much." She leaned over and kissed the spot where his jaw met his ear, still damp from his evening shower. His clean-shaven skin felt soft beneath her lips.

Brown hummed. "I know what you mean. We've had great times here, but I know we'll make even more memories in the new house. What's this?" He picked up the sheet of paper with his free hand and read, "The Wish and Will of Lina Thompson-Mitchell..."

"Some thoughts I wanted to share with whoever takes our unit," she explained. "Anything to add?"

Brown read over the letter, considered the question, then reached out for the pen. In the chicken scrawl she loved to tease him about, he added, *100% agree. Something about this place is magic. Enjoy it to its fullest. Brown F. Mitchell.*

"Short and sweet," Lina commented.

"Like someone else I know." He kissed the bridge of her nose, then hovered his lips inches away from hers. "See you in a minute?"

She closed the gap. "In a minute."

After Brown went into their bedroom, Lina reviewed the letter once more. There was a bunch of space left on the bottom half of the paper, but she figured what they had written was approaching the acceptable limits of sentimentality. She tucked the paper into an envelope, sealed it with chevron-patterned washi tape, and wrote on the outside: *To the new tenant! Welcome to #305!*

She stood, shook the crick out of her knees, and surveyed the apartment, zeroing in on the cabinet above the kitchen's built-in microwave. It was too high on the wall for someone five-foot-nothing like her to use, but practically at eye level for anyone else, especially someone who was just moving in. Teetering on the edge of her office chair, she lay the envelope on the cabinet's freshly dusted surface and tapped it lovingly for good measure.

"Someone will find you; I know it," she murmured.

As she snuggled against Brown's warmth, she thought of the moment she'd had with Mara after dessert. On the sidewalk in front of The Blind Pig, Lina had reached for her best friend's hand and gripped the fingers tightly. Mara turned to look her expectantly in the eye.

"This *isn't* our last PDP," Lina had stated emphatically. "It just isn't."

Many unsaid things passed between the friends in that moment. Gratitude, mostly, and the acknowledgment that, in some ways, they were lying to themselves. They were in their late twenties now; they knew the false promise of someone saying they'll keep in touch with you, meaning they'd drop a standard greeting on your Facebook wall on your birthday. They knew that even in the same town distance can feel insurmountable at times, especially when you've had someone right downstairs from you all this while.

"No," Mara agreed. "It isn't."

And it wasn't.

Not just yet, and not for another two years.

CHAPTER
TWO

A month ago

Early fall in Jacksonville is like few other climates on Earth. The city is far enough north on Florida's Atlantic coast to anticipate cooler breezes and sweater weather a month later, as well as maybe a frost and the accompanying, panicked reminder from local news anchors to leave your taps dripping for the one post-Christmas freeze of the year.

But mid-September is an eternity away from that. In downtown Jacksonville on the day Lina Thompson-Mitchell stepped out of her lawyer's door and ran into Freddie Morales, it was downright balmy.

Employees of the banks and logistics companies fortressed in riverside high-rises queued at food trucks in James Weldon Johnson Park, sweating under the aegis of the Main Library's owl-and-key statue. Those passing under Chamblin's awning entered the bookstore café not for pumpkin spice but for iced lavender lattes, the summer clinging with impressive stickiness to the corners of the afternoon. In the green space where a down-at-the-heels mini mall once stood, runners and dogwalkers could see the 1940s vertical lift of the Main Street Bridge halting traffic so some millionaire's tall-masted yacht could travel farther up the river.

Lina had been pushing open the firm's employee entrance, bracing herself for the wet wool blanket of Florida heat, when she bumped into Freddie for the first time in, God, she didn't even know how many months. She swung the door open and nearly ran right into them as they were heading west on Adams Street.

"Lina Thompson-Mitchell? As I live and breathe!" She heard in a familiar countertenor, velvety smooth but with a knowing energy. Lina fought the impulse to squeeze her eyes—which she'd just confirmed, in the corporate bathroom, weren't puffy or mascara-smeared—shut tight.

Freddie doesn't know, she told herself. *You're a lawyer; remember that no one has to know anything that you don't want to tell them.*

She instead opened her deep brown eyes wide and hugged Freddie's tall and bony frame. She pulled back to study them. They looked fantastic in a cream linen suit; the pant legs were rolled and cuffed over black-and-white penny loafers, and the blazer was worn over a graphic T instructing its reader to 'Pack the Court.'

"Oh my God, Freddie! How are you, babe? It's been, what, a few months?"

And please, please don't ask me why I'm coming out of a lawyer's office, she thought to herself.

As Freddie launched into their response she realized that, duh, of course they wouldn't ask. She worked for this law firm, and since they hadn't kept in touch as much as she'd hoped after she and Brown moved out of the building, Freddie had no way of knowing that, post-lockdown, Lina did most of her case prep from her home office, about ten minutes away.

"It has been a while," Freddie agreed. "How are you? How's our favorite boy, Brown?"

Lina placed a hand over her denim jumpsuit and tried to calm her pounding heart. "He's fine. Busy at the speakeasy. If you're dropping in there, you probably see him more often than I do." There. A lie, but not really. She pivoted away from it as she smoothed any stray hairs that may have escaped her ballerina bun. "But enough about us! How are you? I'm getting excited to go out with you all when Mara comes through this weekend."

Freddie had always worn their heart on their sleeve, along with amazing thrift store finds like a vintage slap bracelet or an heirloom Patek Philippe, depending on their mood. As a heart-sleever, they weren't one for social niceties, and if the answer to "How are you?" was "Not so good," you were going to find out.

"Not so good," Freddie said then, and Lina steeled herself for whatever came next. "Well, *mostly* everything is fine, especially with my other property, but there are some things going on with the old building." They hooked their thumb up the block, in the direction of Lina's former apartment.

Lina clucked sympathetically. "Renovation? It is an old building, so I bet that's pricey."

Freddie shook their head, tossing their box braids as they did. "Reno I could handle. No, I'm going to have to give the old girl up. I can't afford to keep managing it, the way pricing is going around here. I'm trying to be fair and keep my tenants' rent controlled, but the market is in-*sane* right now, and the cost of basic upkeep against what I'm charging them means I'm losing money every month. Even if I pulled the mean old landlord card and upped their rent, I wouldn't really have a choice..."

They slumped against the exterior brick of Lina's law firm and cut their warm, honey-colored eyes at her. "There's this big real estate guy from either New York or Boston, somewhere bougie up north, who was interested in buying it out from under me. It was the only option that made sense, so..." They blew out a breath. "My tenants are in the process of moving out —they have to be gone by this Friday. I own the building till right after Halloween, but then I'm out too."

"Oh, that's awful!" Lina said, shifting her bag to her other side and folding her arms. "I hate that for you."

She kept to herself the important question of where Freddie, who had bought the building off its former owners and operated as its live-in super, would go. She figured they were already stressed out enough as it was.

"Thank you." Freddie paused, sizing Lina up. "Say, would you like to come in? Just for old times' sake. If you aren't doing anything, I mean! I was running out for lunch, but I've got time to show you around."

Lina cursorily checked her phone for the time. Her meeting had wrapped up early, and she had a good hour and a half to kill before her standing Wednesday afternoon therapy appointment —an appointment that had become increasingly important over the last few weeks.

"I've got plenty of time; I'd love to come up."

It was incredible how even sounds could elicit memory. The slight creak of the heavy, oaken front door sent a shock wave through Lina's brain, and she suppressed a goose-bumped shudder.

"You know there have been times that I'd visit Brown after work and, on autopilot, still head for the front door of this place?" she asked. "It's like, 'Wait, I don't live here anymore,' and then I toddle off down the block to find my car."

She took in the tiled entryway, the mailboxes to her right. "Oh my gosh, it looks just like I remembered."

"Yeah, I made some improvements over the last year,"

Freddie said, "as many as I could on a budget, mostly cosmetic stuff in the units."

They made an 'after you' gesture, and Lina headed farther in. The pair walked by the elevator, which was currently out of order, and she touched its old buttons affectionately. "Hey, Otis." On a particularly punchy Tuesday evening, she and Brown had named the lift after its manufacturer. They had giggled on and off for hours about their in-joke.

It felt bizarre being back, like she was walking around the abandoned soundstage of her favorite childhood TV show. Without realizing she'd walked to it, again on autopilot, she found herself and Freddie standing in front of #305, her old apartment. Her eyes pricked with tears.

"It's empty," Freddie murmured into the silence. "Want to go in?"

Lina squeezed her hands into fists and nodded. Then Freddie was opening the white front door, and they were standing in golden patches of sunlight, streaming, as they always had, onto the blond hardwood. Her tan slide-on sandals echoed as she stepped across the floor and smoothed an impressed fingertip along the new butcherblock countertops. Lina remembered two other times her feet had made such echoes: when she had moved in and when she and Brown, full of such hope and promise, had moved out.

Freddie stayed leaning in the doorway, surveying their friend with arms folded, as she took in her old apartment.

"I'm sorry." She snorted in confusion, dabbing the back of her hand under her eyes and hoping her concealer didn't run. "I don't know why I'm so emotional today. I didn't think I would be, but God, this *place*." She walked farther in. "I remember when I had just started at the firm, I would come home for lunch sometimes. We had our big dining table set up right here, remember? In the middle of the main space? And I could see into the office building across the alley. One time, it was pretty clear someone over there was having a birthday, so Brown and I went out and got party hats and taped a birthday message to this window." She tapped its glass with a long fingernail. "They were thrilled when they noticed it."

She could hear Freddie chuckle from the entryway. "You two are always so creative. Like the way you leaned into your characters for Mara's murder mystery PDP. What even was the theme again?"

"'Wild Cards of the Wild West,' I think." Lina laughed, too, as she remembered Brown in a fake mustache and a horrible Texan accent, herself in a feather boa with the alias 'Miss Kitty.' "That was a fun night."

She continued into the apartment, past where she and Brown had spent many a lazy Sunday snuggled up on the couch, sharing a bottle of wine and groaning at each other's silly jokes. She rounded the studio wall into the semi-private bedroom and waved hello to her big, beloved tree in the court-yard, the one she had often found herself smiling at, tucked into Brown's arms as they stayed in bed for 'just five more minutes,' usually to the detriment of her arriving at work on time.

Her chest felt heavy, so she coughed and distracted herself from further memories with the impressive upgrades Freddie had made to the bathroom. The cabinetry had been still more blond wood and particle board when she lived there; now it was white with stainless steel fixtures, and the laminate atop the bathroom sink had been replaced by imitation granite. If Freddie was keeping their tenants' rent stable with upgrades like this, it was hardly surprising they were losing money.

A thought struck her then. "I wonder if it's still here..."

"If what's still here?" Freddie followed her through the loop and back into the kitchen, where Lina was raised up on tiptoe. When she still couldn't reach, she hopped her bum up onto the butcherblock counter—forcing herself not to think of the times

Brown had helped her up there for far less PG-13 reasons—and opened the cabinet above the microwave.

She held out a 'one sec' finger to her friend, then used the other hand to root around the floor of the cabinet. She felt only a giant dust bunny at first, but then her finger tapped something that made a grainy, rustling sound. She grasped it and pulled it down.

Freddie looked a little grossed out by the dirty, dusty envelope Lina had in her hand. "What is that?"

"My wish and will!" she exclaimed. "You know, like when you go to camp and at the end of the summer, you leave a note for the campers who will be in your bunk next year?"

Freddie tetched. "Do I look like I've been to summer camp?"

Lina giggled at them calling out her white-bread upbringing. "I know, it's corny, like you're wishing them all the gooiest smores and willing them the joy of having the top bunk or whatever, but anyway, I wrote one two years ago, right before Brown and I moved into our house. I can't believe it's still here!"

She opened the envelope and saw, below her blue-penned wishes and Brown's addition—*This place is magic. Enjoy it to its fullest.*—that two other tenants had added their thoughts.

What they said! a hand in black fine-point Sharpie whispered. *I have met so many cool people living downtown, and thanks to the low cost of living, I've saved enough to move out west. I'll be bunking with friends in Denver and then... who knows? Sayonara, Jax!*

Agreed, the final one, scrawled in pencil, read. *This place has meant so much to me. New friends, new experiences. Plus, the money left over at the end of the month let me afford healthcare and may have saved my damn life. I'm sorry this place is going away. There are so few like it left.*

Lina was officially bawling now. What had been a personal letter commemorating her happiest memories had become an emotional connection to strangers who had also found, within these four walls, what they hadn't known they'd needed.

This place has been a gift, she'd written back in 2020, meaning it in an ephemeral, figurative way, like when people call a trip to Lisbon heaven or post about their expectant child with the hashtag #blessed. In other words, her privilege was showing. For some tenants the building really had been a gift, the difference between the creature comforts of downtown living and the kinds of public housing she saw being lambasted on the news for poor, roach-infested living conditions. Affordable housing like this building had helped so many people, and places like it were rapidly vanishing.

Lina suddenly slapped her wish and will onto the counter, spooking Freddie. "We can't let them do this," she said between gritted teeth.

Apparently they hadn't been ready for her Leslie Knope levels of cry-then-rally. She got that; it wasn't the first time her vigor had been reacted to with surprise and misgivings.

"We can't let them do this," Lina reiterated as she hopped off the counter. "Not to you. Someone from out of town isn't going to buy this place to keep it the way it is. I bet this sleazy real estate guy will develop it into luxury condos, then charge through the nose for each unit."

"You think so?" they said.

"I practically know so." She snorted. "And if that's true, he shouldn't be buying you out with one lump sum. That's highway robbery! You should be given a seat on the condo board —with stock options. Ideally, we also can't let him do this to your tenants. They need the kind of rental opportunities we had five years ago, the kind that are going the way of the dodo and the cronut."

"Okay, so far I'm with you," Freddie said slowly, still not sure if Lina was having a psychotic break or not. "But who's we?"

"*Us!*" she said. "You know, our old friends. We'll get the band back together! Mara will be back in town this weekend; we can discuss it with her then."

"But, Lina, I've already agreed to sell it to him. I don't know what we can do to change the purchase price. There's no way David beats Goliath." They shook their head. "Not this time."

Lina considered that. "Well, if he decides to raze the building and replace it with condos, he'll need the local government's permission. Then we can go protest his rezoning hearing." She could feel herself getting excited again. "Freddie, we have to at least try to voice our opinions, you know? City hall might not be considering the impact this sort of deal has on affordable housing, and, if you're lucky, the developer might offer you more money to stop the protest. It ain't over till it's over."

Freddie sighed, still sounding defeated. "*Mira*, babe, I really appreciate your fire-and-brimstone fervor, I do. But it just sounds like some old hope-and-change shtick: fabulous in theory, hard to vault over the red tape in practice."

"Come on, Fred!" she pleaded. "Don't you at least want to try to fight for the building? Not just for your tenants, but for all the happiness you've had living here?"

Maybe they were giving in to pacify her, but after a moment, and an extremely suspicious squint, Freddie conceded. "You know, you're right. I got that luxury condo vibe from this guy the minute he brought three lawyers onto our phone call—no offense."

Lina held up her hand. "None taken."

"So yeah, if he does go that route, I'm on board with telling city hall why this is wrong." They straightened the cuff of their blazer. "Besides, those stock options don't sound bad either."

Freddie's gap-toothed grin was contagious. As they headed back down the stairs together, Lina felt buoyant. She had been in desperate need of a project to focus on, and this one was for an especially worthy cause.

"Hey, it was so good running into you," she told Freddie when they reached the sidewalk in front of the building.

"Same," they agreed. "I hate to admit it, but it feels nice, feeling hopeful again." They blew her a kiss as they turned down the block. "Tell Brownie I say hi!"

Lina tried to maintain her mask of enthusiasm as she called after them, "Oh, you know I will."

Despite her earlier buoyancy, Lina couldn't help wondering what she was getting herself into. Like a good attorney, she questioned her own motives, and when she came up with nothing better than how powerful a drug nostalgia could be, she figured it was a point to file away and bring up again at therapy.

If nothing else, she thought as she unlocked her car, this fight for affordable housing was going to provide a superb distraction from her divorce.

CHAPTER
THREE

Later the same day—while discussing that bombshell in therapy.

If Lina had come out with her divorce news to Freddie, they inevitably would have asked what happened.

You and Brown always seemed so solid! What went wrong? That was what her lawyer—a coworker who had known Brown for some time—asked when Lina told them. The question had come quickly on the heels of a cursory *Oh my God! Are you okay?*, and Lina didn't savor the idea of that knee-jerk reaction coming from one of her dearest friends.

If Freddie *had* asked what went wrong, she wouldn't have known how to answer. One fine summer day, she and Brown had been brilliant, perfect even. Then she blinked, two years had passed, and she didn't feel like she knew who she was living with anymore. Could this really be the guy she had fallen head over heels with, laughed till three in the morning with, had incredible sex with, cut out all romantic prospects for? Worse yet, was he thinking the same thing about her?

Where had the magic gone?

She supposed that what had happened to them was the

same thing that happened if someone bought a mint-condition classic car but didn't check the oil or tune the engine each time they drove it. They had let their relationship run on its own, assuming it would tick along like always, until one day it didn't. Brown had stopped giving Lina the emotional support she'd come to rely on, and as a result of his silence and her angst, they had fallen apart.

They fought more and more, until one night he didn't fight back, didn't seem to care if there was an *us* to be part of. In fact, he didn't care so much that he picked up his keys and walked out the door. She didn't know where he went, didn't know all through the night as she stared, dry-mouthed and dry-eyed, at his cool, untouched pillow. She continued not to know when he didn't come home the next morning. By the time she saw him again the following evening, she'd already begun the process of filing for divorce. She remembered feeling a still, smooth stone of certainty drop into the pit of her stomach as she checked the oven clock that morning. Better to quit while they were ahead than to keep circling the drain, she decided. *Time of death, 8:17 a.m.*

Sure, it was a cliché. And Lina hated being a cliché.

"Why do you think you're a cliché?" her therapist, Jill, asked. She took a sip of peppermint tea, pushed her tortoiseshell glasses up the bridge of her nose, and waited patiently for Lina's response.

Lina liked that Jill had a sturdy name. The best therapists, in her experience, seemed to have sturdy old lady names like Carol or Jill or Susan; they wore their hair in no-nonsense, graying styles paired with Teva sandals and drawstring linen slacks. She mulled over her response as she swirled her chamomile tea in a clay mug fired and glazed by Jill herself. Her therapist's question seemed anodyne on its surface, but Lina knew that, before long, Riptide Jill would have pulled her fifty yards from the shoreline of her comfort zone, until she was breaking through wave upon wave, thinking, *How the heck did we get there from here?*

"Well, splitting up over irreconcilable differences? Isn't that a cliché at this point?" Lina responded. "It's the blanket excuse for, 'We tried, maybe not hard enough, but in the end, it just didn't work out. Oh well.'"

Jill leaned forward, a telltale cue that Lina was onto something. "Do you feel like you didn't try hard enough?"

Lina jolted upright. "Hm?"

"You said that you tried, but maybe not hard enough. Do you think that's true? That you wouldn't be filing for divorce if you and your husband had both tried harder?"

There it was, the sandbar slipping out from beneath her feet.

"It's different than it is for people who have a clear reason to get divorced," Lina deflected, "like infidelity or their spouse using their kids' college fund to buy a boat or something. That's all I meant."

"Hm," Jill said again. She wasn't the sort of therapist to scribble on her legal pad during their session, but when she typed up her notes after Lina had left the building, Lina had a feeling that 'hm' meant there'd be an entire section devoted to this tangent.

She set her tea down on a side table, next to the Kleenex, and self-soothed by folding and unfolding her hands in her lap. "A lot of the books I've been reading since I filed the papers," she ventured, "tell me that I can't blame myself for the divorce. Doesn't matter that I'm the splitter-upper; it's the same as if you're the splittee. If a victim of something traumatic isn't supposed to blame themselves if they want to heal, and if divorce is traumatic, then, *ipso facto*, I shouldn't blame myself. *And* I shouldn't blame Brown. Sometimes, a marriage holds fast, and sometimes, it doesn't. We tried; we failed. That happens. And we move on."

"Moving on," Jill mused. "Is that why you're putting such emphasis on saving your old building?"

Lina unclenched her hands. "I wouldn't say 'emphasis.' I don't know yet how my friend Freddie will need me to help. But I think having a project like this, if I can call it a 'project,' would help me focus less on the divorce. The fact that I could help some people, like my friend and their tenants, would be the incredible cherry on top."

Jill searched the ceiling for how best to phrase her next question. "Will you feel like you've failed if you *can't* save the building?"

Lina frowned. What was she getting at? "Well, obviously. We would have failed our cause if that happened. Is that what you mean?"

"Yes and no," Jill said cryptically. "The perceived failure I'm asking about could be in regard to anything. The surface-level project, as you called it, or... regarding something deeper. What you might feel you have failed in is less important to my question than the feeling of failure itself."

When Lina continued to squint at her as if she were the Delphic oracle, Jill gave in and explained. "I'm wondering whether you might not want to save your old building, at least in part, to save your *marriage*—or else to preserve the site of happier times in the face of your divorce. It seems to me that you and Brown were happy in your apartment, and so it might seem to you that, after you left, everything fell apart. Sure, there's the issue of affordable housing, which is an admirable cause, but perhaps, consciously or unconsciously, you want to save the building to try to save your marriage?"

Jill extended one hand to the side as though to demonstrate how clear this was, a psychological *ta-da*.

Lina looked at Jill.

Jill looked back at Lina.

Lina blinked.

"No," she said quickly, crossing her legs as she added, "I don't think that's it at all."

Jill sniffed. "If you say so."

"I mean, I don't *think* so," Lina doubled down, then pivoted to, "I just wish I knew why I got so emotional about everything today in my attorney's office, then again at the old building. I don't think it's because of self-blame or guilt. Is it—is it regret? I don't think it is. I mean, I'm the one who filed for divorce, so shouldn't I be fully happy that it's happening?" She back-pedaled a bit to clarify. "I'm not happy per se; I'm *relieved*, but I'm also feeling a lot of negative emotions."

She smoothed a wrinkle out of her jumpsuit. "You asked about failure," she ventured. "Okay. I just said all that crap about moving on, marriages failing, and I get that objectively, but *sub*jectively, I feel like I've failed a relationship I thought was going to last forever. I don't want to save it, but I think I'm allowed to mourn its loss, you know?" She looked up as though she hoped Jill would give her an answer, maybe a thumbs-up to indicate she was on the right track, but Jill seemed to be expecting the same from her. Lina deflated. "I don't know if it's that either. I guess I just have to work through this like every-thing else, huh?"

Jill nodded in agreement. "Sometimes, when it comes to a sticky situation, there's no way around but through. Before our next session, I think it would be helpful for you to sit with your feelings. If you find yourself getting emotional about the divorce, pause and try to identify what triggered it. You might even keep a trigger journal. That could help us identify your root emotions and what you need to do to move ahead."

An alarm on Jill's smartwatch went off, the signal that they had five minutes left.

"What do you want to use our last few minutes to discuss?" she asked. "Is there anything else for today?"

Lina cleared her throat. "Well, our old friend Mara is

coming through town this weekend. She's staying in our—well, I guess *my*—guest room. Brown and I have agreed to wait to tell our friends... maybe until after the divorce is finalized? At the very least until after this weekend."

"And why is that?"

"I don't know," Lina hedged. "We're both really close to the same old group of friends, closer in some ways than family, given the experiences we've shared with them. Frankly, I didn't have many friends or much of a life outside work before I moved into the old building. Meeting the gang there changed everything for the better."

"That's sweet," Jill allowed.

"It is, but our friends...? It's like the old adage of too many cooks spoiling the broth. Divorce has enough messy emotions involved without each of our—love them, but—*highly opinionated* friends putting their two cents in."

"They're allowed their opinions," Jill asserted, "but at the end of the day, it's your decision."

Lina snorted and uncrossed her legs. "Clearly you haven't met *my* friends. They're tenacious. A bunch of meddlers, Mara especially. Even if we told them we didn't want their input, they'd give it. Forcefully. This one time, Mara insisted on knowing who we were all voting for in a primary election. She wouldn't rest until we filled out our sample ballots in front of her.

"So yeah, we're keeping it to ourselves because it feels weird, like our friends might get contentious. I think we both worry they might at best pick sides and at worst take this from a fairly amicable divorce to something drawn out in court if we tell them too soon. Even amicable divorces get ugly, you know. I've seen it happen."

"Hm." Jill raised a thinly plucked eyebrow. "Hasn't Brown moved out? How are you going to keep that from your friend?"

It was a valid question, one that had Lina's stress levels at

DefCon 1. She hadn't slept the night before thinking about how she and Brown, as a couple, had had a reputation for being handsy. Even when things were falling apart between them, physical touch had been a gloss, a shorthand they used to seek comfort from each other. Freddie had lovingly told them to get a room on more than one occasion.

To keep them and Mara in the dark this weekend would mean to fake being cuddly with Brown. Maybe even hot and heavy with Brown, a thought that broke Lina out in a cold sweat.

"He has moved out," she finally acknowledged Jill's concern, "but he's agreed to stay over that night. After Mara goes to sleep, I'm going to go downstairs and bunk on the couch."

Jill must have sensed the anxiety wafting off Lina like a bad pheromone because she replied, "That seems like an awful lot of pageantry to keep an inevitable truth from your friend."

"Sure, but what's the alternative? Derail Mara's weekend by making it about me? Plus"—she scratched an itch on her elbow—"I'm kind of scared to come clean."

"What makes you scared?" Jill asked. "Your friends' meddling?"

"Not really. I'm not sure." Lina studied the pattern in the carpet. "Whether they meddle or not, it's probably more about what our friends will think." She looked up. "I mean, they watched us get married. They thought we were endgame. I don't know how to tell people who rooted for us like that that we failed."

Jill pursed her lips in thought. When she lifted her arms in a shrug, her collection of bangles clacked against one another. "You know I hate to give answers that feel woo-woo. That's not why I went to an Ivy for my doctorate. But, Lina, I don't think there's one right answer here. The circumstances will all be so variable. You intend to tell your friend eventually, so don't feel bad if you lie by omission to help her have a good time while she's in town. It'll be up to you and your intuition, your emotional feeling about it, whether you tell her now or after everything is finalized." Jill checked the time again, then nodded curtly. "Yeah?"

Lina returned the nod. "Yeah. Thank you," she said as she gathered her bag. "I'm really looking forward to having her here. I'll focus on that."

She was able to keep that promise at least for the next few minutes, as she clopped down the hall and into the parking lot. At that point, Lina's thoughts returned to the prospect of helping Freddie.

Mara had been her closest friend nearly as long as Lina had lived in the building. The memories they had made in those old apartments, especially during their monthly dinner parties, had gotten her through some rough times.

Regardless of whether she was right in calling it a 'project' or a 'distraction from her divorce,' this was just one more reason Lina wanted to help save the building.

CHAPTER
FOUR
OCTOBER 7, 2016

Six years ago

The thing about the first ever PDP was that, like all great ideas, it came about organically—thanks to a hurricane, a hair dryer, and some collectively inconvenient sell-by dates.

"What a welcome to the building this is," twenty-five-year-old Lina muttered.

She stared down at the rainwater that was rapidly spreading across her pristine hardwood floors. She had been waiting out the hurricane on her couch, thankful for the electricity to stay cool and dry while marathoning a true crime series, but when she got up to make some tea, she'd stepped her stocking-clad foot right into this puddle. The only source for the leak she could see were the gaps between bricks in the building's ancient exterior wall.

She'd been living on her own in #305 for a month and, while she'd adored the building for its old-school fixtures when she toured it, she'd never considered what living *with* them would be like. The landlords had historical preservation rules against things like replacing older windows with newer, more energy-efficient ones, but apparently there weren't any rules about making sure your walls were doing their job.

She rummaged in one of the kitchen drawers for the welcome packet she'd received on move-in day, and she texted the number belonging to Freddie Morales, who was listed as the building's live-in super.

Sure thing. Be right over, Freddie texted back.

Five minutes later, a tall, lanky, dark-skinned person who should have been moonlighting as a model, not a maintenance worker, was standing in her doorway. "Hey, I'm Freddie, he/they," they said, then held up what looked like a paint can, a trowel, and a hair dryer. "Where's the leak?"

"Hey, um, Lina, is, is me," she replied, not used to having to give her pronouns, not to mention perplexed by the items Freddie was toting. "She/her, I guess, and it's back through this way."

Against one of the outside walls, there was a mound of beach towels sopping up as much of the dampness as they could.

Freddie squelched them out of the way before they got down on their hands and knees.

"God, a beach day sounds amazing right now," they said, opening the can, which held not paint but a powdery, gray substance that turned to thick mud when applied to the wet wall. "I always plan to go to the beach in the summer but somehow forget to do it before the weather gets rough."

"Same," Lina commiserated. "The summer always looks wide open, but then work gets in the way."

"What do you do for work?" Freddie asked conversationally before sitting up and assessing the layer of spackle. Some water was still beading through. "The rain's going to keep coming unless we can glob it on and dry it fast." They reached behind them. "Hand me that hair dryer, will you?"

Lina carefully plugged it into a socket far down the wall

from the puddle and handed the dryer to the super. "I'm a law clerk at one of the firms here downtown. Hoping to get on the partner track before long."

"Law clerk? That's chill. I'm between jobs right now. Hand me more spackle?"

Lina crouched beside them and dipped her hands into the grayish powder before smearing it on the wall. "Oh, that's okay," she said. "I'm sure you'll find something soon."

"No, hon." Freddie chuckled good-naturedly. "I'm literally *between* jobs right this minute. I work three of them, including this handyperson routine, and I need to head out in twenty to get to my next shift."

Lina's jaw dropped. "During a hurricane?"

Freddie tsked. "Not all of us have cushy law clerk jobs, okay?" They turned on the dryer and heated up the spackle while Lina pressed more of it firmly against the chipped mortar. After about five minutes, the exposed brick didn't look as pretty as it once had, but the leak had stopped.

"There," she said with a wink. "And you've got another ten before you've got to head out."

"Joy of joys." Freddie rolled their eyes. "Anyway, this is a temporary patch. I'll come check on it after the storm blows through, see if we can't do anything more permanent within the building codes."

They were coiling up the hair dryer when the power went out.

"What?!" Lina said. "The landlord told me the building never lost power during hurricanes."

"Usually we don't," Freddie muttered. "I feel bad for the folks up at the hospital. We're on their electrical grid, so if we've lost power, so have they."

This made Lina feel all the more privileged when she said, "And I had a beef Wellington I was going to pop in the oven tonight!"

It was still light out enough that she could see Freddie crease their forehead. "You regularly make yourself beef Wellington? What, is Mr. Belvedere your uncle or something?"

"No," she sniffed. "I do have student loans, you know. I just like to make one really nice recipe each week, then live off the leftovers."

Freddie's forehead creases subsided as a knowing smile lit their eyes. "I get it. I like to make nice food too. A lot of us in the building do actually." They packed up their things. "Hey, I have to run, but do me a favor, keep your fridge door closed. Things are less likely to spoil that way. Assuming we have power, have that Wellington ready for about six thirty tomorrow night, okay?" They took their great loping strides to the door and out into the hallway.

"Six thirty?" Lina called after them. "Why?"

Freddie called over their shoulder, "I'll tell you all about it tomorrow."

At six o'clock the next day, the power was back on; the smell of mushroom duxelles and seared pancetta coated Lina's apartment; and a knock and a note were left at her door.

Drinks in 201. Come join. xx

She set a timer on her phone so that the puff pastry wouldn't burn in the finicky oven, then slunk downstairs. There was a burst of laughter, welling up and dying like a wave on the shore, just before she knocked and let herself in. There was Freddie, holding court over vodka gimlets with a short, stout, brown-haired woman. The woman introduced herself as Mara and had Lina hiccupping with laughter in five minutes flat.

There was another girl as well, Sophie—tall, leggy, full of ambition.

"I'm a receptionist for now, but who cares about that? My big plan is that I've got an Instagram account for each of my interests," she explained, when Lina asked what she did for a living. "I'm going to keep posting to them until one really starts to take off. Instead of assuming that my public wants, say, my thoughts as a fashion influencer, I'll see which one becomes a success and *then* devote all my attention to it."

Freddie snorted. "You have a *public*?"

Sophie tapped her smartphone and said in a singsong, "We all do, if we actually try to find it."

Freddie looked skeptical, but they settled further into the couch. "Sounds like me with all my jobs. For sale to the highest bidder."

Sophie drank to that.

With the help of Freddie's cocktails, Lina was confessing things she only ever thought she'd share with her diary. "You know the bartender downstairs? The tall one who likes to wear bowties, Brown something? Anyway, I think he's cute," she intimated to her host.

"Oh! You mean Brown Mitchell. Yeah, I invited him. He's on his way up," Freddie said.

Sure enough, the bartender in question was walking through the door, wearing what Lina would soon learn was his afterhours uniform of the softest cotton T-shirt and worn-in black jeans. It felt like kismet, or else summoning the devil; she'd uttered his name and he had appeared.

"I love him, though tragically I'm not his type," Lina could hear Freddie saying over the sound of her own heart beating. "But, hey, I don't see the harm in you asking him out."

"That's what I just told her!" Mara hissed as she walked by.

Brown strolled over when it became evident they were talking about him. "Hey," he greeted Lina. "Come here often?"

In the corner of the kitchen, Mara waggled her eyebrows,

and Lina felt the abrupt, thrilling embarrassment of being thrown into a spotlight's beam.

"Oh my God, that's such a line," she replied, cheeks flushing.

"Yeah, well"—he gave a thousand-kilowatt smile—"my dad always said I wasn't that quick on my feet."

Lina bashfully plucked the Vidalia onion out of her cocktail and surveyed Brown from under her eyelashes. He was perfect, even if he had an unfortunate James Dean vibe with his ink-black moto jacket and the long, blond curl on his forehead. He was the first boy—*man*, Lina corrected herself—she'd met who could hold a conversation about literature and music for more than a minute. Even so, she wasn't ready to make her move. Because he was perfect, *she* had to be perfect too. She had to plan some things, lay some groundwork, but give it time, luck, and some reciprocity, and they would be beautiful together.

There was soon a call of 'I'm hungry! Who has the appetizers?' and behold, there was the birth of PDP.

It would grow throughout the years, true to its name, progressing beyond more than just the miracle food—the ceviche, the Wellington, the chocolate lava cakes—they each would have otherwise had to throw away. The meals would become more impressive until it seemed like each chef in each apartment was racking their brain and poring over old family cookbooks to outdo the next.

Though they wouldn't always be together, though a hurricane very similar to this one would nearly pull them apart in five short years, they were together now, as Lina pulled the golden-brown pastry out of the oven and basked in the first *oohs* and *aahs* her cooking had ever received.

And for her and Brown, it was the start of something wonderful.

CHAPTER
FIVE
SEPTEMBER 16, 2022

Last month—at the outset of all the chicanery

On Friday, Lina emailed a new brief to her assistant, scooted out of her home office, and rushed upstairs at four o'clock to change out of her work clothes into a graphic T and casual skirt combo. Mara would be there in an hour or so, and there were things Lina needed to do around the house before she arrived.

Typically, if a houseguest was on their way over, Lina would be eager to make the guest suite and common areas as clean and fresh as the big reveal on a home design show. In this case, though, her prep was less eager, more anxious to convince Mara nothing was out of the ordinary. Who knew what she would do if she learned about the divorce?

This not-knowing kept Lina awake and dyspeptic most nights. Mara was best friends with her, but she was friends with Brown too. Lina had to put on a convincing show, one that said she and Brown were still living together and—*Of course, why would you even ask that, Mar?* she practiced saying in the mirror, with a smile she hoped didn't look demented—still happily married.

Are you on your way? she texted Brown from the upstairs bedroom, then responded to Mara's message—*ETA 5:15!*—with a GIF of Amy Poehler and Tina Fey break-dancing.

When Brown's response wasn't immediately forthcoming, Lina huffed a breath through her nose. She could feel her anxiety alchemizing into frustration with her soon-to-be ex-husband. He made it so easy, Mr. I'll Get to It When I Get to It. He'd better get his butt over here before Mara did, or there would be consequences. Lina hadn't come up with them yet, but they would exist and be meted out with swift justice for sure.

She set her phone down and scrounged around in the top drawer of her dresser. Her fingers hit a stubby black velvet box, and she felt relief that she hadn't done the impulsive thing and thrown out her engagement ring and wedding band. It felt weird putting them back on, just as it had felt weird taking them off. Throughout the week since she'd filed for divorce, she'd gone to fidget with them with her left thumb and been startled when she was met with bare skin.

Rings back on, she rehung their wedding picture, the one she'd shoved into the walk-in closet at the top of the stairwell until she could figure out what to do with it. In its gilded frame, she and Brown stood in a casual suit and a pure white shift dress in the apartment courtyard. Though it had only been two years ago, they looked so young. Big, coat-hanger grins were pasted across their faces as they looked, him down, her up, at one another, so eager and mirthful and excited for the future.

What a pair of idiots, she thought.

Her phone buzzed. Brown, finally.

Here. Did you change the locks?

Shoot. She'd done that on Monday and forgotten to tell him.

Be right down, she responded instead of acknowledging his question. As she turned to go, she noticed the picture was hanging at an angle. She straightened it, only for it to shift to the left again. She pushed it to the right. It rasped against the wallpaper and defiantly moved back to the left. She sighed. It would have to stay wonky. She tried to ignore the irony and hustled down the carpeted stairs.

"Hey," she greeted Brown as the door swung open.

He was standing to the farthest side of the small, stylized brick porch, cuffs of his red-and-black flannel rolled to show his toned forearms. The years since Lina had first met him had been kind to Brown. He now wore his Botticelli-angel curls closely cropped, and what little baby fat he'd had in his twenty-five-year-old face had melted away into a well-built jawline that showed off his handsome, full-lipped mouth.

Which was currently pouting.

"Hey, yourself." He hooked a thumb at the front door. "So, the locks?"

She blew out a breath. "Okay, yes, I changed them. Sorry you had to find out like this, but we're burning daylight. Come in. I've prepped your bag for you."

The bag in question was a gym duffel that had seen better days. It crouched like a kicked dog at one end of their Pottery Barn sofa, on the sisal rug, packed to its brim with a week's worth of Brown's clothes. It was part of the reason Lina had urged him to show up early—that and, completely conversely, to help her convince Mara he still lived there.

"Did you pack more underwear this time?" Brown asked as he hefted it. "You know, to avoid any more incidents."

By 'incidents,' he was referring to last Tuesday night, when he had shown up at her door at eleven o'clock, begging her to throw down more boxer briefs. Apparently, the concept of stocking up at any Target, Walmart, or department store had missed his brain completely. This was typical Brown and, Lina reminded herself, one of the reasons they were breaking up. She was done being this grown man's mother.

Moreover, she couldn't believe he had the gall to ask her about her packing methods. "It's all in the bag," she said tersely.

As though he didn't believe her, he unzipped the duffel to check. He nodded when he saw the eight pairs of briefs she'd thoughtfully folded. "Bless you," he said with true gratitude, then added, when he saw the sour look on her face, "What's got your goat?"

Lina refused to engage with him. She crossed her arms and pressed her lips together before blurting out, "Until Mara gets here, we don't have to talk about anything important. No emotions, no heart-to-hearts; nothing. Beyond logistics and what the weather's doing, I don't have anything to say to you, and you don't have anything to say to me. Anything you need to say to me can go through our lawyers."

Brown's mouth gaped open as his eyebrows rose in disbelief. Then his entire face closed in on itself. Too late, Lina realized her comment had gone too far, and she followed as he stalked out to his white '92 Chevy Blazer and stowed his satchel in the wayback.

She was trying to find a way to apologize for her tone when she took in the detritus—wrinkled work shirts, an old tube of sunscreen, beach sand, and no fewer than six lottery tickets—littering the floor of the compartment.

"Jeez, you keep this thing messy," she said, unable to resist one last jibe.

"Thank you," he bit out, choosing the high road of taking her gripe as a compliment.

She finally relented, bracing her hand against the old SUV's paneling. "Look, I'm sorry for grouching at you about our lawyers. I'm just nervous about this, that's all."

He eased himself onto the lip of the trunk with a sigh so that he was looking up at her. "Why? Because we're about to lie to one of our best friends about our marriage, a lie that will for sure have consequences if we're ever found out? Can't imagine why that'd make you nervous."

She halfheartedly returned his smirk.

"Anyway, it looks really nice in there." He indicated the house with a jerk of his chin. "Would be a shame if someone were to... mess it up."

She wasn't sure why he was extending her this olive branch, but she accepted it with a nod, keeping to herself that it looked nice because his magazines, socks, used coffee mugs, misplaced wallet, and general bric-a-brac weren't clotting every surface. *Grown Man's Mother: Exhibit A.*

He stood, gripping the doorframe as he did, so that his hand was close to her own. She noticed the tan line around his left ring finger, the absence it marked. He caught her gaze, held it for a moment, but then he turned around, digging into the cavernous wayback and surfacing with two six-packs of his favorite lager.

"Shall we?"

Her messiness expert started his mission in the spotless kitchen. He cracked open two cans of beer, poured them down the sink, and left the empties crumpled on the counter.

"What are you doing?" Lina asked, observing from a safe distance.

"Exactly what we planned." He offered her one of the remaining beers and, when she declined, opened another for himself. "Trust the process, Lina. There's a method to my madness."

Unable to help her organizing compulsion, she toted the rest of the drinks to their designated shelf in the refrigerator.

"I figured we'd just muss the place up a little," she said, watching Brown free-throw old receipts onto the work surface, "not totally destroy it."

"Destroy?" He sniffed. "That's a strong word, isn't it?"

He moved into the living room, where he put his beer can, sans koozie, sans coaster, directly onto the reclaimed wood of her coffee table.

"Well, I mean, you seem really into it," she continued with a flinch. "Is this about the locks? Or my lawyer comment? Like, some sort of sick revenge, making me clean up after you one more time? I said I was sorry..."

"Apology accepted," he said coolly, "but I also want Mara to buy that I still live here. She's my friend, too, you know."

Lina watched Hurricane Brown wreak havoc on her perfect living room. "What do you have to be afraid of if she finds out? You're not even the claimant in our divorce."

Brown executed an impressive pile driver onto the couch, denting the cushions with his bum, then flopping onto his back and rocking violently from side to side. "To make it seem more lived in," he explained as he popped up, then unfurled a blanket from the back of the couch and draped it haphazardly across the furniture.

"Brown," she demanded, the context implicitly being, *Answer the damn question.*

"Doesn't matter if I'm not the claimant," he finally said. "When a couple gets divorced, people always assume it's the guy's fault. Mara will go from my oldest friend to my biggest enemy real quick."

He looked up then and his gaze softened. He'd spied their vinyl collection, nestled in wire crates below the television.

"Hello, lovers," he cooed, as he drifted over to them. "Oh my God, *Rumours*! I forgot we had this." He cradled the record so that Stevie Nicks and Mick Fleetwood were pressed against his dark blue cotton T-shirt. "I missed you guys so much."

Was Lina jealous of the attention her ex was lavishing over an inanimate object? Of course not; that would be ridiculous.

The spike of frustration pulsing through her veins was

clearly about how Brown could be so gentle with something he cared about seconds after he'd trampled over all the things she loved. Sure, this time it was intentional, requested, but it was serving only to bring back all the times she had asked for precisely the opposite and gotten no help, or the opposite of help, from him. Only disrespect for her things, their shared possessions.

She'd taken Jill's advice to keep a trigger journal. When she'd gotten off work that afternoon, she'd opened a new note in her phone's app and typed: "Friday, 4:04 p.m. ANGER. It took me all last weekend to scrub and buff and sage him out of the place, including three full hours learning how to install a new door lock on YouTube, and in fifteen minutes flat, it's going to look like he never left. A mess, garbage everywhere, Brown annoying me constantly. How did I ever marry such a slob?!"

It was frustrating to think about; their differences had once brought them closer together. Why had that changed? How had they become a rift instead?

Brown misread the line forming between her eyebrows and carefully returned the album to its plastic slipcover. "Sorry. You're right. Time's a-wasting; we've got to keep going."

"Keep going?" Lina balked, her eyes wide. "Don't you think you've done enough?"

Brown smiled mischievously. "One thing left to do. The pièce de résistance—always pissed you off when I lived here!" With that, he dashed up the stairs.

Lina flumped down on the dented couch cushions and took a swig of warm beer to fortify herself against whatever fresh hell was coming.

Ignoring the ring of condensation discoloring the coffee table, she focused on how excited she was to catch up with Mara. It'd been months since they'd seen each other, and she couldn't recall the last time they'd successfully planned a Skype date. There was no way she could spoil the weekend with her divorce news.

But what if, after all Brown's disastrous efforts, they were caught in their lie? What if Mara noticed his gym bag was being used as a duffel? What if Lina slipped and said something to Freddie while they were out tonight?

She was saved from her thoughts by the sound of a car pulling into the driveway.

"Mara's here," she announced.

Brown had returned downstairs with some dirty socks he must have retrieved from his old hamper. He was artfully balling them up and tossing them in a smelly heap on the coffee table. He spread an arm toward the piece of rejected performance art as if to say, *Eh? Am I good or am I good?* A scuzzy piece of lint dangled from one, disgustingly close to the water ring.

"Very nice," Lina said, though she groaned internally. She did a double take at his bare ring finger. "Hey, just in case, shove your hand in your pocket."

Mara Jilcott was the Romy to Lina's Michele, inseparable since the first PDP. Not long after the hurricane, they had started getting together for what they called 'W(h)ine and Cheese' sessions, kvetching about how the real world was in no way like it had been advertised and polishing off cheap bottles of red on the floor of Mara's apartment.

Their joined-at-the-hip-ness had ended, Lina guiltily supposed, the day she and Brown moved out of the building. She made herself feel better by considering that Mara had moved even farther away to work at a political nonprofit in Georgia the year before. They kept in touch over FaceTime and in person on the weekend of the Savannah 5K, which Lina loved to participate in. Now, thanks to Mara landing an executive position at the nonprofit, she was driving through Jacksonville on her way to Orlando to celebrate at the Epcot Food and Wine Festival.

Lina could not be more excited for her best friend. As she closed her front door behind her, Mara hopped out of her lime green Prius, her short, brown curls and leopard-print blouse mussed from two hours on the road.

"Mara!" Lina cheered from her stoop, then hurtled down the steps.

"Lina! Is that you?" Mara said, squishing her face into a wizened old lady expression. "You don't call, you don't write..."

She dropped the pretense and her weekend bag to wrap her arms around the rapidly incoming Lina. Mara self-described as 'bagels-and-blintz thicc,' and her voluptuous frame turned heads every time they had a girls' night out. It also gave the best hugs in the world, which Lina knew from all the times she'd cried on Mara's soft shoulders. Having her best friend here this weekend, with everything that was going on, made the world feel steadier under Lina's feet.

"How was your drive? How are *you*? Oh my gosh, it's been *way* too long!" Lina squeezed Mara, inhaling her vanilla-and-lemon scent, and then pulled back to pick up her bag. "Whoa, when did you get this filled in?" she asked, taking in Mara's sleeve tattoo.

Mara had been collecting ink on her right arm since Lina had known her, but the vines and tendrils of flowers, dotted with delicate honeybees, seemed to tie the random lot of them together.

"Up in Savannah," Mara said, her dimples showing. "But I asked for orange blossoms so I'd never forget my Florida roots."

"Love it!" Lina enthused. "Hey, come inside. Brown can't wait to see you, though I'm sorry the place is such a mess," she added out of habit.

She then realized how weird that sounded, given that she and Brown had spent the last half hour making it that way.

With a fair amount of misgiving, Lina pushed open the front door and gestured for Mara to step through. They were greeted by Brown, who was standing awkwardly at the foot of the inside staircase. He had clearly taken Lina's note about his wedding ring to heart, as he stood with his left hand very obviously shoved into his back jeans pocket, his right hand resting not at all casually on the newel post, and a forced grin on his face. In theory, the pose was a good idea. In practice, he looked like an old oil painting of a country squire, if the country squire had been painted by an artist cranked out on meth.

What the heck is he doing? Lina wondered, plastering a matching smile onto her lips and hoping Brown wasn't going to give them away in the first five minutes. She was *not* letting the odor from his sweaty gym socks seep into her newly steamed carpets for no good reason.

Mara either didn't notice Brown's kookiness or was too excited to see her old friend to care. "Brownie! How are you?"

When she reached up to give him a hug, with his hand still firmly ensconced in his back pocket, his reciprocation was more like a lean into her body than anything else.

"Doing great!" he cheered. "It's good to see you, Mars Bar."

"You too." She gestured at his side hug. "What's this, some new bartender thing?"

"Gouged my hand on the Y-peeler last night," he said, face suddenly grim as he fibbed. "I'd better keep it in my pocket. It's not pretty."

"Yikes," Mara cringed.

"Y-yeah." Lina used the lie to her advantage. "It's so bad he can't even wear his wedding ring. We were just changing the bandage when you drove up."

She turned to Brown, hoping her desperate eye contact would be translated as, *Stop standing in the foyer like an idiot.*

Let's move into the living room, but her message was drastically lost in translation. He instead seemed to interpret it as, *Come, my darling, stand diagonally behind me, with your left hand still in your pocket and your left elbow touching the small of my back like a weird, pointy hand substitute. Oh yes, that'll pull the wool over our friend's eyes for sure.*

Lina tried to keep the frustrated huff of breath through her nostrils subtle. In an attempt to make Brown's gesture look less stupid, she edged to the side and looped her right arm through his left, clasping his flannel-clad bicep.

Mara took in their pantomime with a quirk of her pierced eyebrow. "Long week?" She chuckled nervously as she looked between Lina and Brown. "You guys are acting... well, 'strange' doesn't even begin to cover it."

The truth of that statement must have struck Brown, and struck him dumb in the process. When he didn't say anything, Lina gave his bicep slightly too hard a squeeze before relinquishing her grip.

"Why don't you stow your bag in your room, Mara? Then we can pick up Freddie and get the evening started. I need to talk to Brown about something, and then I'll be in right behind you."

Mara took her bag into the guest suite, leaving Lina and Brown alone in the front hall.

"What are you doing?" Lina hissed at her ridiculous partner in crime. "You look like a crazy person!"

"I don't know why you'd be mad at me," Brown sniped back. "*You're* the one who told me to keep my left hand in my pocket!"

Lina pinched the bridge of her nose and forced herself to take a deep, not-at-all-soothing breath.

So help her, she and Brown were going to survive this weekend.

Even if it killed her.

CHAPTER
SIX

One butterfly bandage for a fake Y-peeler injury later.

After Mara had a chance to freshen up, they all headed out for their reunion evening.

"An escape room? Really?" Freddie asked. "What are we, doing corporate team-building exercises?" They had been excited to see Mara, but in light of this announcement, they resignedly buckled their seat belt in the back of Brown's Chevy.

"Hey!" Mara protested loudly from up front. "I think they're fun. Besides, this place was able to get us in last minute for dirt cheap."

"There's a tiki bar afterward," Lina said, hoping to tempt Freddie into a team spirit.

"Well, thank goodness for that," they muttered, flipping down their vintage Ray-Bans. "Sure we can't hit it before?"

After they were escorted to their escape room, it became clear how they'd scored a last-minute reservation. The four friends stood in a cramped and garish chamber with white-washed walls. It held a tatty chaise longue; an armchair whose pleather was cracking open; and a large wooden desk littered with tobacco pipes and treasure chests. In one corner, a book-shelf held maybe ten titles; beside it a cheap plastic wall clock was stuck at a quarter past eight. A poster of a giant, very phallic Rorschach test dominated one wall; a poster of the Eastern Alps another, just beside the countdown timer and the exit door with its own very obvious knob.

"Twenty-five bucks a head for this?" Brown said. "What's the theme again? Insane asylum?"

"No. It's Freud," Freddie said, holding back a laugh between pinched lips. "The theme is *Freud*."

Brown choked. "Really?"

"Yep," Mara said, no nonsense. "And we've got an hour to solve it."

"So long as I don't have to go in depth about my relationship with my mother," Brown joked.

"Or leave a positive Yelp review," Freddie added, dissolving Brown into a fit of giggles.

"Guys!" Lina said, hands on her hips just behind Mara. "Do we want to waste our money or solve this escape room?"

"Are you kidding?" Brown asked.

"I don't kid about escape rooms," she replied. Lina had been in exactly one before, but the thrill of nearly solving the puzzle was a major reason why she'd been open to Mara's idea in the first place.

"Well, look," Brown said, turning to the girls with a forced smile. "Should we try the knob?"

Why was he being so infuriatingly glib about everything? Lina could only imagine this was retaliation for her lawyer comment, the changed locks, the boundaries she had put up earlier. The next hour was going to be a metric ton of fun, she could tell.

"The knob?" Mara stated. "To the very door we're trying to exit?"

"Yeah, why not?" Brown asked.

"Humor him," Lina suggested with an eye roll. "If we don't, he'll keep bringing it up. See, Brown?" she said after jiggling the handle. "Locked."

He shrugged. "Worth a shot. You should always start with the simplest solution first."

Lina's dentist was going to make a killing off all the divorce-related tooth grinding she'd been doing lately.

"Oh, look! A clue!" Mara said. She pulled a rolled-up piece of paper out of one of the pipes and brandished it proudly.

Lina and Brown glared at each other, and the game was afoot.

If Lina had known an escape room would serve as a perfect metaphor for her failed relationship with Brown, she would have joined Freddie in pleading to go somewhere else.

The room was literally inescapable. They were nowhere near solving the puzzle, and the claustrophobic, whitewashed walls were closing in. Lina felt grateful for the digital count-down clock, which told her she had just five more minutes left of this torture. It was the only way she could convince herself she wasn't trapped for eternity in this tiny room with her ex and their best friends, her own personal definition of hell.

Of course, there was one fringe benefit to the escape room: she could get out all her Brown-focused anger in public with no one being the wiser. She had already yelled at him several times for jumping ahead on clues.

"Wait, wait, *wait!*" she had snarled at minute twelve. "You keep skipping ahead, Brown. We need to focus on this letter. I think there's a cipher in it."

"Well, you work on that," he simpered. "I'm going to focus on the bookshelf."

Lina balled her hands into fists, crumpling the letter in the process. "If we split our focus, we aren't going to finish faster,

Brown! You're doing what you always do—racing ahead, never having a plan—and so even if we're going faster, we're wasting more time!"

Brown stopped what he was doing with the bookcase—apparently trying to see if pulling down any of the books opened a secret compartment—and turned to face her. "Well, maybe if you're so worried about wasting time, you shouldn't analyze everything into the ground, *Lina!*" he snarked. "You're so pathologically detail-oriented, you couldn't see your way out of this escape room for the penis-shaped trees!"

"Hey, umm, guys?" Mara meekly held up an open treasure box. "I figured out the combination lock."

But their vigorous in-fighting had continued, escalating to the point that, at minute fifty-three, Mara had given up on her own game and joined Freddie on top of Freud's desk to watch the smackdown.

"Wish I'd brought a snack," Freddie complained as she hopped up.

Mara wordlessly pulled a granola bar out of her backpack and handed it to them.

Lina was shoving a cheap piece of printer paper into Brown's face. "No, no, no," she asserted. "This letter from Carl Jung says that tea will be served at *one* o'clock! We need to move the minute and hour hands to reflect that! Maybe that will unlock the secret compartment."

"Lina!" Brown barked back with exasperation in his voice. "We tried the clock thing already. Put down the stupid note and move on to the next clue." He thrust out the clue—a blue, plastic parakeet they'd discovered in a desk drawer—in his bandaged hand.

"*Next* clue?!" Lina demanded. "We already tried the para-keet! And its beak didn't unlock squat!"

"You have to imagine the escape room workers," Mara intimated to Freddie, "just making a killing off this content on YouTube…"

Lina shot them a glare.

"Jesus," Freddie mumbled around the granola bar. "How are you two still together?"

"I have no idea," Lina and Brown chorused in response.

There was a pause.

"Mara," Lina added, as sweetly as she could, "when you came up with this plan, was bowing out of the game and starting a fight between me and Brown on your agenda?"

"Um, as a matter of fact, no, it wasn't," Mara blustered. She held up her hands in surrender. "Okay, fine! There's no way we're winning in the next two minutes, but sure, we'll help."

"We?" Freddie asked, crossing one leg over the other and moving around some notes on Freud's patients. "I'll continue watching the Friday fight night from up here, thank you. I'm realizing I like the way people break down in escape rooms more than I actually like escape rooms, you know?"

"You are one sick and twisted human, that's what you are," Mara laughed.

"Evil incarnate, more like," Lina agreed.

"Thank you," Freddie preened.

"Wait." Brown pointed to the letter Lina had been shoving in his face for the last fifteen minutes. "Are they misspelling 'ceiling'?"

She flipped the paper around to face her, only to realize swapping the *i* and the *e* would solve the cipher. "You've *got* to be kidding me."

Lina had intended not to drink—it would be the easiest way to keep her head on a swivel, the lies in check—but after the inherent frustration of the escape room, the cocktail list at the tiki bar was too enticing.

It didn't help that for every question she asked Freddie about work and for every question Brown asked Mara about Savannah, there were three fired back at them about married life. When Freddie started impersonating her mother (aka asking her and Brown when there'd be grandkids), Lina excused herself and muscled her way up to the bar. Brown was driving; she could afford to tie at least a tiny one on.

She ordered a Jungle Bird and enjoyed the tartness of the Campari and the pineapple as the drink hit her tongue. Finish one of these and her anxiety would be in check; to be honest, that was so much harder to control these days than the lie. She scowled across the room at Brown, where he sat laughing with Freddie at their table. If she and Brown couldn't even be civil to each other in an hour-long escape room, then maybe they *should* tell Mara about the D-word.

She took another slurp through her straw. It wasn't the worst idea. After all, Mara was such a sweetheart; she wouldn't be one to take sides.

Lina turned to rest her back against a bamboo chair and saw that Mara had joined her.

Mara nudged her full hip in against the bar next to Lina. She looked gorgeous, filling out a pair of black jeans and leaving little to the imagination in her V-necked leopard-print blouse. "It's so good to see you, Leen," she said, cheeks flushed from her own umbrella drink. "I know I've been bad about keeping in touch lately, and it makes me feel so guilty not knowing what's going on in your life."

"Aw, don't feel bad." Lina rubbed her thumb against her tiki mug. "As they say, the phone rings both ways. We've all been busy."

She couldn't bring herself to say with what.

"Well, I'm just glad to hear you and Brown are doing well," Mara said. "Remember my friends up in Georgia I told you about, Jason and Kelly? The ones I thought would be together forever? Guess what? *Separated*." She took the look on Lina's face—one of horror at the synchronicity of it all—for horror over such a sturdy couple going sideways. "I know, it's nuts. And I was so close to Kelly. Like this." Mara held up and crossed two purple fingernails. "But she's been such a royal pain in Jason's backside that, honestly, I think he's winning friendship custody of me. It just hurt so much to see him hurt, you know? Like, Lina, I don't think you're getting this, but Kelly? She is dead to me."

A snap from Mara accompanied each of the last three words, which resounded in Lina's brain: *Dead. To. Me.*

"You and Brown *are* okay, aren't you?" Mara said when Lina remained silent, dazed. Absolutely mortified.

Lina wavered then. Should she tell Mara the truth? Surely her best friend could handle it; she wouldn't choose sides, right? Never. Not when it came to Lina and Brown. Kelly was some old so-and-so from Savannah; of course she would be on the chopping block. But not Lina. Lina was Mara's joined-at-the-hip best friend for life. Such things demanded loyalty.

Mara grabbed her forearms. "Lina, please say something," she blurted. "Please tell me you and Brown are okay. If something was wrong with you guys, I wouldn't be able to take it. Was it the escape room? Are you guys in a fight over the escape room?" She relinquished Lina's arms to shove her hands through her hair. "Oh God, if I caused a rift in your relationship by suggesting that as tonight's activity, I would lose my freaking mind!"

Mara's response was so strong that all thoughts of telling her what was going on got sucked back up into whatever corner of Lina's brain bad ideas occupied. She took an enormous gulp of her drink.

"Whoa," she crooned. "Overreact much? Don't put yourself in a tizzy worrying over us. We're doing just fine."

She mustered the energy to boop Mara's nose. In response,

Mara slowly, gingerly, lowered her hands back to her sides, and Lina relaxed back into her lies.

"In fact"—she thanked the bartender from the bottom of her heart for bringing over extra shots of rum to accompany her next drink—"in fact, we're happier than ever."

After dinner, Brown found a parking spot close to the old building, and they all hopped out to walk Freddie home.

There was an unpleasant surprise waiting for them. Lina stared, baffled, at two posted bills on the door. Any warm feelings she had stoked with her friends over drinks that evening were plunged into an ice bath at the sight.

"Hey, these weren't here when I stopped by on Wednesday," she said.

"Or when you picked me up today," Freddie added, mournfully pulling their key out of their fanny pack.

One was a 'Sold' sign, which Lina supposed meant that Freddie had accepted the developer's offer, but the one below it was a notice for a public hearing to discuss the future of the property. Just as she'd feared, some Richie Rich was going to scoop up their building and enact whatever dastardly plans he had for it. Rezoning it into a block of condos with a rooftop garden, probably.

"It's just like we talked about, Fred," she murmured.

If Lina had tied a tiny one on at the tiki bar, Mara had laced up a giant's sneakers. She zigzagged over to join them by the door. "Wait, what's happening? Freddie, what is this?"

Freddie turned to their tipsy friend with a sigh. "Some real estate developer is buying me out, babe. I don't have any choice. I can't afford to keep going. I have to either raise my tenants' rent or sell out. Unfortunately, though, I'm now realizing they ripped me off, 'cause it looks like they're turning the old place into luxury apartments."

"What?!" Mara said. "That's awful. We can't let them do this, guys! We lived here." She whirled toward the entirely sober Brown, who caught her before she could tip all the way forward. "Lina and Brown got *married* in the courtyard for cripes' sake! They can't just turn it into luxury apartments. Guys," she said, eyes wide with realization, "we have to save the building."

Apparently, white women approach the point of 'we have to do something' in many different ways: some from residual, divorce-related emotions; some from too much wine at dinner.

However, even as Mara was approaching that point, Lina was starting to have cold feet. She cut her eyes at Brown, who was now propping Mara up, and saw that he shared her doubts. Their friends often brought up the fact that they had gotten married in the building's courtyard. If they became an integral part of this whole rah-rah 'Save the Building' thing, Lina was quickly realizing they would have to keep up the 'We're in Love and Our Marriage is Perfect' charade—for who knew how long.

She flashed back to the claustrophobia of the escape room. The walls were closing in.

"I don't know," she hedged. "I mean, the building is important to all of us, but I don't see how anyone can go up against some rich guy these days and win. I mean, who's even going to save it?"

Freddie turned to her, equal parts puzzled by her response and hyped for Mara's enthusiasm. "Come on, Lina. Us! *We* could save it. You, me, Mara, Brown—and maybe Sophie. Like we discussed on Wednesday."

"Yeah," Mara echoed, from within Brown's friendly embrace, "like you discussed on Wednesday."

Brown shot her a look.

"I just—" Lina clasped one elbow in her opposite hand, trying to think of the kindest way to put it. She could feel Brown's presence just over Mara's shoulder, his doubts buoying hers enough to say, "I've had some time to think about it, Freddie, and I just don't know if the opinions of five thirty-somethings will make any difference to this developer, much less to city council."

"Lina, you *promised*," Freddie said. "Remember? For my tenants and everyone who needs affordable housing on a living wage?" They jabbed their keys at the second sign, advertising the zoning hearing. "We have to go to this and make our voices heard."

"Yeah!" Mara hiccupped woozily. "About afforgeable mouse things. On a—what they said."

As Lina stood on the gum-scarred pavement, staring at her friends, her heart melted. Huddled outside the old building, Mara and Freddie looked so vulnerable. Mara's face blazed with naive optimism, and Freddie stood, framed by the big, oak door, fondling their keys like prayer beads, ready to go in and enjoy what time they had left in their home.

Lina's mind flashed to her wish and will; to laughter spilling out of the stairwell as they hopped from one apartment to the next during PDPs; to Brown's fingers stroking her hair in bed on countless Sunday mornings. More than anything, it was the look in their eyes—the confusion in Mara's, the way Freddie's wavered on the edge of betrayal—that made Lina stand on the diving board of a pool of guilt, about to jump in.

"Y'all really want to save this place?" she asked doubtfully. "Like we're in an eighties movie, saving an orphanage? What do you think's going to happen? Our friendship and tenacity and a little spark of hutzpah will beat the big, bad rich man and win the day?"

"Don't forget Sloth and a pirate ship full of treasure," Brown chipped in.

"Exactly!" Mara nodded, clearly missing his *Goonies* reference. "This has to work. We have to do it. Be-Because—"

She was reaching for words she couldn't quite grasp, but

Freddie had her back. They whispered it aloud, almost to themselves: "Because we're the orphans without it."

Lina could feel tears welling in her eyes. Freddie had hit the nail on the head. Without the building, without this beautiful, supportive group, what was she but alone, untethered, without a family?

She snapped herself out of it and muttered, "I can't believe I'm friends with you weirdos. Look, Freddie's right. I did promise to help them out. But Mara's beyond tipsy, and Brown and I are tired. If this is so important to you, we can confab about it at brunch tomorrow, okay? I'm going home to bed."

"Yes!" Freddie thrilled in relief, clearly only hearing the part where Lina hadn't flat-out rejected the idea. "We're going to save the building! You'll see, Lina. Just you wait."

On the ride home, Mara talked their ears off about rhetorical strategies, citizen petitions, and the best ways to fight zoning committees. Lina shared a look with Brown, both across the front seat of his car and later, in their once-shared bedroom, where they waited for Mara's snores to cue Lina to sneak down to the couch.

"Oh, um, sorry," Brown said.

They were both lying fully clothed on top of the sheets, arms rigidly at their sides for fear of touching the other. Even so, he had accidentally brushed his left foot against Lina's right calf, and now he was awkwardly clearing his throat and mumbling excuses like a compromised vicar in a Regency-period romance.

Lina sighed and sat up, wrapping her arms resignedly around her knees.

"No, *I'm* sorry. For snarking at you so hard, back in the escape room," she explained. "I was looking for clues in the puzzles that just weren't there."

"Hm. Why does that sound familiar?" Brown asked.

She reached behind her for her pillow and lightly thwacked him with it.

"Ow," he deadpanned. "Anyway, admitting you have a problem is always the first step. Hey, how do you feel about all this 'save the building' stuff?"

"It's a really lovely sentiment," Lina whispered. "And I'm impressed Mara could spout so much information about community organizing while three sheets to the wind."

"Try five," Brown chuckled. "Yeah, that was impressive, but Lina, you know why we can't be part of this."

Lina hugged her knees more closely to her chest and paused, pretending to listen out for her friend. In reality, she didn't know what to say. This was the textbook definition of being between a rock and a hard place. She had meant it when she offered Freddie her support earlier in the week, and she had hated to wound them by starting to retract her offer tonight. Was there any way to be part of this campaign without having to lie about who she and Brown were to each other? Was there any way to keep her friends?

"Yeah," she finally uttered, eyes fixed on the tag of the pillow. "We can't."

As much as she hated to admit it, Lina couldn't help wondering if Brown was right.

CHAPTER
SEVEN
SEPTEMBER 17

One neck-cricking, sleepless night later

Lina passed a rough night on the couch. She startled awake every few moments, thinking the air conditioner cutting off or a rustle outside was Mara waking up to discover her. She contemplated creeping upstairs and sleeping on top of the covers, but finally she drifted off around three in the morning, with her neck at a weird angle.

When she woke up after a few unsatisfying hours and toddled into the kitchen, there was a crick in it. As she waited for the coffee maker to brew, she gingerly slipped out of her pajama set and into a linen sundress she'd brought down the night before. She folded the blanket and stowed her pillow in the hall closet, then settled onto one of the barstools at the kitchen island with a cup of life-giving joe.

Brown soon tiptoed downstairs to join her. "Hey," he whispered huskily. "How'd you sleep?"

"Hey, yourself." Lina looked up from the article she was reading on her phone. "There's coffee."

"Great. When are we meeting Freddie for brunch?" His

white T-shirt rode up, separating a bit from his pajama bottoms as he reached for a mug in the cabinet. Lina did her best to ignore the domestic normalcy of it—not to mention the clean lines of muscle tapering to his waist.

"Half an hour," she said, then pointed at her phone. "Hey, I've been reading up on housing insecurity. Remember the rent moratorium early in the pandemic? Apparently, that made a lot of mom-and-pop landlords have to sell out to corporate ones like this guy Freddie's up against. Then those corporate landlords bundled their properties into stock portfolios that *have* to raise rent every year to meet their shareholders' promised return on investment. This had a snowball effect, and now a lot of tenant-minded landlords like Freddie are getting edged out. Really fascinating." She scrolled a bit more. "I can share the article with you if you like."

Brown leaned into the steam wicking off his mug and leveled her with a frank stare. "Lina, you know why we can't help save the building," he reiterated his position from the night before. "I'm faking all this with you for one weekend only, remember?"

"I know, but I hate to see Freddie hurting." She sighed dramatically and set her phone on the counter. "I guess I'll have to break it to them at brunch that I just can't help them save their primary means of income."

Brown wasn't hopping aboard this particular guilt trip. "Speaking of brunch"—he nodded at the guest room door—"should we wake her up?"

"Maybe. I was thinking—" Lina interrupted herself, patting Brown's arm frantically. "Oh! Oh, here she comes!"

Mara stumped blearily out of the guest room, head down, short hair spiked around her head in a frizzy halo.

Lina quickly wrapped one arm around Brown's waist and used the other hand to cup his face, like this was a totally normal pose in which they could be caught on any given morning. Brown let out a noise somewhere between a laugh and a cough.

"Good morning, Mara! How'd you sleep?" he asked, cheeks smooshed between Lina's thumb and forefinger. She winced and eased up a bit.

"Mnnh." Mara came forward to rest her forehead on the cool granite of the kitchen island.

"Went a little hard last night, did ya?" Brown said. When Lina glared at him, he shrugged—*What? Couldn't resist.*

"Aspirin?" Mara begged.

"Sure thing," he replied, chipper as can be. "I think we have some around here somewhere..."

Lina released Brown from her death grip so he could rummage through the cabinets. Thank goodness she hadn't rearranged those since he'd moved out; Mara didn't look like her head could tolerate more drawers opening and closing than were absolutely necessary.

"Here!" He tossed Lina a bottle of aspirin.

Mara looked up groggily, so, in a panic, Lina said, "Thanks, babe," and gave Brown a perfunctory morning kiss. She ignored the way her mutinous body wanted to curl its toes at his warm smell, and slid the bottle across the island to Mara. Mara gave them a thumbs-up and trundled back toward the bathroom.

They stood with frozen smiles plastered on their faces until the door shut.

Brown pulled away from Lina, rubbing his hand over his mouth. "Ugh!" he said in disgust. "Your morning breath should come with a hazmat warning."

Lina breathed into her hand and sniffed. "It's not that bad, is it? I didn't want to sneak upstairs and wake you by brushing my teeth."

He waved a dismissive hand. "Whatever. Anyway, listen, I'll drive separately so I can go home right after brunch."

Home? Oh. His apartment.

Lina, still self-conscious of her morning stank, spoke with her hand in front of her mouth. "As much as I'd love that, you should ride with us. More convincing that way."

"Why? If they ask, we'll just tell Mara and Freddie I have to work after."

"But what if she—"

There was the flush of the toilet, then the sound of the sink running. When Mara peeked her head out of the bathroom door, Brown was snuggled against Lina from behind. Lina could only picture them as a deranged stock photo, probably labeled something like 'Unmedicated Couple Having Breakfast.'

"What's the dress code?" Mara asked.

"Casual," Lina said, as casually as she could with her ex's hips pressing into her rear and her neck crick flaring up. "I'm wearing this, but shorts and a tee would be fine."

Mara grunted again and trudged into the guest room.

"Ow!" Lina hissed, rubbing her neck when Mara was back out of earshot.

"You okay?" Brown asked.

"Yeah, fine. Just my stupid neck, from sleeping on the couch."

"I don't even know why we're doing this," he said, moving back to his seat. "She's clearly too hungover to pay any attention."

Lina shook her head so hard the crick made itself excruciatingly known. "What if that's what she *wants* us to think? But okay, all right. You can drive separately. Just stick to the story, and when we all leave the restaurant, head to the bar first before you double back toward your apartment. Otherwise, it'll look suspicious." She walked her mug to the sink to rinse it.

"Yeah. *That'll* look suspicious." Brown exhaled heavily as they both climbed the stairs, him to get dressed, her to brush her teeth. "Jesus, Lina, this is getting more elaborate than a Secret Service maneuver."

. . .

Waiting on the couch for Brown and Mara to finish getting ready, Lina found two minutes to add to her trigger journal.

Saturday, 10:23 *a.m.,* she typed. *FEELING CONFUSED?!? It's beyond frustrating to pretend to still be with him, have to kiss him and touch him around M. All while still being furious with him for all we couldn't be.*

She thought of the primal reaction she'd had to his scent—if she was being honest, to his body pressed against her—and was glad she hadn't given in to the impulse to sleep upstairs.

Ask Jill, she added, *do people ever have last-time farewell sex with their exes, WITHOUT FEELINGS ATTACHED? Wonder if Brown would be into it.*

The very idea infuriated her, so she deleted the last sentence and added in its place all the reasons she refused to be with him: *Can't believe I'm still lusting after a messy, sarcastic, know-it-all jerk who will never amount to anything.*

Just then, Mara exited the guest room, looking a bit more human. "Ready?" she asked.

"Yep!" Lina chirped, pocketing her phone and grabbing her keys off the end table. "Brown's going to drive separately. He has to go to work later."

As they walked down the sidewalk toward her sedan, she found that she understood why other people kept personal diaries. The private, no-consequences outlet was, at times, all too humanly necessary.

At brunch, Lina was riding high.

Her group had scored a pair of comfy outdoor couches on the rooftop of a popular Five Points spot, the restaurant jutting like a ship's prow out over Margaret and Oak streets. She and Brown sat on one couch, with Freddie and Mara across the way.

Sure, the crick in her neck was deepening from leaning into Brown's side just enough to look friendly, not enough to press her skin, through her skimpy halter dress, against his, but wasn't that what masseuses were for? After all, Mara's visit was nearly over, and she didn't seem to suspect a thing. She would head down to the food and wine festival, and Lina's charade—and the twinge building in her trapezius muscle—would blessedly be over. The elderflower cocktail and the eggs benedict she had ordered were her just rewards for the weekend going off without a hitch.

Mara, meanwhile, was not having a good time. "Why is it so bright?" she moaned. The aspirin she'd taken earlier clearly wasn't helping.

"Are you going to be okay to drive to Orlando?" Lina asked. She hoped the concern in her voice read as worry for Mara's well-being, not anxiety that she'd have to spend one more minute than necessary cozying up to Brown.

"I will be," Mara said, to Lina's great relief. "Hey, do you think they'd get mad if I sprawled out on this couch and took a nap?"

"Yes. We would," their server said, standing over them. "Please don't put your feet on the furniture." She served cocktails for Lina and Freddie, a local beer for Brown, and a strong, black coffee for Mara, who winced as she stirred two sugar packets into it.

"Well, Mara's epic hangover aside, I'd call last night a success," Brown said.

"Really?" Lina rejoined. "We lost the escape room and Freddie learned their building's getting demolished for luxury condos."

Freddie toasted her sardonically with their drink.

"Correction: You nearly *murdered* me in the escape room." The hand Brown had draped around her waist reached out to goose the top of her thigh. "Good thing I have fast reflexes."

"Fast reflex *this*, Brown Mitchell." She pinched his side until he flinched away from her. That'd teach him to get handsy again. "Anyway, if I almost murdered you, you probably had it coming."

She turned to their friends and tried to keep an appropriately straight face despite the visual that met her. Freddie was sitting upright, draped in peppy, purple-and-blue parachute pants, while Mara lolled in a rumpled, white T and severe, black Bermuda shorts beside them.

"How are you feeling about all the building stuff, Freddie?" Lina asked, putting her hand on Brown's and hoping it looked like a natural thing to do.

"Decent, actually." They sipped a Bloody Mary with a hearty garnish of celery, fried pimento olives, and bacon. "I was pretty blue when I went in last night, but by the time I went to sleep, I was feeling better. That's all thanks to you guys being on board to help save the building." Their smile wavered as they looked at the others. "You are still on board, right?"

"Totally!" Lina said, no thought needed. The article she'd read that morning had convinced her to push aside her worries from the night before. Speaking of... "Right, Brown?" she asked, then squeezed his hand to elicit his agreement.

Brown made a strained humming noise in his throat and sipped his beer.

Though Lina's hackles were raised, it seemed like a good enough answer for Freddie, and so three pairs of eyes swiveled to Mara, who was currently trying to cut the tiniest possible piece off one of the pumpkin spice crullers she'd ordered for the table. She finally retrieved the scrap of donut and looked up to realize everyone's eyes were on her.

"Well..." she hedged, and the callbacks erupted.

"Aw, Mara, why not?" Lina said.

Freddie shook their head. "Child, you are one hot mess this morning."

"What happened?" Lina demanded. "You were all-in last night!"

"Well, yeah," Mara said. "But I was *drunk*. I wasn't thinking of the logistics involved." She sighed apologetically. "Challenging city hall isn't something you can do in a grassroots way anymore. The only people who ever make waves have political and financial backing. I'm really sorry, Freddie, but it's not feasible for me to drive two hours down from Savannah for a snowball's chance in local government. I don't even know if work will let me come in remotely after this promotion. And, Lina, are you the best person to help Freddie out? You know you have a penchant for biting off more than you can chew…"

"Do not!" Lina protested.

She wanted to spill the beans entirely, to tell Mara that friends make sacrifices for each other, like two-hour drives and lying about their relationship status, but she pressed her lips together and swallowed her pride.

"Do too," Mara insisted. "Remember when you took on too many cases as a junior associate? You figured it would get you on a promotional track, which worked great until you had to take a month of part-time work to recover from the burnout."

"It's true," Brown said, nodding.

Lina had kind of blocked that out, but it was clear what her soon-to-be ex-husband was saying by taking Mara's side: *Are you sure you want to take on this challenge while we're getting divorced? Seems like a horrible idea to me.* She removed her hand from his and ran it through her dark hair.

"Okay, fair," she admitted, "but lobbying against the rezoning is such an important cause. And if we're all in it together, there's less chance of me getting burned out! Come on, Mara. We have all benefited so much from the building." She pointed around the couches. "You couldn't afford to get out from under your parents' thumb until you found the building and its rent control. Freddie went from working multiple part-time jobs to having one job with great security." She reluctantly took Brown's hand again and, trying to keep emotion out of her voice, muttered, "And we found each other there, I guess."

He gave her a wry smile as though to say, *And we see how that turned out.*

Mara was sitting up now, looking both green and guilty. "Freddie, are you okay? I'm really sorry I can't do more. Maybe I could help out online from Georgia?" she suggested.

"I'll be okay," they said. "Even if it's just me, I'll say my piece to city council, but to be frank, the developer getting to gentrify the building felt less like a done deal last night, when I had you all by my side." They looked up. "You may think this cause is really important to you, but I feel that in spades. I don't think I've ever told anyone this, but before I moved into our building, I was living out of my car."

Lina's thigh was still pressed against Brown's, so she could feel the moment when Freddie's words hit him and he stiffened. She looked up and saw her ex's heart breaking for the younger version of their friend they'd never known.

"Freddie, we had no idea," he murmured.

"I know. I don't tell a lot of people, and I'd prefer to keep it that way," Freddie said. "Otherwise, they do this pity thing with their faces." They smirked. "You're all doing a pretty good impression of it right now."

Lina felt her eyes misting but forced herself to stifle that emotion. She kept silent, too, holding space for Freddie's story; there was nothing she could say that would do anything besides make her feel a little better, and that wasn't what Freddie needed.

"It wasn't as bad as it sounds," they explained. "Right after college, I had a really unforgiving student loan repayment plan, and after I paid the minimum each month, it was like I could afford food or I could afford an apartment. I guess that's not much of a choice..."

They got overwhelmed for a second, then steadied themselves with a drink from their cocktail. "Okay, it was still bad. But look at me now. I got the resources I needed to climb out of that place. This is why we need to fight for affordable spaces like the old building, you know?"

"Fred, I totally agree with you. I know tons of people, myself included, who've had to couch-surf at some point or another. If it were up to me, that story alone would convince city council to save the building. But I think Mara's right," Brown said gently. "If we don't have backing to fight The Man, as it were, then The Man is going to take one look at our marches and rallies and petition signatures, say, 'That's cute,' and then demo the building."

In that moment, Lina would have said anything to wipe the dour look off her friend's face. "Doesn't mean we aren't going to try. Right, Freddie?"

"Right," they said, and the table lapsed into a thoughtful silence.

A passel of young couples in bright dresses and seersucker laughed as they breezed by, prompting a light bulb to go off for Lina.

"Mara, you said people with financial and political backing can contest city hall," she mused. "Would that sort of influence extend to... minor internet celebrities?"

"Well, yeah, if we had someone like, say, *Sophie* on board, then we'd be going places." Mara clutched her coffee cup and looked wistfully over the industrial modern rooftop. "Too bad she's too good for us."

Lina sat back, deep in thought. Finally, she said, "If Freddie and I can get Sophie on board, will you consider helping?"

"I mean, sure, but that's a big *if*," Mara said. "She doesn't talk to any of us anymore."

"Yeah, she's been MIA in our group chat for, what, nearly two years?" Brown said.

That was true. Once Sophie had moved to LA with her grandmother's inheritance and made it big as an interior design influencer, all her Jacksonville friends had become personae non gratae.

"Work with me here," Lina growled, as she nudged Brown in the ribs. "I get that it'll be hard to reach out to her, much less convince her to come. Forget all that. Let's say we *can* get through to her, get her on board. Then would you come down to help save the building?"

Mara took a tentative bite of cruller. "It would feel good to help, if I could," she admitted, "especially saving a building that once saved all of us." She looked at Brown and Lina. "And brought some of us together." The enthusiastic Mara from the night before peeked out for a moment. She tipped back her head and said, "*If* you can get Sophie van der Wahl, count me in."

Lina whooped and gave Freddie a high five.

"All right then," Freddie said. "Challenge accepted."

Brown kept markedly silent as their waiter returned with a tray steaming with chicken and waffles, shrimp and grits, corned beef hash, and light, fluffy biscuits. As the plates were passed around, he met Lina's eyes, and she could see he was frowning.

She did her best to enjoy the eggy ooze of her benedict, though her stomach was now churning. When it came to helping Freddie, it seemed Mara wasn't the only one she would have to convince.

CHAPTER
EIGHT
THE SAME DAY

After a self–pep talk in the parking lot of Brown's apartment complex

The challenge she had accepted, Lina thought later that day, after giving Mara a sendoff hug and telling her she'd keep her posted, wasn't so much protesting the rezoning of the building. The challenge was balancing this do-gooder project with her major life decisions.

Lina knew she would feel much happier after the divorce was finalized. But moving ahead with said do-gooder project, with friends who thought she and Brown were together, would necessitate pretending they were still married. If Mara knew they were getting divorced, much less that Lina was the filing partner, last night's conversation at the tiki bar had made it pretty clear how she would react.

However, the hope that Lina had seen on Freddie's face when they talked about saving the building, about giving younger versions of themselves the sorts of opportunities that were dwindling in both their county and their country, made it non-negotiable that she'd, nevertheless, persist.

Which was how she found herself driving to the address Brown's lawyer had listed on his rejoining papers as his current residence. It belonged to a nice apartment block on the South Bank of the river, and she was low-key, begrudgingly proud of Brown for being able to afford this place on his own. She took the elevator up to the twentieth floor and knocked twice on the door to #20C.

After a pause, she heard her husband's familiar footsteps coming to the door. It felt so odd waiting there for him, to see if he would even let her in, and she realized guiltily that he had likely felt this way the evening before when he arrived at what used to be *their* house.

He must have checked through the peephole because she heard a long-suffering sigh before the door swung open. "Lina," he deadpanned. "What a surprise."

"Hey," she said. "I got your forwarding address from the filing papers. Can I come in?"

He closed his eyes and shook his head. "Freaking filing papers." When he opened his eyes, they were full of determination. "No, you may not come in. Anything you need to say to me can go through our attorneys. You've made that much *very* clear. Well, except for putting on one hell of a show for our friends, apparently."

"That's why I came here," she said, trying to sound upbeat and completely not like she was grinding her back molars. "I really want you on board for this! With all the people you know from the bar, you could do so much to help save the building."

"More than Sophie?" he sniped.

Lina balled her fists at her sides. "Please, can I come in? Just for a minute."

"Fine," Brown relented. "If you can't keep your voice down while you're yelling at me, come inside so you won't bug my neighbors."

"Gladly," she ground out, giving in to her frustration,

though she was pleased that her inability to keep a steady volume was working in her favor for once.

She strode past him and cursorily assessed his bachelor pad. The one-bedroom apartment had clearly come furnished, with particle-board couches, tables, and chairs she could only describe as 'Grown-Up Dorm Room chic,' and motel art on the walls. Past the kitchen, though, his balcony featured an impressive view of the river. She hated that he had a great view.

When she turned around, Brown was leaning against the wall of his living room, one strong arm folded over the other. "Well?" he asked. "Did you come over just to snoop? How are you finding the apartment you forced me into renting?"

"Tolerable," she sniffed.

"Funny," he responded. "That's precisely the word they used in the leasing brochure."

Lina couldn't help it. She cracked a smile. Brown was genuinely one of the funniest people she knew, and divorcing him wasn't going to make that any less true. He had a dark, dry wit that often, at one and the same time, made her burst out laughing while feeling like a horrible person for doing so.

Brown's lips curled up in muscle memory too. Then he remembered who was standing in his new living room and scowled.

"Why does our stupid old building mean so much to you anyway?" he demanded. "It's a place where we lived, and yeah, it used to be important to us, but now it isn't. I don't get what the big deal is."

Lina threw her hands in the air. "We went over all that at brunch, Brown, but since you asked so nicely for a recap, it's not about you. It's not about me. It's about people who barely make a living wage, who deserve to live in decent places."

"I don't buy that do-gooder crap for one second. Not from you. It sure sounds like it's about us," he said, coming to sit on his cheap, new couch—Or was it a futon? Oh God, it was—a few feet away from her. "And I'm not agreeing to help until you tell me precisely why. Lina, really, why are you doing this? Why are you setting yourself up to get hurt?"

She looked away from his demanding face, out the window to where a couple of jet skis were tooling down the river. She racked her brain for an argument, any argument, that would persuade Brown to do this one last thing for her. Maybe it was the way his supposition that she would get hurt echoed Jill's that she would fail, but her therapist's proposed explanation leaped back into mind. Lina wasn't sure if she bought it yet, but what the hell? Maybe *it* could buy *her* Brown's agreement.

"Okay, so maybe it *is* about us," she admitted. "Not us now, but us back then. Our time in the building was special. And because of that, I really want it, and the building, to be"—What was the word Jill had used? Ah, yes—"preserved."

Lina flitted her gaze back from the river to her ex, where he sat on the futon. The look on his face had softened into something more receptive, and, feeling motivated by it, she continued.

"Just because we don't care about each other anymore shouldn't negate all the years that we did," she said. "We shouldn't write off the good memories just because things are ending. You're right, helping Freddie out is just a bonus that makes me feel less selfish. But you're also wrong—the building still means a lot to me. It's where I met you, where we fell in love. Brown, it's where we were *happy*. For all these reasons— and yes, the do-gooder crap, as you so beautifully put it—that building should still mean a lot to you too."

She looked down at his face, the furrowed brow, the pursed lips, and tried to remember when they had last had a conversation this deep.

"Okay, I give," Brown said. When her body language indicated excitement, he held up a hand. "Not about the project. I give in by admitting that the building still means a lot to me. I see it every day when I go to work. I see how hard Freddie has worked on it, and I'll admit it makes me mad that the place where we have all those memories is going to be redeveloped and made into some overpriced, antiseptic crap like this one. But I still don't understand why we have to lie to our friends about our marriage to be part of this."

Good, Lina thought to herself. It was a good sign if Brown was starting to muse about how to relate to his friends in the context of this effort, not about coming on board itself. She almost had him.

"Believe me, I know how weird it feels, lying to our friends about this," she said, trying to help him see that they were on the same side. "I feel it too. I just feel like bringing it up now would derail the momentum this campaign needs to get started. We wouldn't be lying to them at all if this hadn't come up over the weekend, but it's too late to change that. Why don't we go along with it for now and, when the campaign is underway, when we find a natural opportunity to tell them, we will?"

Brown planted his palms on his knees and hinged up to standing. "But when is there a natural opportunity to tell someone you're getting divorced? It's not like they make a greeting card for it."

Lina snorted in appreciation. "True. But we'll find our moment." She tilted her head to one side and stepped closer to him, so close that she could smell the clean sharpness of his soap and feel the warmth coming off of his flannel shirt. "Come on, Brown. Find it in your heart to do the right thing. Besides, if you help me with this, I'll give you something you want."

His blue eyes roved over her face, dipping lower for a second before coming back up to meet hers. "Oh yeah? What's that?"

She leaned toward his ear and whispered, "The vinyl collection." She pulled back enough to assess whether the bribe had landed. Judging by the way his cheeks had flushed, it had.

"I saw you ogling it at the house yesterday. Go along with this little white lie until the campaign's over, and Bowie, Bad Brains, Wings? It's all yours."

His eyes searched hers. "All of it?"

She nodded. "All of it."

"Even *Rumours*?"

"Even that."

He seemed like he was about to tip over into agreement, but then his walls were back up. Brown breathed hard out of his nostrils and bit his lip. "God, Leen, what do you want me to say? Sometimes you can be a real pain in my ass, you know that? This is, like, the textbook definition of a harebrained scheme." He looked like he was about to say something he would regret, and Lina wondered if it would wound her ego or break her heart. He waved a dismissive hand instead. "Fine. I'll do it for the record collection. But I'm going to need that added to the divorce agreement in writing. You're not getting a takesie-backsie on this one."

With that incredibly mature sentence pronounced, he forced himself back against the futon's thin padding, and Lina couldn't help thinking of their comfortable, overstuffed chester-field sofa at home.

"Besides," he said, as though to comfort himself, "we'll just be doing community organizing. We won't have to pretend to be super lovey-dovey doing that."

On the elevator ride back down to the parking lot, Lina continued thinking about their sofa at home in Avondale, the one she'd gotten a few hours of sleep on last night.

Just before she'd crept down, she'd turned to Brown and given him a genuine smile. "Hey, I know I gave you a hard time today. But thank you for coming. It's been a big help."

"Isn't she going to know? If you take the couch, I mean," he asked as she got up and headed for the microfleece blanket she'd stacked in an armchair in the corner of the bedroom.

She shook her head. "I've set an alarm to make sure I'm up before she is."

He stood then too. In the semidarkness cast by a streetlight, she could see his hands on his hips. When he said, "Well, thanks for letting me have the bed. I guess you've got it all figured out," it wasn't done with harshness but with sad, solemn —would fatalism be the right word?

"I guess I do," she murmured, slipping the sateen border of the blanket through her fingers. She heard the snick of Brown's belt buckle, the whisper of his work pants slipping from his legs down to the floor, and wondered with an ache when those sounds had become foreign to her. In only the space of a week? That couldn't be right, could it? "Well, good night, Brown."

"Good night, Lina. Sweet dreams."

He'd wished her sweet dreams every night they were together, whether by her side in their big, cozy bed with an embarrassingly juicy kiss before lights out or via text message with about five hundred accompanying emojis on nights he was working late. The wish made her realize, as she settled with her phone and her blanket on the couch, that he wasn't feeling entirely positive emotions about the divorce—much less fully negative emotions toward her. It had kept her tossing and turning that night, along with the crick in her neck, so that her alarm was superfluous.

They were doing the right thing, weren't they? Before he'd moved out, all they'd done was argue—or else sit in sulky silence. They'd tried everything else. This was the only recourse left.

Even so, she thought as she stepped out of the apartment block and took her phone from her bag, their conversation last night made her feel a little less alone in her mixed emotions.

Sophie, hey, Lina typed. *Long time. Are you free to talk? Lina xx*

She crossed her fingers and would've crossed her eyes and toes if she could. Then she tapped the 'Send' button and her message was winging its way across the country, hopefully reaching a late-model iPhone somewhere in Malibu. Whether to her or to Freddie, she dearly hoped Sophie would respond.

For one thing, she stood by what she'd told Brown. They had had so many happy moments in that building that if it were lost to them, demolished to make way for something newer, more perfect, then some irrational part of her felt their memories would be bulldozed and carted off to the landfill along with it.

On the other hand—she worried her lip as she turned out of his complex—she was apprehensive as to what he meant by saying she might get hurt. Who exactly would be doing the hurting, hm? Not him, she hoped; at least not by revealing the truth about their relationship to their friends.

She supposed she'd have to do the thing she had grown worst at and try to trust him. As he had once told her, though under very different circumstances, you could never know someone.

Not all the way.

CHAPTER
NINE
JANUARY 21, 2017

Five years ago

The thing about risotto was that you had to cook it low and slow, a good while longer than your run-of-the-mill Minute Rice —the only other kind twenty-six-year-old Lina had cooked at this point in her life.

Long hours at the firm had forced her to dispatch her habit of making one nice meal per week. Nowadays, she usually made some sort of quick and easy pasta if she was fixing dinner for herself, something she could crank to medium-high and stir until al dente while she scrolled through Facebook. But in addition to being a slow burn, risotto was high maintenance. You had to add the broth, made of chicken stock and white vermouth and tons of butter and all things good, to the long-grained rice, one ladle at a time. This allowed the rice to slowly but surely absorb all the beautiful flavors and to develop its rich and velvety texture.

As such, Lina had rushed home from work to prep, slice, dice, and get everything ready for that night's PDP entrée. It was ambitious, but she aimed to impress. And if she left soon after appetizers had been served in Mara's apartment, she would be serving up piping-hot mushroom risotto to her friends right as they walked through her door.

At least, that was the plan right up until she walked into Freddie's lounge area, where they were hosting cocktail hour. Mara sat on the couch, spreading her arms over its back. Ever since she'd gotten a tattoo of an upside-down triangle—a symbol of the divine feminine, apparently—just inside her right elbow, she'd found every excuse to show it off. On the couch beside her sat a tall, handsome guy with curly, blond hair and a deviously crooked nose. He was all clean lines in a chambray button-down and tight black jeans, and though Lina had seen him a billion times before in The Blind Pig, her heart was yet again skipping a beat.

"Hey, Lina, you remember Brown Mitchell. He works at the bar downstairs," Mara said with a knowing wink, crossing one black-and-white Air Jordan over her knee.

Did Lina remember Brown?! Of course *she remembered him!* She'd only mooned over him from across the bar every Saturday for the last fifteen weekends. (And yes, she'd counted.) At this point, it would be more of a surprise if she *didn't* have the cadence of his voice memorized, the way his lips twitched a moment before he broke into a grin at a customer's joke.

Brown didn't move a muscle, yet somehow his posture on the couch had become deliciously inviting. "Mara, you're being ridiculous," he said. "How could I ever forget Lina Thompson?"

There it was, the lip twitch. Then the megawatt smile.

Oh, God, she was a goner.

"Yes, this is Brown, and he's making me *very* nervous to be hosting cocktails," Freddie admitted as Sophie helped them carry over a tray of coupes filled with something milky green.

Sophie took a glass from the tray and handed the other to Lina. "May I interest you in a Death in the Afternoon?"

"Or my attempt at it at least," Freddie said nervously.

"I'm sure it's great, Freddie," Lina reassured them. They all clinked glasses and took a sip. It wasn't long before Lina was coughing on the licorice fumes of absinthe.

She wasn't the only one.

"Whoa," Mara said, wiping tears from her eyes and setting the high-proof concoction down. "Who died and made you Ernest Hemingway?"

Freddie leveled her with a look, and she held up her hands as Brown kindly said, "It's really not that far off, Fred. Your ratio is tipped a little too evenly between champagne and absinthe, that's all. More champ, less absinthe next time."

"Yeah, next time. I should have known when it came out all Emerald City," Freddie confessed, laughing.

Lina took one more bracing sip from her coupe before setting it down for good. She couldn't have addled wits if she wanted her risotto to be a smash hit, but she needed a little liquid courage around Brown. She could only keep up with his quick wit when she was a bit tipsy and her mind wasn't doing its patented Overthinking Routine—which, of course it was tonight. It had been, ever since Mara hinted that Brown might make a cameo appearance at their January PDP.

She must have been staring straight at him because he waved his hand in front of her face and whistled like he was getting her attention. "Eyes up here, Ms. Thompson." He settled back into the couch with a laugh. She blinked and tried to rejoin the real world by smoothing the hem of her bright red skater dress.

"Well, cocktails are a success. Shall we move on to Apps?" Mara suggested. "Give us some time to soak up the green fairy? I've got just the freshly baked bread and charcuterie board for that."

Lina sat back on her heels, testing her balance. Sturdy as a hundred-year oak—she stood up and got a head rush—though less so when she was fully upright.

"I can only stay at Apps for a little while, guys. I've got the Main Course to cook up and impress you all with!"

"Ooh, tell the risotto bambino I say, '*Ciao!*'" Mara crowed.

Thanks to cocktail hour, the evening was gathering steam. There was a point at every PDP where Lina felt like the switch that controlled all the lights in Downtown Jax flipped on, becoming a spotlight for her and her friends, one they basked in, young and incandescent.

They were spilling out into the hallway, feeling its warmth, when Brown said, close behind Lina, "Hey, don't worry about coming to Mara's. I'll bring you a to-go plate, then come help."

"Sure, come on!" She beckoned their newest dinner guest up the stairs, fully aware of the extra swish she put in her step. "They say something about too many cooks spoiling the broth, but I think those folks are just spoil*sports*, more like. The door will be unlocked, number 305—see you in a sec."

She opened her apartment door, and the golden aroma of the broth on the range welcomed her. She had just set her keys down on the laminate kitchen counter when Brown joined her. He toted a paper plate loaded with warm sourdough, a big hunk of melted brie, and something stinky and blue that Lina was determined to avoid.

"Smells good in here," he said, casting his eyes around her apartment.

"Thanks. The base has been cooking low and slow for about fifteen minutes. Now it's time to add that rice."

"Add that rice!" Brown punctuated, to the tune of "Whip It."

"Hey, I love Devo," she enthused before nibbling on a corner of the bread. She was grateful for his casual banter. From any other guy, it might have come off as meaningless chatter, but something told her Brown could sense her nerves. Instead of taking advantage of them, his easy conversation was trying to tell her, *It's all right. You're safe with me.*

"Same. So underrated," he said. Lina looked up from the rice she was adding to the pan to see him checking out her apartment. "Nice space you've got here. Is it just you?"

"Yep! Just me. Been that way for a *loooong* time now." She stirred the rice vigorously, enjoying the sizzling noise it made in the pan and hoping he, in turn, got her subtext.

"Long time, huh?" His voice sounded a little closer now. Its innuendo made her shiver. "You've never seemed too lonely at the bar."

She shrugged, turning to the cheese plate. "That's mostly because I've got you to talk to. I mean—and the other bartenders. And the occasional Tinder date. Most of those are duds, by the way."

Brown leaned against the counter directly beside her. "I hear you. It's the same way for me. I'd much rather have someone I can talk to."

Her heart was sizzling now too. She wished she had some broth to ladle over it, like she was doing to the rice. She made sure the stovetop was on medium-low heat and gave the pot a quick stir before turning around and biting the bullet.

"I hope you mean me when you say that," she said.

He looked her up and down like he was seeing her for the first time. "You know, come to think of it, I do. Huh. Lina Thompson knows me even better than I know myself."

She fortified herself with a bite of brie, which melted on her fingers and felt like heaven on her tongue. This was her moment. She was being adventurous with the risotto, and she'd be adventurous with her crush. She wiped her fingers on a kitchen towel before smoothing her hands across his shoulders, playing with the buttons of his chambray shirt.

"I suppose I do." She quirked her lips to one side and made full eye contact with his baby blues. "I love that we're on the same page, Brown. You may not know this, but I've liked you for a while now."

His eyes danced. "I knew."

"You knew?!" She flashed back to all those moony Saturdays, but still couldn't help asking, "And you let me dangle all the same?"

His hands were on her hips and moving lower, into swooning territory. "It was fun to watch you squirm a little."

"I'll show you squirm—" She paused as they heard a roar of laughter from Mara's apartment a couple of doors down. "I should really watch the risotto. They'll be texting us to see if it's ready before long." She turned in his embrace and stirred another ladle of broth into the rice.

"Don't worry about them." She could feel Brown's smirk on the shell of her ear. "I had a feeling we were on the same page, as you said, so I gave Mara a tenner and told her to keep the others distracted." He traced his rough fingers down the inside of her elbow, past it, until they reached her own fingertips. He gently took the ladle from her, replaced it in the broth, and took her hand, palm to palm, shooting sparks deep into her abdomen. "We've got time."

He turned her around and moved even closer, if that were possible, before cupping the base of her neck with his other warm hand and kissing her low and slow.

Low and slow. Low and slow...

Something else was meant to be done low and slow tonight, she thought absentmindedly as Brown hitched her thigh up against him, if only her lust-addled brain could remember what it was. She checked that the knob was at the right heat—yep, medium-high—and led Brown around the corner to her bedroom.

.

"Luckily, the fire was contained to one room of one apartment. Number 305."

An hour later, the gang, all the bar's patrons, and the few

other folks who lived in the building were camped grumpily, frostily out on the January sidewalk. They had been for the past forty-five minutes. At some point in their canoodling, Lina and Brown had been rudely interrupted by the shriek of a fire alarm and had dashed out into the night, laughing giddily and pulling on clothes after Lina had switched off the offending stove. Neither of them—and no one else in the PDP crew—had had the foresight to bring jackets or coats with them when they rushed out of the building. Thankfully, Jacksonville Fire and Rescue kept a few itchy, gray woolen shock blankets large enough to drape over a baby elephant in their truck.

That was who was standing in front of them. Lina had been privately relieved that her cheeks were the only thing ablaze, but when the firefighter mentioned her apartment number, three pairs of eyes swiveled in her direction. Brown, cheekily and a bit embarrassed himself, stared straight ahead.

As if this wasn't enough, the firefighter continued. "We identified the source of the fire, which was this." She held up with two hands what looked like a chimney sweep's crockery. What had once been Lina's pride and joy—a Mediterranean-blue melamine and ceramic Dutch oven—was now covered in ash. A melted metal whisk sprouted out of the middle of it, held in place by a claggy, grainy residue.

"Oh no, your bambino!" Mara said, unable to keep her laughter in.

At this point, it was clear even to the firefighter that the girl with the mussed, dark bedhead had something to do with the brick of risotto she held in her hands.

"I—I'm *so* sorry," Lina confessed. "I got, um, distracted and totally lost track of time."

The firefighter strolled over and stopped directly in front of her, staring into her eyes without saying a word.

Finally, she said loud enough for them all to hear, "You are very lucky that the smoke detectors in that unit were functional.

I wouldn't have put it past you to have gotten 'distracted' and forgotten to replace the batteries. Cooking is not a good time to get distracted, people. If you're ever using an open burner, stay on top of it. Especially in an old building like this."

"Yeah, Lina, gosh," Brown said. When she glared at him, he winked winsomely.

"I won't be telling JSO to press charges *this time*," the fire-fighter said. She surveyed the crowd once more. Then her radio squawked, and she bade them all a good night before clambering back onto the truck and zooming off to her next call.

The show was over, so the patrons went back into the bar to finish their drinks, leaving the five friends standing out on the sidewalk.

"So... pizza?" Freddie said, breaking the silence.

It was impossible for Lina not to laugh. She felt someone giggling beside her and turned to Brown, pretending to punch him in the stomach like she was actually mad at him instead of high on life. To his credit, he did a good job of pretend-reacting to being punched.

"'Yeah, Lina, gosh'? That's all you can say when you're as much to blame as I am?" She stood back and looked him up and down, taking in the way he hadn't properly lined up his shirt's buttons on the rush out the door. "You think you know somebody."

"Oh, you can never know anybody all the way," he countered. "But it was totally worth it."

"Worth it?" Mara quipped. "What were you two doing?"

Sophie tetched. "We all know exactly what they were doing. Can we go inside? It's freezing out here."

The others quickly agreed and headed back into the building, already discussing whether to order takeout for the entrée or skip it and head straight for dessert and a nightcap.

Brown took Lina's hand again. When she turned to him this time, she dropped all pretense. She hoped her eyes said exactly what she wanted them to: that she was vulnerable, that she was open, that she was all his if he wanted her to be.

"Hey," he opened. "Fire scares aside, are you okay? I really enjoyed... *distracting* you tonight. Want to do it again sometime? But, you know, with dinner and a movie first?"

"Absolutely I do. You know where to find me. Just follow the smell of scorched risotto." She pulled him in for a kiss.

"I think," he said against her lips, "you're going to be very good for me."

CHAPTER
TEN
SEPTEMBER 20, 2022

Three weeks ago—twenty-five minutes and five dollars after arriving at the airport

"We don't have to keep doing this, you know," Brown said.

Then he tipped back in his rocking chair in a way that made Lina's blood boil. She wasn't sure *why* it made her blood boil. Maybe because his flip-flops slapped the tile floor of the arrivals lobby whenever he rocked forward. Maybe because it was ridiculous for the arrivals lobby to have a fleet of rocking chairs in the first place. Or maybe because, on the way here, Brown had sung along, off-key, to every instance of Steely Dan, Hall & Oates, and Fleetwood Mac the classic rock station had to offer, to the point that she had forked over the hourly fee for the airport parking garage—only for him to be annoying outside the close quarters of his SUV too.

She grabbed the arm of the chair and put a halt to his movement.

"I can't focus on what you're saying when you're rocking back and forth like that," she snarled. "*What* are you saying?"

"The charade, pretending to still be together," he said. "We don't have to do it. Sophie's already on her way here. She's not going to fly back at the drop of a hat just because we tell her the truth."

Lina had been surprised when Freddie texted her that Sophie was in. They went on to intimate that Lina and Brown's love story had been the big hook for their big ask—*And she wants you and Brownie to pick her up!*

Lina had flooded the chat with heart emojis as Freddie sent over Sophie's arrival time and flight number; she had kept her frustration that her and Brown's lie would now be under greater scrutiny to herself. What was that old line from *The Godfather*? "I try to get out, but they pull me back in"? For perhaps the first and last time in her life, Lina identified on a molecular level with Michael Corleone.

And what about such a small-potatoes project had made Sophie board the flight from LAX? Surely not their love story? It seemed suspicious if Lina thought too hard about it, so she focused instead on the fact that their campaign now had Sophie's clout, backing, and celebrity connections. This was great news. Sophie and her 500,000 Insta followers were, in short, too big to fail.

In light of all this, Lina had posted about protesting the hearing on her own social media, with its own much less impressive following, though the posts got a decent number of shares and likes. Mara, now convinced by Sophie's participation, was driving back down for the zoning committee meeting that evening. Thankfully, she'd be staying in a bed and breakfast on the river this time. It would give her space to work from home when they weren't doing things for the campaign, she said, before also admitting that Lina and Brown's soft guest room mattress gave her the worst back pain. Lina had teased her about getting old before they hung up, conveniently omitting her own lingering neck crick from her night on the couch.

She nervously checked the tunnel that connected the

airport's main hall to the terminals past security, then zeroed back in on Brown. "Why are you going on about this now? Why are you suddenly Mr. Truth Guy?"

Brown sighed as though it were obvious. "You're clearly very upset to be spending any amount of time with me, and to be honest, that, in turn, is making me pretty upset. Couldn't we just come clean?" he asked. "Like, we're not even staying together for the kids. We don't *have* any kids. We're lying about staying together for our friends, who are full-grown adults. They'll understand, or if they don't, they'll get there eventually, and in the meantime, they'll still support this cause. The building is bigger than you and me. I mean, literally, but also—"

"Hold that thought," Lina said. "Here comes Sophie."

By this point, Sophie had exited security. In her wake trailed a weary-looking airport employee Lina hoped was being tipped enough to lug a rolling cart laden with half a dozen matching Louis Vuitton suitcases.

Sophie herself was carrying nothing, so she was able to fling her long, sculpted arms wide, smacking a larger man in a bucket hat and a TSA agent in the process. When they realized they'd been struck by a tall, white-blonde model-slash-goddess, neither person seemed to mind.

"You guys! I'm here!" she declared in a clear soprano to Lina, Brown, and the rest of Jacksonville International Airport.

"You're here!" Lina cheered, as she accepted Sophie's hug. Though she was more elbows and angles than Mara, Sophie smelled unbelievably good; like artisanal rose water and bespoke honeysuckle, if those were even things. Lina relinquished Sophie so she could greet Brown.

"And you have so many bags! Welcome home," Brown added with a grateful smile for the airport employee, who had unceremoniously dropped all six bags on the floor. He tipped the man a ten-spot to say thanks on Sophie's behalf.

"The beauty of gate-checking," Sophie said with knowing

green eyes. "Well, I don't know if I'd call this place home anymore, but I'm glad to be here and help you out. Now, let me look at you." She held Lina and Brown at arm's length and studied them with a dazzling smile on her face. "How are you guys?! It does my heart so good to see my little Bellini still so very much in love. To be completely honest, if it wasn't for you two and how important the old building is to your love story, I *literally* would not be here to do this. But what are favors for, if not to give to old friends?"

Brown was about to rebut her when a couple of travelers, a man and a woman, halted near them.

"Oh my God," the woman squeaked. "Are you Sophie van der Wahl?"

Sophie bit her lips together and nodded enthusiastically. "I am!"

The woman nearly sank to the floor before oh-my-God-ing again. "I check your Insta feed, like, *every* day. No! Every hour! At least every time I take a break at work." She was staring at Sophie and Sophie alone with an intensity that was either admirable or terrifying. "I have learned so much about luxury home design from you. Your guest interview on the Goop podcast about doing a little bit of spring cleaning every day? Life. Changing."

The man nodded. "It's true. Heck, she bought half your home goods line the day it came out." He looked haunted as he added, "She would do literally anything Sophie tells her to."

"Like even sign a petition to save a building?" Brown asked sarcastically.

"A petition? Yeah, sure." The woman turned, fully serious, to Sophie. "Is the link in your bio or...?"

"See?" Lina muttered to Brown as Sophie and her fan took a selfie. "She's got the clout we need to get the word out. That lemminglike following is *alllll* ours."

Brown still seemed doubtful, so Lina really put the screws to him.

"Look, mister." She prodded his chest. "A deal's a deal. Keep playing along with this or you can kiss the record collection goodbye."

He stared down at her finger until she sheepishly retracted it. "My record collection," he said. "Right."

After her fans moseyed into TSA Pre-Check, Sophie zoomed back over to her friends. "God, sorry, guys," she whispered. "My public can be a bit much sometimes."

"No idea why," Brown snarked.

Lina shot him a look, one that advised him to say *hasta la vista* to Fleetwood Mac on vinyl, which he seemed to understand.

He cleared his throat and gently put his hands—his left one now sporting his wedding band—on Lina's shoulders. "Well, Soph, whatever your reasoning, we're glad you made it." He nodded to her luggage. "Can I give you a hand?"

Sophie rolled her eyes in gratitude. "Oh my God, thank you. Chivalry isn't dead!" She foisted her carry-on and oversize purse into Brown's arms, swiped open her phone, and soon had its camera pointing in their faces.

"Say hello to the world, Bellini!" She hopped around to walk in front of the so-called couple. "I'm going to get a little B-roll, so act natural."

Lina looked at Brown, shrugged, and did her best to smile kindly when he leaned over and kissed her forehead. Surely that would sell this love story her friends kept begging them for, she thought, but then Sophie looked up from her screen with a frown.

"Don't smile so big, Lina," she cooed. "The camera adds ten wrinkles."

· · ·

"Bellini," Brown snorted a while later, from behind a stack of suitcases. He and Lina were riding a creaking elevator down to the airport's garage level. "I'd forgotten our celebrity couple name."

"Can't wait to forget it again," Lina said to the brown-and-white monogram in front of Brown's eyes.

Sophie's flight had been delayed, so the plan was to head straight to the city council hearing. Taking none of their hints that she should come with them into the garage, Sophie waited, scrolling through her phone at the curb, as Brown and Lina pulled his dilapidated Chevy Blazer around to pick her up.

"Bucket seats," she said as she clambered in. "Charming."

"Glad to see you haven't changed, Soph," Brown mumbled.

Lina hated the feeling of suddenly seeing things through another person's judgmental eyes, the very phenomenon she was experiencing as they squeezed themselves, Sophie, and her flotilla of suitcases into Brown's vintage SUV. She hadn't noticed before Sophie said something, but the vehicle had a distinct undercurrent of stinky work boots and old seat leather that had baked in the Florida sun. Brown must have noticed, too, because he tried as subtly as possible to flick life into the evergreen air freshener hanging from his rearview mirror. When that didn't work, he cracked a window.

"Isn't this the car they caught O.J. in?" Sophie ribbed him. "Why do you even drive this thing, Brown?"

"It's still running, and it gets me from A to B," he said in his defense. "Why would I need anything else?"

Sophie pivoted to her next nitpick. "And no bottled water for the guests, I see. Hm. Nice touch."

"Sorry about that," Brown simpered. "Oh! You know what? I think there might be one rolling around under the seats. Leen, could you reach under there and grab it?"

She winced at his bare-knuckled comeback, but with a stagy shake of her head, Sophie muttered, "I've been in better Ubers."

Brown grinned wickedly. "One star?"

"Totally," Sophie laughed, and Lina was surprised when Brown's low chuckle joined hers. She had forgotten how these two used to badger each other back and forth, like siblings, but it seemed they remembered and had picked up right where they left off two years ago.

Sophie slipped out of her sandals and propped her dark red toenails on the dash. "But honestly, thanks for picking me up. It's been ages since I've driven on these ridiculous roads, and I doubt Jacksonville's rental car center has the caliber of vehicle I'm used to."

Lina suppressed the urge to roll her eyes at that last comment. Hopefully, the gentrified Sophie could still relate to their anti-gentrification campaign.

By now, Brown had merged onto the highway. Sophie wasn't wrong, at least not about the roads. Depending on traffic, the airport was a fifteen- to thirty-minute straight shot to downtown. Of course, that was a huge 'depending.' The highways in North Florida were continuously, notoriously under construction. The frequency of crashes and the magnitude of rush hour traffic were no spectator's sport.

"Anyway, thanks for hitting the ground running," Lina said, trying to move past her shock at her ex and her old friend's repartee.

"No sweat, babe," Sophie said. "I figure you guys can drop me off at my hotel after the meeting. It's out at the beach, but I got a heck of a deal since I'm a promotional partner with their parent company."

"Out at the beach?" Brown asked, for once dropping his joshing tone to hint at the extra hour that would tack onto his commute that evening, but Lina cleared her throat.

"I'm sure it'll be no sweat," she echoed Sophie's phrasing.

"Sure. *Babe*," Brown said, with a sarcasm only Lina grasped.

"So, what's the plan at this subcommittee thing?" Sophie

asked, scrolling through a trendy-looking app as she did. "What's our angle?"

"We're meeting Freddie and Mara outside and heading in together," Lina said. "We'll go in, hear the developer's plans for our old building, and then they'll ask if anyone dissents. That'll be us. We'll air our grievances, show city council why this rezoning is wrong, and motion for a referendum vote on low-income housing in Jax."

"Sounds straightforward."

"I think so," Lina agreed. "Mara doesn't, though. She's been all, 'Big issues like this don't get solved in one meeting.'"

"Ugh, typical Mara," Sophie said. "Doesn't she know we have a bona fide lawyer in our midst?"

Lina kept mum on the fact that she practiced a very different kind of law than housing rights and real estate legislation. Instead, she looked out the window to admire the city skyline.

Heading southbound on 95, one of the city's seven bridges gave drivers their first view of downtown Jacksonville. It never failed to make Lina's heart race when she was coming home from a trip, and in that afternoon's sunlight, the view was particularly gorgeous. This city wasn't perfect, Lina thought, but it was trying to get better. She and her friends were going to help.

"Ugh. This city gets dumpier every time I'm back," Sophie muttered.

Lina focused on the golden-hour light forming a halo around Brown's head, his strong jawline clenched as he focused on driving, and kept her mouth shut.

CHAPTER
ELEVEN

One 'agree to disagree' conversation about Jacksonville's dumpiness later

The highway views merged onto Union Street, and soon Brown was navigating downtown's one-way interchanges. He found a parking spot a mere two blocks from city hall, and they hoofed it over.

Mara and Freddie stood on the low, stone steps waiting for them. Mara had covered up her tattoos with a bell-sleeved, olive blouse and gray capris. Freddie stunned in a floral and black velvet blazer, bolo tie, and tuxedo pants. Brown's flip-flops were all the more obnoxious by comparison.

"Unbelievable," Lina huffed at him, as Sophie barreled past to embrace Freddie.

"I'm so sorry this is happening to you," she murmured as she smooshed against their shoulder.

"Why are you sorry?" they said, cupping her head with their hand. "It's not your fault."

She squeezed them one more time, then turned to Mara, who already had her arms outstretched.

"So glad you could come," she said. "I have a little background in local politics, but the world runs on social clout these days. It's incredible to have your know-how on our side."

Sophie accepted her embrace. "Well," she joked, "one does one's best." More seriously, she added, "I'm glad I could be here too. When Freddie called, I moved my schedule around right away. I couldn't stand by and watch this happen—not to the place where we all met." When she pulled back, she puffed out her cheeks. "Oh my gosh, two whole years! I can't believe I've been gone that long. How is everybody? I try to follow along in the group chat, but things are just so busy, you know?"

"We're all good." Brown looked down at his feet, then up at the group. "Am I underdressed? Lina thinks I'm underdressed."

Freddie paused to assess his appearance. "You're not, um, *over*-dressed," they offered.

Lina sighed.

"I'm sure it'll be fine," Mara reassured Brown. "Shall we go in?"

"Let's!" Sophie said.

Mara turned toward the entrance to city hall. "Okay, so. The trick to these subcommittee meetings is to listen carefully to—"

But Sophie shook her head. "Mara, this is small-town politics. You just said so yourself. The bush leagues. I wouldn't worry too much about it. We'll be fine—just like Brown's flip-flops!"

Mara froze in place, her finger cocked up into the air. It seemed her plans for a quiet and orderly civic effort, supplemented by social media clout, were rapidly being steamrolled in favor of Sophie's operational philosophy. Whatever that might be.

Lina gripped Mara's finger and wiggled it gently as she and Brown walked into the building. "Don't worry, Mar. We've got this!" She leaned in closer. "Remember, you're the one who demanded she be here."

Ahead of them, Sophie went live on Instagram, and as they queued for the metal detector, she said into her front-facing camera, "All right, kiddos and kiddettes. Time to make hers-story."

"Ma'am, no live recordings without a press pass," a beleaguered security guard said. He waved for her to put her phone down and step through the machine.

"Oh my God," Mara muttered under her breath.

Lina suppressed a chuckle.

Despite the corny line and Sophie's general extra-ness, she was riding the tide of her enthusiasm. Here was a daughter of Jacksonville who'd gone away, made a name for herself, and, despite all her quirks, had come back to help others less fortunate than she was. With Sophie, they had hundreds of thousands of likes and shares and retweets; they had a global community on their side; they could not go wrong.

Scratch that. Yes, they could.

Turns out that Tuesday evening zoning committee meetings for buildings no one has ever heard of are historically poorly attended. There were maybe two other people there to express opinions against the building's redevelopment, thanks to Lina's social media posts. (Sophie's seemed to have reached a primarily West Coast audience, which was great for online petitions but horrible for in-person participation.) When these protesters realized the rally they'd been promised was nonexistent, they gave their condolences and left.

"I—I figured there'd be more of an uproar," Lina said to Mara, as they filed into the wood-paneled council chamber. They had their pick of seats in the audience gallery, which faced a dais holding six of the fourteen city council members.

"Me too. There were so many comments on your posts," Brown added.

Apart from them, there were two other gentlemen in the room, seated at a table near the front, with a microphone in its center. One was middle-aged, with a full shock of white hair, and the other was younger, fresh-faced, likely in his twenties. He had 'I'm running for Congress in five short years, and I approve this message' stamped all over his silver-spooned, cleft-chinned face.

The gang was startled to find that the older gentleman, who was wearing a Polo with a pastel tennis sweater tied around his neck, waved at Sophie. She waved back.

"Who is that?" Freddie hissed. "And, by the way, 1980 called. It wants its fugly fashion trend back."

Mara snickered.

"Freddie, meet your buyer," Sophie replied. "That's Bob Nickerson, commercial real estate developer."

When Mr. Nickerson didn't stop staring at them, Freddie waved back, which seemed to spook him into turning around. "And how do you know dear Robert?"

Sophie said dismissively, "Oh, you know, all the home redesigns I do... His third wife is from out my way. We travel in the same circles."

Before Lina could follow this line of questioning, the meeting was gaveled into order by a severe-looking woman on the dais.

"I hereby declare this session of the zoning subcommittee in order," she stated. "This evening, we are hearing presentations for, and any that may be against, the rezoning of parcel 505B."

Mr. Nickerson turned on his microphone and spoke into it. "I highly doubt there will be any against," he said in a plummy voice.

The council tittered politely at his joke.

"Mr. Nickerson," said the head councilwoman, "the floor is yours."

"Thank you, Madame Chairwoman," he replied. "I've flown here from Manhattan specifically for this meeting, so I appreciate your and the council's attention"—he turned briefly to the back—"and that of my friends with us here tonight. I—"

"Objection!" Freddie interrupted.

The word had burst from their lips, seeming to surprise them in the process given the way they covered their mouth. But they couldn't stuff it back in; it was echoing off the vaulted ceiling and up to the dais.

"Um, Fred. That's totally not how this works," Mara whispered.

"I beg your pardon?" Mr. Nickerson said into his microphone.

Instead of demurring and waiting for the public comment section, which Mara and Lina were frantically trying to convince them was a very real part of the plan, Freddie doubled down. "I said I object," they iterated as they stood.

"Oh no," Lina groaned into her hand.

"What's happening?" Brown said. "Isn't this what we're here to do?"

"Yes, but they're speaking out of turn," she explained.

Mara nodded. "They basically just took the meeting hostage."

"Guys, don't worry," Sophie winked. "Freddie and I have watched *Legally Blonde* literally dozens of times. They've got this."

Freddie was riding the momentum of their momentously bad decision. They strode to the front, where a podium stood, negating any protests that were coming their way from the dais or from their friends.

Lina winced. "Oh, I can't watch." She covered her eyes and buried her head against Brown's shoulder. Despite the increasingly downward spiral of the situation, the familiar smell of his fabric softener comforted her.

She could hear Freddie clear their throat and begin.

"Hello, my name's Freddie Morales, pronouns he/they, and I'm the current owner of the property proposed for rezoning. I'm an ordinary citizen, so I don't really know how any of this works. Sorry if I'm going out of turn or whatever."

Not a bad start, she thought. She peeked out from between her fingers to watch them have their say.

"Anyway," Freddie continued, "my friends and I are here because we are extremely concerned with the state of affordable housing in this city. While I have tried to keep my units affordable, prices are rising all around us. This year, I had no choice but to sell my building to Mr. Nickerson here, who becomes its owner on November 1. In four months of negotiation, redeveloping the building into luxury condos was never brought up once. I accepted what I now realize is a considerably lowball offer, essentially in the dark.

"Personally that stings, but the issue is bigger than me. We have tons of luxury condos going in downtown, a neighborhood that five years ago Mr. Nickerson wouldn't have touched with a ten-foot pole. Now? Now it's gentrifying. That's all well and good for those who can afford it, but what about those who can't? Where do they go when the condos come in? Where do *we* go?" They drummed their knuckles on the podium. "Your constituents are not okay with this. In fact, they are aggrieved" —they awkwardly took in the empty, cavernous space—"even if they couldn't be bothered to show up tonight. I hereby request that you table your vote and move the rezoning of this property to a citizen referendum, to be added to the ballot this November." They ended by muttering a soft 'thank you' before rejoining their friends, eyes wide with embarrassment.

"Great job," Brown murmured, prompting a shaky smile from Freddie.

To his credit, Bob Nickerson adapted quickly to the turn this meeting had taken. "Mr. Morales," he said into his microphone. "Is it all right if I call you 'mister'?"

Freddie shrugged as though to say they didn't love it, but sure, fine.

"Mr. Morales, I'm sorry to hear that our business conversation left you, as you say, 'in the dark' on my true intentions. When you spend as much time in real estate investment as I do, you sometimes forget that what may be obvious to you may not be to the person on the other side of the table. You forget the human interests of the transaction."

He smoothed his pompadour and turned back to the council. "Please rest assured that I have not forgotten the human interests of this project. My firm plans to redevelop the current property into a set of classic sixes. There are plans for more handicap-accessible facilities, a hydroponic rooftop garden—"

"I knew it," Lina groused.

"—and a bee sanctuary that will connect this new building to the property next door. This is all being done so not just young, single people, but actual two-income families can live and grow in your downtown community. Thank you."

At the end of his remarks, the head of the committee conferred with her co-members. Lina found herself holding her breath.

When they turned around, the chairwoman's microphone squeaked with feedback. "Thank you, Messieurs Nickerson and Morales," she said once it leveled out, "for bringing your concerns to our subcommittee. Mr. Morales, though we are sympathetic to your points, we would like to highlight that there are, indeed, several important nonprofits in town already doing work on affordable housing. Moreover, we are of the mind to approve the parcel for rezoning, given all the business it will bring downtown."

Freddie deflated, as did Lina, though she gripped their hand in solidarity.

"However," the chairwoman continued, "in light of the fact that there is such... *colorful* opposition to this measure, I hereby propose that instead of taking an in-committee vote on the rezoning of this parcel tonight, we take it before the full city council in two weeks' time. All for?"

Four hands went up.

"All opposed?"

Only two dissented, both with apologetic glances at Mr. Nickerson.

The committee head banged her gavel. "The final vote on rezoning parcel 505B will take place in full city council chambers on the evening of October 11." She peered over her rimless spectacles at Lina, Brown, and their friends. "To our vociferous dissenters, if you want us to reconsider Mr. Nickerson's proposal, we'll need to see at least a thousand petition signatures and much more community support than you've shown tonight. Pretty speeches are one thing; numbers are more important."

"Hydroponic rooftop bee sanctuary. I hate how cool that sounds."

Lina elbowed Brown in the ribs.

"What?" he cried. "It *is* cool!"

"That isn't even what it was called." When he didn't break eye contact, Lina conceded. "You're right, though, it does sound cool. Ugh, we're in over our heads."

She leaned against his shoulder and, despite every internal warning not to, found herself inhaling his familiar and comforting musk for the second time that day. God, why did he always smell so good?

They sat on the steps of city hall with their friends, looking south of Weldon Johnson Park toward their old building. The sun had set while the committee was in chambers, and the wrought-iron streetlamps lent something Dickensian to their exhaustion. Lina was frustrated and feeling hopeless. Sure, Freddie hadn't followed protocol, but they had brought up some fantastic points. Even so, the subcommittee had steamrolled them like they didn't matter. To Lina, this offer for them to come back and plead their case in front of the full city council felt like nothing more than a consolation prize.

"I told you!" Mara was saying. "I totally told you. If my nonprofit marched into government buildings like this, expecting pretty words to get things done, I'd be out of a job. This is not how local government works."

"Okay, yes, that's true, I get that now," Freddie griped. "But did you hear the way he said, 'Your community?' Not *ours*. Not *mine*. That's what pisses me off more than anything. He'll come down here, supervise the renovation of the building, then set up a property management firm to run it while he sits on some white, sandy beach, raking in dough." They twisted one of their box braids round their finger. "And somehow all this pissing me off just makes me want to save the building more."

A car whooshed past while the group processed Freddie's determination.

"You're sure, hon?" Lina asked. "It broke my heart to see them deny you like that. Mara's right. We're up against a whole bunch of red tape and people motivated by money, not emotions. You're sure you want to move forward with this?"

Freddie took in the huddled masses of their friends and gave their signature gap-toothed smile. "I am. It got all of us back together, didn't it? Even Sophie."

Lina smiled against Brown's warmth, then pretended it wasn't the weirdest feeling in the world to hook her chin on his shoulder to survey the others. They were all looking around at each other bashfully, as though cautiously optimistic that they hadn't been beaten yet.

"Yep, even me," Sophie said. She stood and stretched to her full and impressive five-eleven. "Listen, it's late, and I flew a one-stop route from Malibu this morning. Let's all regroup after work tomorrow. Lina, Brown, can you guys host?"

"Um, sure," they said at the same time, without really thinking about it. Lina suppressed a miserable groan. If the hopeless look on Brown's face was any indication, then he, too, immediately regretted his decision.

"Great!" Sophie said, oblivious to their inner turmoil. "See you little community advocates tomorrow at five. Now, Brown, how 'bout that ride?"

CHAPTER
TWELVE
SEPTEMBER 21

After a night and a day of feeling kicked while they're down

"At least I got out of driving Miss Sophie," Brown said as he adjusted the brim of his favorite navy blue ballcap. "Chauffeuring her to and from the beaches every day? No, thank you."

He and Lina were back in her driveway half an hour before they and their friends would meet to regroup. After the failure of a hearing, Brown seemed to need further enticement to go along with the plan, so Lina had incentivized her vinyl collection bribe. She'd offered to give him a couple of his favorite records now as a good-faith gesture, and he'd sped over to the house in a jiff.

She laid a sympathetic hand on his arm. "That would've been awful. So she got a rental car?"

Brown's eyes moved down to her hand. "Yeah, I guess so. Maybe from someone she's a promotional partner with. 'This community organizing brought to you by Lincoln.'"

Lina chuckled, then licked her lips. She couldn't help but stare at her hand on his arm as well, couldn't help but feel the muscle straining up to meet her beneath the cotton tee.

Brown cleared his throat.

"Sorry," she said, as she snatched it away. "Force of habit."

Her memory snagged on the other night, when she'd hooked her chin on his shoulder; another force of habit, she thought bitterly.

"Listen," she ventured, "this separation is all so new. Even for me. I'm sorry if I forget myself and reach out to touch you. It used to be the most normal part of my day."

"Yeah, no, I get it," Brown said. "Especially when we're in front of our friends for"—he puffed out a breath—"the next two weeks."

Lina wasn't sure how they were going to keep up this charade for the next ten days, much less two weeks, but she kept this doubt to herself.

"Yeah, well, if you want the rest of that vinyl collection..." she teased him to try to lift the mood.

When she peeked up into his eyes, it looked like something behind them cracked open into vulnerability. She wished she could fix her gaze on his, assure him that these two weeks would fly by, that they wouldn't have to do more than light PDA, since most of their time would be given over to phone banking and canvassing, but it was too much for her to crack herself open too.

She was saved from further emotional confusion by the hum of tires on her brick driveway. Mara and Freddie waved enthusiastically through the windshield of Mara's Prius, and Brown worked quickly to tuck *Hunky Dory* and *Armchair Apocrypha* into the back of his SUV before glomming his bony hip into Lina's waist as tightly as he could. If Jack and Rose had shared space like this on the dang floating door in *Titanic*, Lina thought, there would've been no third-act tragedy.

"What are you doing here so early?" she asked Mara from within Brown's stranglehold.

"We were both done with work ahead of schedule, so I gave

Freddie a ride." Mara looked casual in a paisley caftan and slides. "What are you guys doing out in the driveway?"

"Oh!" Lina racked her brain for an excuse. "Brown just got home from running out to get food for our meeting. Right, babe? You know, pizza, cheesy bread... brain food."

"Brain food, right!" Brown said.

Freddie cocked their head to one side and surveyed the SUV's trunk. "I'm seeing a lot of junk back here, but unless some old lotto cards, an empty energy drink can, or this mysterious vacuum attachment"—they held up a long, thin nozzle with a brush on the end—"are brain food, I'd say Brown had a brain fart and forgot the pizza. Wait, is that a suitcase?"

"My gym bag," Brown blurted, as Lina broke out of his hug and excitedly snatched back the vacuum attachment.

"I've been looking everywhere for this thing!" she cheered. When Mara and Freddie looked perplexed, she said, "It's really good for reaching into the dryer's lint trap, getting it all nice and clean again for, um..."

"Optimal dryer efficiency," Brown supplied.

"Y'all are so weird," Freddie said.

"Made for each other," Mara surmised.

"Anyway," Brown cut them off. "You're right, I spaced on the pizza. Better grab it before Sophie gets here."

He clambered back into the driver's seat and, after he turned the ignition to get the air going, hand-cranked the window down. Lina was close enough to smell his afternoon musk, though she was determined not to be bowled over into emotion by it this time. She was very aware of their friends watching them from the front porch, though, so she leaned in to give Brown a peck on the cheek, her lips grazing against his five o'clock shadow.

When she stood up, she was still close enough that she could hear his next words, uttered beneath the rumble of the engine.

"Still worth lying to these chuckleheads?" he asked, blue eyes flitting to Mara and Freddie.

"Well—" Lina began, heart hammering, hoping she didn't have to convince him here and now, in this very public venue.

"I'm joking. See you in a bit."

He winked at her from beneath the brim of his baseball cap before backing out and driving away.

"It's not over till we say it's over," Sophie declared. "They're trying to beat us down. They're trying to tell us our needs don't matter as much as theirs do. That affordable housing doesn't matter as much as a condo developer's bottom line. Well, to that, I say, 'Tough.' They could have picked any old building to tear down to get even richer, but the one they picked is ours."

She stood on Lina's back deck, a weather-treated, cedar-planked affair that led from the open-plan kitchen down to the swimming pool Brown had insisted they put in. A living situation, Lina had just underlined for her friends, that would never have been possible if living in the old building hadn't let her pay down her student loan debt with a quickness.

Sophie was speechifying not to her friends, but into the smartphone she had stabilized on a tripod. She had tried to coerce Mara into holding it while Freddie steadied a reflector disc just out of camera range, but they had both said there was no way in hell.

Instead, they were off to one side at a wrought-iron patio table, trying to eat pizza as quietly as they could without snarking.

"Yes, my babes," Sophie continued into the camera with Valley Girl vigor. "My friends and I lived in that old building. We met each other there before Jacksonville became an attractive market for real estate investors. Before rent flew sky-high, we were able to be young twentysomethings, still broke, but with an opportunity to better our circumstances"—here she spread an arm to indicate Lina's backyard—"and to do so while affording a roof over our heads. Without help from a parent or benefactor. Without a white-collar job. But what about the people who don't have Mommy and Daddy's money? What about people who can't get office employment? Ronald Reagan once said..."

Freddie gagged on their slice of pizza.

"...that the money of America's wealthiest would trickle down to the rest of us. That as they got wealthier, they would help us all out. That it was the economy, stupid."

"Did he actually say that?" Brown muttered to Lina. "I thought that was Bush I."

"I think she's half right, but she's on a roll," she replied.

Sophie jabbed a finger into the air. "And I say that's *bull*."

Freddie relaxed a bit.

"We need more buildings like the one I spent my twenties in. We need more affordable housing in all areas of our country. Yes, I see you hitting that like button! I see you agreeing with me! In the words of Jimmy McMillan, the rent is too damn high. In the words of Sophie van der Wahl, when the going gets tough, the tough get mobilized."

If Lina had been paying attention, she would have seen Sophie's gaze soften as it looked off camera, toward her friends.

"Before I go," she said, "I want to introduce you to two people near and dear to my heart."

But Lina barely heard this. She'd just nabbed a cheesy breadstick, still tantalizingly warm from the pizzeria's woodfire ovens, and dipped it into their signature marinara sauce, a medley of tomato, sauteed onion, and roasted garlic so rich you could eat it as gazpacho. She did, though, clock Brown beside her as he muttered, "Oh no."

"Mm?" she questioned, taking a bite of the breadstick.

"Bellini time," he hissed just before a French-manicured

claw gripped Lina's underarm. Another snagged Brown's forearm and, with preternatural strength Lina assumed Sophie had procured at an LA Pilates studio or else in some underground training bunker owned by Elon Musk, hauled them into the camera's range.

"These," Sophie said grandly, "are my friends Brown Mitchell and Lina Thompson-Mitchell or, as I like to call them, *Bellini*. Say hi, Bellini!"

Brown gave a faint, deer-in-headlights wave. Lina did the same and noticed the cheesy bread was still in her hand. Unsure what to do with it while she and Brown were bookending Sophie's live shot, she chucked the offending carbohydrate off her deck.

Sophie continued. "They met and fell in love in the building, and during the pandemic, they actually got married in our courtyard! I'll share some exclusive snaps of that to my Stories later."

Out of the corner of her eye, Lina saw a stream of red hearts go up Sophie's phone screen, a clear indication that her viewers were vibing with this romance angle.

Sophie put a soft hand on each of their shoulders. "So listen, even if you don't care about affordable housing—which, like, rude—but if you don't, surely you care about love, right? If you won't do this for the common good, do it for my friends. Do it for Bellini." She turned and gave first Lina on her left, then Brown on her right, a thousand-kilowatt grin.

Lina made the mistake of catching Brown's eye and almost choked on the now sodden glob of cheesy bread when she realized he was telepathically screaming, *Kill me now.*

"Okay, babies!" Sophie said. "Watch this space, follow the hashtags #SaveTheBuilding and #Bellini4Life, and check out the links in my bio to learn more." She blew her viewers a kiss before hitting a button to end the livestream.

Lina finally gulped down her bite of breadstick and

followed Sophie back to her patio table. "So, what was that?" she asked.

A quick look at Freddie and Mara's faces confirmed she wasn't the only one thinking it.

"What was what? Oh, your impromptu introduction to the limelight?" Sophie scoffed good-naturedly. "You're the crown jewel of our social media campaign—I thought that was obvious. Every social cause needs a great story to get people to take action, and Brown, Lina, you are *it*. Be prepared for a whole lot more camera time while Old Soph's in town. Thank goodness you have this gorgeous patio for video content, though." She wrinkled her nose. "No offense, but your house is, like, a total wreck. Do you even have a cleaning service?"

Brown gave Lina a proud look, and Lina did her best to scowl and act like she resented the comment.

"Anyway," Sophie said, "let's cut the rainbows and unicorns and get this done."

"Rainbows and unicorns? That was all *you* just now," Mara said.

Freddie agreed. "I figured you were going to quote RBG and ask me to donate fifteen dollars to your reelection campaign."

Sophie waved them off. "Okay, sure, but we obviously need to regroup. We went into that city council meeting yesterday and got completely trampled."

"Yeah," Mara said, "because we were unprepared. We need to get organized before the October 11 hearing."

Sophie shook her head. "We got trampled because no one turned out. And why did no one turn out? Because no one *cares* about city council meetings. No one attends them even if they act all upset on Facebook. You know why? *Because they're boring.* We need to meet these people where they live: online." She selected a slice of Veggie Lovers' pizza, as well as a napkin to blot the grease.

Mara looked doubtful. "How? Webinars or something? Thousands of eyeballs on your posts aren't going to help us with city council."

"Ugh, webinars," Freddie said. "Those never work on me."

"Well, right," Sophie said, avoiding Mara's glower. "Because webinars are the worst. No, we need to organize a protest that people can be part of on their couches, in the time it takes to double-tap a post. Something fun, a no-brainer, with minimal clicks or effort between them and signing our petition."

"That sounds great!" Lina enthused, trying to pivot away from Sophie and Mara's bickering. "What did you have in mind?"

Sophie beamed at her. "So glad you asked, Lina. I was thinking we could do a 'Live-In.'" She flashed her hands in the air to emphasize her point. "Basically, we go back to the old building, document our stay to show everyone what a wonderful, safe, stable space we had for a reasonable rent."

"We'd be squatting in the building for signatures and donations?" Mara asked, even as Lina's heart dropped into her stomach. "And posting about it on social media?"

"Yep!" Sophie said. She wiped off her hands to scroll through her phone again. "And Bellini? Look how many likes and comments we got when I brought you onto my livestream just now. Like I said, you're clearly the media darlings of our campaign."

Lina had some sort of positive-looking line graph foisted into her face, but all she could see through her sense of queasy apprehension was a haze of bluish-white. Going back to the old building on her own would be fine, but the others expected her to share her old apartment with Brown. Beyond that, Sophie clearly expected them to parade their ersatz relationship in front of Jacksonville, not to mention a half million Sophie van der Wahl fans—and those women were scary, charismatic MLM types. A quick look at Brown's lips, which had gone so thin and pale as to retract on themselves, showed he felt largely the same way: in way over his head.

To her horror, as Lina tuned back into the conversation, she heard Freddie crowing about how great an idea this was. Even Mara seemed up for trying it. "I guess I can still work on my version of the campaign while we're doing the Live-In," she mused. "It's not like we'll be constantly in front of Sophie's iPhone for that."

God, Lina hoped not, though her chances of avoiding that fate seemed slimmer by the minute.

Then the meeting really got away from her. Like a deranged reality television host, Sophie revealed that she had already put in some calls to her regular sponsors, and they had set up next-day delivery to make the old building their home again. There would be gorgeous furniture, some from Sophie's own line; a week's worth of meals from a grocery subscription service; and some sort of fancy-schmancy cooling mattresses.

Sophie brushed her white-blonde hair out of her face. "They're made from used avocado husks sourced by unwed teenage mothers in the Amazon or something."

"Wow, that's awesome," Brown choked out eventually. "But while this might be easy for your followers, it sounds like an awful lot of effort and staging and production cost for us. Maybe these sponsors could contribute some money to saving the building instead? Or give Freddie a grant to support their tenants in a new building?"

Sophie rolled her eyes. "That's not how it works, Brown. Nowadays, it's all about the production value. Also, we need to return the furniture gently used at worst, so don't eat on the couches or beds—and spread a napkin down before you use the tables."

Lina knew she could at least abide by that rule. All that was coming her way had kind of spoiled her appetite.

As the others excitedly plowed through the remaining pizza

slices, they wrapped up their meeting and planned to move into the building that Friday after work. Soon after, they said their goodbyes, leaving Lina feeling like she'd survived a whirlwind of positivity and can-do spirit.

Brown was the last to leave.

"Good thing I'm already packed," he mumbled, looking up from under his eyebrows to gauge her reaction.

"Yeah," Lina said faintly, studying the brick paving under her ballet flats. "Good thing."

What had she wanted to say to him about two weeks of light PDA? That fooling their friends for this cause would be a breeze? Forget it. Moving back into the building, things were about to get a lot more personal and a lot more complicated. She groaned and shoved her fists into her eye sockets to stave off the coming anxiety headache.

"Well, Leen," Brown summed up, lounging against the hood of his Blazer, "we've just yes-and-ed ourselves into a whole world of trouble."

CHAPTER
THIRTEEN
SEPTEMBER 23

One ill-fated regrouping session later

When Lina told Jill about the Live-In, she could have sworn Jill almost dropped her professional veil of mystery and detachment to tell her, like they were friends sitting at a bar, that she was making a certifiably Terrible Decision™.

"Lina," she said, then opened and closed her mouth twice before saying, "are you certain you know what you're doing?"

"Yes. I'm squatting in my old apartment as part of a protest demonstration for affordable housing. I just happen to be moving back into it with my husband, whom I'm in the process of divorcing."

"A situation which your friends know nothing about."

"Yes, there's also that." Lina shifted in her seat. "It's kind of the most important part because we wouldn't be in this situation if it weren't for those friends. At least one of them, a very important one, wouldn't be helping us out if it weren't for our relationship."

"And moving back into your old apartment with your husband, whom you're in the process of divorcing, means..."

"Right. Sharing a bed," Lina pronounced.

"Sharing a bed," echoed Jill.

"Yep! Sharing a bed." Lina nodded.

There was a pause.

"We're both adults. Surely we can share a bed without any drama." She considered this before adding, "Unless there's a couch. In which case that's a good backup option."

Jill leveled her with a stare, as though she expected Lina to back down from her self-assurance or else come to some related breakthrough, one that Jill herself could see clearly but didn't want to come out and give to Lina that easily. When Lina didn't reach that point, Jill sighed and stared at her hands folded in her lap. "Okay, great. Just wanted to make sure we were clear on all that."

Now, it was Friday afternoon. A very tired Lina stood next to an annoyingly chipper Brown, tapping one toe in the lobby, waiting for Otis to trundle down to the ground floor. They'd just waved hello to Mara, already in her old street-facing apartment, as she popped her head out the window to loop a banner over the balcony. The banner listed a website for more information and their ad hoc Venmo account for any donations. Apparently, a local reporter had already asked if they could interview the group early next week.

"If we're gonna be famous," Brown had jokingly posited, as they unlocked the front door, "when do we get a personal assistant to carry our luggage?" He gestured to the two weeks' worth of clothes he had crammed into his gym bag. "I feel like a pack mule."

"No kidding." Lina readjusted the strap of her duffel and leaned forward to jab the elevator call button again. Otis seemed to have gotten even slower in his senescence, and she wondered if it wouldn't be more efficient to throw in a leg workout and take the stairs. "This elevator is ancient," she grumbled. "Did we really used to deal with this all the time?"

"I guess we were used to it? I dunno," Brown said with a shrug. "Hey, remember the time I got all the groceries into the apartment in one trip?"

Lina snorted. "Yeah, I do. You practically cut into your palms with all those plastic bag handles."

Brown puffed out his chest. "Worth it."

"You're such a dork."

She rolled her eyes at him affectionately, and he smiled back.

Otis finally made it down to the ground floor and opened his doors with a weary chirp. One short ride up—"Thanks, Otis," Lina said out of habit—and one long, weighted walk down the echoing hall of the third floor, she was unlocking the door to their old apartment.

Before the building was converted into individual units in the early 2000s, it had lived many lives. It was originally constructed to be doctors' and dentists' offices in the 1920s, and each one-bedroom studio featured some of the original fixtures. Each entryway segued into a kitchen, which led into a multi-purpose living space before going behind a frosted-glass wall to a semi-private bedroom. The loop was completed by a full bathroom with a sink, toilet, shower stall, and two doors, the only actual closed-off room in the whole place.

Lina cut through to the bedroom to place her bag on her preferred side of the bed, next to the window. Meanwhile, Brown flopped his gym bag down in the apartment entryway with a heavy thunk.

"What do you have in there, bricks?" she wondered aloud. Then, after catching a breath, she added, "I have *got* to get back to the gym."

Brown followed her into the bedroom and starfished his arms and legs out across the mattress, flopping facedown like the human equivalent of his gym bag.

Lina primly moved her suitcase to an uninhabited corner of the room. "Do you need me to bring your stuff in here or what?"

"Or what. I'll get it in a minute," he said, turning over onto his back to look at her. "It just feels nice to get off my feet."

"Right." She examined her nails. "And get them all over the clean sheets."

He sat up, suddenly on the alert. "What's that supposed to mean?"

Lina checked herself. He was right. They were getting divorced. There was no longer a need for this passive-aggressive song and dance, the adult equivalent of holding your breath like a stubborn child until your partner acknowledges you. Toward the end, they'd both been tiptoeing around each other, afraid one would say the magic words to send them hurtling into their latest fight about nothing in particular.

Well, Lina was tired of walking on eggshells. She figured Brown was too. In a weird way, getting divorced had its fringe benefits. With no further consequences to her words, she could finally say what she meant to the man in front of her.

"It's been a long week," she admitted. "I meant that I feel like I have to do a lot of things by myself, like you assume I'll do them for you. I've felt that way for a while now." She glanced up at the brick wall. "Probably since we moved out of this place."

Brown returned to his back and stared up at the ceiling. "Won't you by definition have to do a lot of things for yourself once you're single again?" he asked.

"That's different," she said.

When she looked up at him, Brown was doing an impressive job of imitating Jill. It was like there was something they could see in the corner of the room, a signpost blaring something obvious in neon, and they were waiting for her to acknowledge its presence.

To which Lina had to say, *What neon?*

"I was there for you tons of times," Brown said, so softly Lina almost didn't hear him.

Her initial reaction was to bluster. "Yeah? Name one."

He sat up on his elbow, creasing the front of his T-shirt. "When it counted, I was. That time you blew out a tire, I got up after two hours of sleep to wait for the tow truck with you. When you got COVID last year, I brought you homemade soup *and* your favorite takeout food. Right to the guest room door. I did it wearing, like, two sets of gloves, a mask, and goggles, but I was there."

She wanted to hold on to her righteous anger; to say, *Anyone can make an effort in a time of crisis. That's expected if you want to meet the basic minimum of being a decent partner. I wanted effort every day; I didn't want to have to remember so hard that you cared.*

But she didn't. After all, he had presented two very good exhibits to the proverbial jury. He had been there for her when it mattered. She shouldn't discount that. He was being there for her now, regarding their friends. If only he'd stop drawing out the divorce proceedings, everything would be square.

"Yeah," she said faintly, returning to the memory of his COVID nursing skills. "I think we joked about you double-wrapping your gloves."

"Double-bagging," he corrected her.

"Oh my God! That's right." She allowed herself to laugh.

"Can never be too careful..." he said with a genuinely flirtatious smile.

Lina tapped his hand in friendly affection, then did a loop around the apartment to check out what Sophie's moving crews had done earlier in the day. Waiting in line for lunch, Lina had watched a behind-the-scenes video Sophie had posted to TikTok, in which men in coveralls moved in fast-forward to assemble furniture and roll out bespoke area rugs. Seeing it in person was something else.

When Lina and Brown had lived here, the place had obviously been furnished with their own tastes and twentysomething levels of affordability: an IKEA bed Brown complained was too low to the floor; a rickety kitchen table with a missing leaf that Lina had bought off Craigslist; an overstuffed couch from a sidewalk sale.

Now, there was a seeming doppelganger effect that Sophie couldn't have planned, unless she recalled their apartment from memory. The layout of the furniture was precisely the same as when they'd lived there, but instead of the low and narrow IKEA bed, there was a plush, queen-size canopy frame with deep purple sheets and two walnut end tables. There was a six-person oak trestle set against the self-same east-facing windows the rickety old four-top had. Instead of the overstuffed couch, a sleek, emerald sofa perched over an oriental rug, playing host to a tasteful mix of throw pillows in mustard and teal.

She checked the tag, still attached to the couch by a plastic fastener. "Are we allowed to cut this off, or does it negate the whole 'Don't mess up our loaners' thing?" She turned the tag over to see Sophie's smile beaming up at her. Above her confident pose, a cursive script read *Van Der Wahl Home Goods.* "Oh wow. Brown, we must be getting a first look at some of Sophie's new stuff."

"I'll say," his voice bounced over to her from the kitchen. When he opened the cabinets, they were full of matching Le Creuset enamelware. "Look, Leen!" he joked. "We're squattin' in style!"

As Lina surveyed Sophie's interior decoration, she couldn't help picturing not only the furniture she'd once had, but the *us* she'd once had. She remembered her first kiss with Brown on her ratty old couch; the excitement she'd felt to make way for his things in the cramped closet; the feeling of warmth and care when she'd opened her eyes one morning to find a to-go coffee and a love note waiting for her on the nightstand.

She looked up at the current Brown, who was making a racket in the kitchen, pulling all the pots and pans out for no apparent reason any sane person could offer. She rolled her eyes. It was good to speak candidly with him as she'd done just now; at the very least, it was diluting the tension in the air from thick pea soup to something less easy to cut with a knife, even if it did feel like too little too late.

In another way, it felt like Lina was entertaining ghosts, superimposed on a beautiful, interior-designed backdrop. Her own furniture had discovered (or rediscovered) the curb, and that shiny, happy version of them was gone. Maybe, like Sophie's decoration, it was time for a change in her life. Lina was glad she wouldn't have to be disappointed by old mainstays for much longer.

Her phone hummed against the kitchen counter where she had left it. She picked it up to see a joyful message from Freddie in the group chat: *Soph!! These meal kits are fire! Dinner and drinks in my apartment in an hour xx*

This was followed by Mara's: *Aw! Just like old times!*

The feeling of being haunted continued, first at dinner with memories; then later, perhaps much more literally. As it turned out, Freddie had mixed and matched Sophie's boutique meal kits. They'd taken a packet of rice from one; lean beef, onions, tomatoes, and peppers from another; and a can of black beans for the use of their broth from a third, before transmogrifying it into what they really wanted to cook. The result smelled drool-worthy as Lina and Brown walked in.

"Oh, yes!" Brown cheered as he greeted Freddie. "I have dreams about your *ropa vieja*."

"Thanks, doll." Freddie placed the steaming stew pot in the center of the table. "I can't believe I had to get in such a tight spot before y'all would attend another dinner party!" They smiled tenderly at their friends gathered around the table. "JK kidding. Thanks again for all your support, guys. You especially, Soph. I know they're forecasting a hurricane in a few days, so you staying here rather than heading back to Cali is so kind."

"It's usually no worse than the earthquakes we have out west," Sophie demurred. "Just a lot wetter."

As they ate, Lina surveyed Freddie's apartment, which looked the same as she'd always known it. A discarded bicycle tire suspended above the kitchen counter held a set of burnished copper pots and pans. Eclectic souvenirs from friends' trips around the world and their own visits with family down in Miami dotted the living room. Since they still lived in the building—or did for the time being—Freddie had insisted Sophie shouldn't borrow furniture for their space. She had agreed, but had given them a case of wine from a subscription website that, judging from the impressive labels, cost about as much as the furniture loan would have.

Everyone had asked for seconds and was scraping up the stewed meat with the last bits of fluffy rice when they heard a voice outside.

"Hey! Hey, you!"

Brown dismissed the group's tilted heads and raised eyebrows. "Probably they had to cut somebody off at The Blind Pig."

"Hey, you, in the apartment building!"

This time, it was clear that the voice was coming through some sort of amplification system—and that it was talking to them. The five friends crowded around Freddie's open windows and looked down onto the sidewalk.

Nickerson's baby-faced staffer was standing on the street with a megaphone. Though the crowds around him were dressed casually for a night out, he was wearing a stuffy suit and tie. The bargoers were reasonably giving him weird looks.

When he saw them sticking their heads out the windows, he

lifted the megaphone back to his lips. "This is a message for Freddie Morales and their friends: Cease and desist with your demonstration. Robert J. Nickerson is fine with pleading his case before the whole of city council on October 11, but this Live-In is beyond the pale. So, again, cease and desist."

"Hey, careful where you point that thing, man!" a passerby sniped as the megaphone nearly hit his head.

Brown folded his arms. "How did Nickerson even find out about the Live-In?" he called down. "We haven't given any interviews."

The staffer held up his phone in his free hand. "I have Instagram, too, you know. My boss is watching your every move."

Lina rolled her eyes. "I'm surprised your mommy and daddy even let you have an unsupervised account."

"I'm thirty-seven," he mumbled, still talking through the megaphone.

She cupped her hand around her ear. "What?"

"I said I'm thirty-seven! I'm hardly a kid."

Another bar crawler saw the banner hanging out of Mara's window. They stopped behind the staffer, fiddled with their phone a second, and then called up, "Just Venmo'ed you five bucks. Keep up the good work! We need more affordable housing in this city."

"Thank you, kind stranger!" Sophie cheered.

Lina settled her steely gaze on Nickerson's staffer. "Look, sir, I'm a lawyer. Does your boss have an official cease-and-desist order?"

"No," the man said sheepishly.

"All right then. I don't have to tell you we have Jacksonville on our side. Run along home and inform your boss that my friend here still legally owns this building until November 1. Until then, it's their private property, and without any official order, you can't tell us what to do. If that's all..."

She turned back into the apartment without finishing her thought.

"Hey—" the staffer called, but they'd already shut the window.

"The nerve of that jerk!" Mara said. "Sending his unpaid intern out to do his dirty work for him."

"You think he's unpaid? And thirty-seven?" Brown snorted. "Poor guy."

"What did he mean about Nickerson watching our every move?" Freddie asked. "What is he, intimidated? By us?"

"Don't listen to him," Sophie advised. "He seems like an incompetent, and he clearly only came out here to try to spook us." Her green eyes widened. "But speaking of spooky, Mara, tell them what you found before dinner!"

Mara gladly accepted the change of subject. "Oh, right! So check out what I found in my old apartment." She reached into her tote bag under the table and retrieved a long, black cardboard box. "Verrrry creeeeeeeeepy, no?" she asked in a bad Bela Lugosi imitation as she held a Ouija board aloft.

"Uh, yeah. Emphasis on the word 'no'!" Freddie crossed themselves. "You found that Ouija board in your abandoned apartment? And y'all want to play with it?! This is how scary movies start, people!"

"Oh, come on," Mara said. "Wasn't this building originally doctors' and dentists' offices? Back in the day when there were still *operating theaters*? If any building is haunted, it's bound to be this one."

Brown gave her a skeptical look. "You just happened to find a brand-new, shiny box... containing a speaking board brought to us by the fine people at Hasbro... in your old apartment? Hm. Interesting."

Mara feigned shock, though she made a great show of peeling the price tag off the bottom of the box. "Brown, my oldest, dearest guy friend! I can't believe you'd accuse me of such a thing. Even if I planted it—and I'm not saying I did!—I figured we could bust out the board after dinner and see what messages we get from the beyond. Come on... you know you want to. Wouldn't be a dinner party without a 'Wild Card.'"

She waved the box at Freddie, who batted it away.

"Not in my apartment," they said. "Take your demon bait elsewhere."

"Okay," Mara said, "in the basement then? But, guys, let's do it! I can't be the only one who's ever felt a presence here."

"There were those three knocks on my ceiling once or twice," Sophie mused.

"And that time Lina thought she saw an old woman standing at the foot of her bed," Mara added.

Freddie shuddered.

"Oh, right," Lina said, "in the same room where I'm sleeping tonight. Thanks so much for the reminder, Mar."

"Don't worry." Brown threw a casual arm around her shoulders. "I'll be right there, getting haunted with you."

Lina was suddenly very aware of his touch, the way she had been when Sophie yoked them up for a quick couples' photoshoot in the courtyard before dinner. She forced herself to clamber back aboard her train of thought.

"This time, you mean," she said. "Besides, Mara, that's not even what happened. I didn't see an old woman. I was drifting off to sleep when I heard a voice just above my—"

"Oh wait, start over!" Sophie blurted. She snagged her phone off the dinner table and held it up, motioning for Lina to continue.

"Okay, um. It had been a long day at work, and I was finally getting ready for bed," she recalled. "I had just lain down, face in the pillow, and was drifting off to sleep, when I heard a voice, just beside and above my ear, saying, 'Heeey, Lina.'"

Freddie yelped and covered their mouth with their sleeve.

"I kept my eyes squinted tight. I was convinced if I opened

them, I'd see something scary. I reached out for Brown's side of the bed, but it was cold. Empty. I didn't want to be alone with... whatever it was. As I started to wake up, I realized he was at work, so I rushed down to the bar to find him."

"In her fall jammies, I might add," Brown said. He looked directly into Sophie's camera. "No, like, it literally said, 'It's Fall, Y'all' across the shirt."

"Sexy," Mara deadpanned.

Lina made a faux-menacing motion across her neck as Brown picked up the thread of the story.

"I remember I was making a cocktail one minute, and the next she had practically vaulted over the bar and was Scooby Doo-ing her way into my arms." He gently squeezed Lina's shoulder. "I think you yelled, 'Zoinks!' at one point."

"She did not!" Sophie laughed.

Lina smiled faintly as their banter continued, giving her the cover to turn and look inward. She was remembering another night that Brown's side of the bed was cold—the more recent night that she'd decided it was better to call time of death than to try to resuscitate their relationship. She turned to Brown now, in the warmth and safety of Freddie's apartment. He returned her assessing squint with a questioning one, his feigned innocence making her feel like she was the only party responsible for all the hurt they'd caused one another. She was starting to wonder if some things were better left un-resurrected.

"Lina? Hello?"

She looked up to realize she'd been instinctively leaning into Brown's touch. Across the table, Sophie peered curiously at her from over the top of her phone.

"Where'd you go just then?" Brown asked. "You looked miles away."

"Maybe she's been possessed." Mara laughed.

"Why?" Freddie demanded. "Why would you say something stupid like that?"

Mara put on a scratchy voice: "There is no Lina; only Zuul!"

Lina roused herself, gently shrugging off Brown's arm under the excuse of a full-body yawn. "I don't know what happened! Zoned out, I guess. Probably just the comfort of being around my favorite people after a good meal. If we want to do the Ouija séance or whatever, we should get this show on the road while I'm still awake." She cut her eyes at their host. "Though if Freddie is spooked already, we don't have to make them more uncomfortable."

"I'm mostly just being the drama for the sake of being the drama." They winked at her. "We can get up to no good if y'all want to. Besides," they added, as they all began gathering dishes to take to the sink, "if this building might be demoed and redeveloped soon, we should probably let any of its remaining tenants say their piece."

CHAPTER
FOURTEEN

One "Hail Mary" from Freddie after that

Freddie had done their best to make the basement more than a dank, creepy storage space for their final tenants. Before the Live-In, there had been a few old armchairs and a borrowing library in a communal corner, but there wasn't much more Freddie could do without adding in expensive upgrades, like flooring and insulation.

Now that Sophie's crew had had their way with it, though, the basement was about as cozy as an industrial space could be. The rough, stone stairs had a thin carpet running down their center, before joining an area rug at the bottom. The rug was held down by an eclectic but matching assortment of armchairs and floor pouffes. In place of the decrepit old storage lockers that had run around the border of the basement, Sophie had put in smart, sleek cabinets.

Freddie halted at the top of the stairs, looking down as the lights flickered on. "Sophie, what is all this?" they asked. "How did you know we'd be coming down here?"

"I didn't," she said, "but you know, I thought I could show

my followers what this building would look like if it had a communal space for its residents." She grinned brightly. "Now I get to show it to them in real time!"

"Come on, guys," Mara urged from behind them. She rattled the Ouija board in its box. "We're burning daylight here!"

Freddie got busy lighting candles in a circle around them, including, Lina noticed, at least one prayer candle to the Virgin Mary and one orisha candle.

"Covering all my bases," they explained.

Brown pushed the chairs back, then settled in cross-legged next to Lina on the rug. He patted her hand. "Hey."

"Hey, back," she said.

Their favorite influencer was chronicling the whole event for her Insta Stories. Lina knew because she'd been tagged in about five of them, each with a call to action to Sophie's followers to donate to their cause or sign the petition.

"Okay, so how does it work?" Sophie asked, after she finally pocketed her phone. "What do we do?"

"Join the circle," Mara said, "and we'll get started."

Things started innocently enough, with the overhead lights out, candles flickering, five hands clustered on the planchet, and your standard slumber party Ouija questions: *Is anyone here? Did you live here in a previous life? How many of you are there?*

It got a little creepier as they thought up more specific questions.

"Oh! I have one," Sophie said. She asked the board, "Have you ever encountered any of the living gathered here tonight?"

There was a collective intake of breath as the planchet tracked its way toward the upper left corner of the board. *Yes.*

In the quiet flicker of the candles, the air felt cool on the nape of Lina's neck, almost as though someone was breathing there.

"Who moved it? Which one of you jerks moved it?" Freddie said, a note of panic rising in their voice.

Sophie didn't answer but instead asked the ghost, "Which one of us have you seen?"

The planchet rasped along the board: *L-I-N-A*.

Mara's eyes were wide as saucers. "Oh my God," she muttered, looking across the circle at her friend.

"It's just a dumb game," Lina tried to tell herself. She welcomed the feeling of Brown's free hand rubbing her back. "One of you is totally moving it."

But no one fessed up.

"Do you have anything to say to Lina?" Sophie asked the spirit with a wicked, candlelit grin.

The planchet began to move, and Lina squeezed her eyes shut. She couldn't look, didn't want to see what either her friends or some spirit from the beyond was trying to tell her.

And that's when things got spooky.

Right outside the high basement window, the white noise of the air conditioner shut out. It must have created a natural vacuum. All Lina knew in that moment was that the light beyond her eyelids went from the warm, reddish-brown glow of the candles to complete and utter blackness.

There was the sound of at least three people screaming at once.

"Oh my god, ohmygod, *ohmygod*!" Lina freaked out, wrenching her hand away from the board and pulling herself into a curled-up, cross-legged position, like a drowned spider. "Sophie, why the hell did you have to ask something like that?!"

"Don't say 'hell' right now!" Freddie warned with a groan. Their voice sounded far away, and Lina guessed through her fright that they had sprinted halfway up the basement stairs.

"I was just playing around..." Sophie muttered.

In the face of her fear, Lina only needed comfort and safety.

Her irrational mind knew Brown was sitting to her right, and she clung with all her might to his strong, warm shirtsleeve. It smelled like him and like the bar and like familiar, safe, bright places. She focused on that and tried to block out the highlight reel her mind was making of all the scariest moments in horror movies she'd ever seen.

Brown could feel her shivering and pulled her closer. "It's okay," he muttered with a gently amused laugh. "Just the wind. Freddie's going to get the lights on, and we'll be fine."

"You're sure?" she whimpered.

She popped an eye open. In what little light there was, she could see his comforting silhouette.

"I'm sure." He hesitated for a moment. Then, when she didn't seem to be pulling away or saying no, he gently pulled her closer, cupped his hand around her jawline, and kissed her.

There are so many different kisses a couple has in a marriage. The ebullient one on their wedding day. The romantic ones on date nights and in the bedroom. Mostly the quotidian, think-nothing-of-it pecks that say things like, 'Good morning,' 'I'm going to work, bye, I love you,' and 'Welcome home, did you pick up the milk we needed?' The drudgery of those kisses made you forget the spark you'd once possessed.

In that unfinished basement, when his lips met hers, all thought of ghosts, real or imagined, fled her mind. All except the ones she'd felt, standing alone in their old apartment earlier that day—the ghosts of their younger, happier selves. Lina didn't believe in ghosts or in time travel, but there in that darkened basement, she wasn't sure if it was 2018 or 2022. It was like she was kissing the sexiest memory.

She gasped raggedly and pressed herself against his chest. His moan vibrated on her lips, and if it hadn't been for Freddie finding the light switch, who knows where they would have ended up.

When everyone stopped screaming, they gawked across the circle at Lina and Brown. They had stopped kissing, but floored by all that had happened, Lina didn't have the energy to pull out of the embrace. Brown rested his forehead against hers, and something low in her abdomen throbbed.

"Gross," Mara said playfully. "Get a room, you guys."

"Yeah, it's not like you don't have one right upstairs," Sophie added, though she definitely snapped a photo or two that Lina figured she'd be tagged in later. ("Look at these lovebirds! Save the building for them!")

Lina tried to calm her racing libido and stop thinking about how they did, in fact, have a room with a nice, plush bed three floors above their heads.

"So, I'm confused," Brown admitted.

"What?" Lina genuinely hadn't heard him, both because his mouth was full of toothpaste and because she was trying to stand as far away from him as the tiny bathroom allowed.

Brown's touch downstairs had been combustible, explosive. Once she'd cooled down, Lina realized she didn't know what would happen if he slept beside her, or even so much as brushed her again, and she didn't want to muddy the waters of divorce even further. The last time they'd cohabitated, it'd been in a house with three bathrooms. The one off their bedroom even had two sinks. She, for one, really missed that creature comfort.

He swished and spat, then dried his hands. "I'm confused," he said again. "You were acting all nice to me at dinner, but since Mara's woo-woo thing downstairs, you're all weird."

"I'm not being weird," Lina simpered. "Excuse me," she added, trying to butt in toward the sink to dampen her own toothbrush.

"Yes, you are. What's the matter? Ghost get your tongue?" He waggled his eyebrows.

Well, *some*one definitely had.

Shut it, she told her inner monologue.

"I've told you before, and I'll say it again. If you have anything to say to me right now," she told Brown, "you can say it through our lawyers."

"Say it through our— Are you kidding me, going back to that old saw again?!" He took a steadying breath through his nose. "That's a fine thing to say after that kiss. Can't really convey *that* through our lawyers." He had to edge his hips backward because, though he was still flossing, she was taking her contacts out.

"Let's get one thing straight," Lina asserted, "that kiss meant *nothing*. You comforted me in an intense moment. That's all." She called back to their earlier conversation, then made her next words a barb. "You were *there* for me."

He wasn't taking that lying down. "'That kiss meant *nothing*'? 'Comforted me in an intense *moment*'? That is such a lawyer thing to say. Even more than the 'say it through our lawyers' line. Why don't you want to talk to me about this?"

Lina shrugged, eager to evade the question. "All I'm saying is that there's no need for embellishments, like that kiss you pulled earlier. The entire reason for any canoodling is to convince our friends we're together to keep this project moving forward. For Freddie. For people other than ourselves. And yes, I guess in your case, for the stupid vinyl collection. To do that, do we need to canoodle? Sure. Hold hands? Fine. All perfunctory and static. But there don't need to be big, showstopping numbers, you know?" She met his stare in the mirror. "Which means no funny business tonight."

"Might I remind you that this whole thing was your idea?" When he didn't get a rise out of her as she daubed retinoid cream onto her forehead, he launched his own barb. "I bet you liked that kiss a whole lot more than you're letting on right now."

Lina clenched her hands into fists. "I *didn't* like it. You may think I did, but I totally didn't! You have no clue what I do or don't like, which is half of our problem. The kiss was nothing; just like me touching you by accident on Wednesday. Stupid muscle memory reflex getting me into trouble."

She nudged him aside with her hip so that he was completely out of her way. In doing so, she knocked over her toner bottle, dousing them both in foul-smelling witch hazel.

"Oh, great. That's just great!" Lina said, snatching up a towel and blotting at her favorite silk pajama set.

Brown threw up his hands at the one-sink-ness of it all. "How did we ever live like this?"

"I have no idea, Mr. Handsy Man!" she said, looking super attractive with her thick, pasty retinoid treatment halfway massaged in. Between this and the witch hazel there really was no risk of anything handsy happening. "Apparently, there's too much space between us down in the basement and not enough space between us at this sink. You know what? This conversation is over. I'll sleep on the couch tonight."

"Oh, no, you don't. I'll do it. That way you can't be a martyr in the morning," he sneered.

She'd expected more of a fight, not for him to give a tight-lipped nod before marching out of the bathroom.

She made sure to give him a soundtrack full of dramatic huffing and drawers opening and closing louder than necessary to fall asleep to.

When she finally flumped into bed, she could hardly appreciate the way the mattress, according to the trifold brochure the movers had left on one of the end tables, supported her lumbar spine in all the right ways. She couldn't think about anything other than the roller coaster of a night she'd had and why, despite all her drawer slamming, it had left her not feeling angry but tender, raw, and unprotected.

She supposed she shouldn't have been surprised by her

sudden, vicious sadness, she thought as she turned the light out and tried to sleep. Wasn't that the case with hauntings? Once you got over the terror of seeing a ghost, didn't its very being, its deep longing to reach out and touch a present it could never access, make you weep?

CHAPTER
FIFTEEN
SATURDAY, 9:56 A.M.

Feeling(s): Sad. Anxious. Frustrated??

Lina cradled her phone, curled up in bed in her old apartment. She touched her lips, replaying the kiss from the night before with the frequency of a looping TikTok—the soft hem of Brown's shirt bunched in her needy fists. His moan vibrating against her mouth.

She moistened her lips and turned back to her screen.

What if I'm making the wrong—

She growled in her throat and tossed her phone against the other pillow, the one that Brown's head wasn't resting on for very good reasons. Namely, that they were getting divorced.

Jill's trigger journal had betrayed her into, what, some inverted Kubler-Ross grieving process? The self-help books said Lina was supposed to be hitting bargaining and acceptance any day now, not getting more and more confused by her own choice.

She wouldn't add to the trigger journal for a while, she decided. It was hurting more than helping.

She pressed her palms against her eyes and then stretched

her arms out, pushing all thought away. It felt luxurious to focus only on the view outside the apartment's wide windows. Early autumn sunshine dripped out of the sky like molasses onto what was probably her favorite view in all of Jacksonville: the court-yard tree bursting into pink and yellow blooms.

She listened out for Brown in the living room.

Silence.

She sighed in relief. She didn't feel like interacting with him yet. Given their recent track record, the conversation would either be a shouting match or a passive-aggressive smug-off. Either would be too confusing right now, when her heart was feeling this vulnerable.

Hm. Not a bad thought to note. She had reached for her phone to add one last bit of context to her latest journal entry when there was a knock on the front door.

She sat bolt upright. Her leisurely morning was over.

"Brown?" Her voice quavered.

"Mmph?" His answer suggested it was coming from a face smooshed against a pillow.

"There's someone at the—"

"Yoo-hoo! Anybody home?" Freddie said in a high-pitched voice from just outside the apartment. From the sound of it, they were drumming their fingernails against the doorframe.

"—door," Lina said as she hopped out of bed.

Freddie lowered their voice to its normal register. "You know, I do have a master key. I'm doing this silly bit as a common courtesy—mostly to myself, since I don't want to walk in on any early-morning nasties you married types might be getting up to."

"Brown!" Lina hissed.

He mumbled in return.

"Freddie's at the door! And you're sleeping on the couch!"

This was apparently the magic phrase to get the crankshaft in Brown's brain turning.

"I'm up!" he announced in a groggy stage whisper. "I'm up! What do we do? What do *I* do?"

"Act! Natural!" Lina said as she power-walked by, scooting into the kitchen to throw open cabinet doors. "And help me find the mugs!"

"I'm putting the key in the lock..." Freddie called.

Brown hurdled over the couch only to almost run into Lina as she flitted around to the trestle table, two white ceramic mugs in hand. He dashed to the entryway, throwing open the doors to the utility room and bathroom and essentially barricading the front door. "To buy us some time," he explained as he *Risky Business*-ed his way back to the kitchen table.

"Good thinking," Lina said.

"I'm counting to five, and y'all better be decent..." Freddie warned.

Lina wiped her forehead and gripped her mug with both hands. Nothing quite like anxiety sweat first thing in the morning. Then she looked down and a wave of nausea came up to join the sweat.

She whimpered. "We forgot the coffee!"

The knob turned.

Lina may have given up, but for whatever reason, Brown still seemed determined to see their ruse through. "Quick, gimme your mug," he said.

"Good morning, starshine!" Freddie crowed. "The Earth— Whoa, door barricade."

It took a second for them to navigate the triangular maze that three doors opening out on each other constituted. Brown used that time to run each of their mugs under the tap and rush them back to the table.

Which was how Freddie finally waltzed into the kitchen to see Lina, manic and wild-eyed, and Brown, hazy and bare-chested, clutching mostly empty mugs, a giant spill of water on the table in front of them.

"Man, they did not plan the way those doors opened very well," Freddie said. Then after surveying them, they added, "Rough night?"

"Hm?" Lina said, her voice an octave higher than usual.

Brown's foot started jittering next to hers.

She took his hand and the jittering stopped.

"Just wondering if you're finding it hard to function this morning." Freddie nodded toward them. "There's no coffee in your mugs. Maybe there was some water, but looks like that all wound up on the table."

"Sometimes," Brown said, still waking up, so that the excuses department of his brain was not yet open, "we like to... *anticipate* our coffee before we have it."

"Yeah," Lina said, "it's, like, a meditation thing. I heard about it on Sophie's podcast."

They turned their lips down in thought. "Cool, cool, cool," they said. "Good stuff. Good stuff." While Lina and Brown were in barely awake disarray, Freddie looked alive, refreshed, and stylish in a matching lilac athleisure set. They put their arms, in their cozy-looking cropped hoodie sleeves, behind their back and strolled around the apartment.

"Um, so, what's up?" Lina called after them. "To what do we owe this visit?"

"Well," their voice came from the bathroom. "I don't know what's up, but *something* definitely is. And Detective Fred is going to find out. Toothbrushes are dry," they observed, "so no one has brushed yet."

"We've been up for a while," Brown lied. "They may have dried since then."

Lina gave him an encouraging smile: *Quick thinking!*

Freddie strolled out to the kitchen. "And yet the coffee pot is cold and empty. Surely your ritual can't last more than a few minutes?"

Lina tried to put on her most knowing voice. "Who said we

were up drinking coffee?" She hoped her bedhead was mussed enough to support this suggestion.

"Hm." Freddie passed back through the bathroom. This time their voice came from the other side of the frosted-glass wall in the bedroom. "For 'something other than drinking coffee,' these sheets sure don't look that rumpled."

"I—we—" Brown hemmed and hawed before settling on, "I got nothing."

Lina slumped her head into her hands. "You know, you're an excellent cross-examiner, Freddie. Have you ever considered law school?"

"I don't mean to pry," Freddie gloated, as they crossed to Lina and threw an arm around her shoulders. "I came in here to let you know everyone else is already awake and waiting for you in Soph's apartment. But is there trouble in paradise, guys?"

"How did you know that?" Lina asked.

Freddie's jaw dropped open. "I didn't," they said, their voice a mix of sympathy for their friends and pride that they had figured it all out. "I saw a pillow and blanket near the couch and thought I'd take a stab at it. But, there *is* trouble?"

"I'm afraid so," Brown said. "Freddie, we're getting divorced."

Lina forced her eyes to keep looking at Freddie, her lower lip to stop trembling. Here was her worst fear realized and said out loud, and she didn't know what would happen next.

"Div—" Freddie clutched the drawstrings of their hoodie with one hand. "*Divorced?*" they whispered. "Why?"

Lina cleared her throat and prepared to perform the answer she'd given her therapist when Brown cut in.

"Well, I'm sure it was for a lot of reasons for both of us," he said, "but at the end of the day, I wanted to have kids and Lina didn't. I guess we each thought the other would change, so when we didn't..."

"Oh man," Freddie said after a brief silence. "That sucks.

I'm really sorry." The other shoe dropped. "But if y'all are getting divorced, why..." They looked around the apartment. "Why all this?"

"We were doing the lie as a nicety when Mara was here last week," Lina said, "and then you all just kept going along with it, and we felt like we couldn't correct you. Especially not after Sophie got on board. She's kind of made our love story the centerpiece of our campaign."

As Freddie processed this new information, Lina wished she could have five minutes alone with her trigger journal. Jill had told her to look out for any strong emotions about the divorce, and boy, was she feeling about fifty right now.

If Brown thought they were splitting up over the idea of becoming parents, then he had no idea why this was happening. Was she making a huge mistake, then, filing for divorce? Should they be talking more, hashing out that last argument that had scared Brown into running away, instead of calling it quits? The kiss last night, the revelation this morning—the whole concept that she might be making a grievous miscalculation made Lina feel like she was breaking out in hives.

"You're right," Freddie finally said. "Sophie is, like, obsessed with the optics of the fact y'all got married in the courtyard. I think if she knew the truth, not only would her followers stop chipping in money and signing petitions, but she'd probably head out herself."

"So you see the predicament we find ourselves in," Brown said flatly.

"Please, Fred?" Lina asked, pulling herself back into the conversation. "Can you keep our secret?"

Freddie spent a long moment sizing her up, and Lina found it difficult to make eye contact. "Okay," they said after a moment's thought, then swiveled to Brown. "Okay, but what were you doing on the floor?"

Brown combed the hair at the back of his head, which made

it stand up even more. "The couch was too short. I got cramped."

"Dang, Lina, you could've at least let him share the bed." Freddie pronounced their judgment with a perfectly threaded eyebrow. "Take one for the team, girl. Anyway, I wasn't joking. This fight against rezoning is important to me, so I'll keep your dirty little secret. And if you want to keep it, too, maybe work on a little more natural of an interaction? Y'all have been acting all weird lately, different than you usually do. Like, you've been plenty touchy-feely, but it felt"—they waved an arm, searching for the right words—"off. Like *Stepford Wives* or something. Anyway, the others are waiting on us. I'll head over. See you in a sec."

They opened the door, then paused. "Guys? I'm sorry you're dealing with this, but please know I'm not picking sides. I love you both and always will. Plus, I'm glad you're back in the building." They ran their hand along the doorframe. "Even if it's just for now, it feels more like home."

Lina gave them a wholehearted smile as they departed. Freddie still cared about them, still considered them friends, despite their failings. Maybe there was hope on the other side of some finalized paperwork. And yet, as Freddie left, the apartment fell into a different type of silence.

Lina couldn't pinpoint what she was feeling. If she didn't know any better, she would call it sadness and guilt that she'd roped Brown into this civic campaign and then forced him to spend the night on the floor. She might also call it regret and shame that she had communicated her needs so poorly that her husband didn't even know why they were getting divorced. She didn't like not knowing the source of these complex emotions, so she shoved them to the back of the closet and selected her old reliable: anger. It was becoming a welcome and familiar feeling, like putting on a pilled and threadbare favorite sweater right out of the dryer.

She yanked it off its proverbial hanger and put it on.

"I can't believe you didn't wake up on time!" she broke the silence, whirling around to glare at her husband.

Brown had apparently been expecting her opening jab and parried it just as enthusiastically. "At what point did we say I had a wake-up time?"

"We didn't!" She followed him into the bedroom, where he rummaged through his suitcase for a change of clothes. "But *if* you'd woken up on time, *we* wouldn't be in this situation. Every person who knows about us is one more liability."

"*Liability?*" Brown straightened with his head halfway through his actual sweater. "Jeez, Leen. The way you say it, it sounds like you're going to put out a hit on Freddie or something."

She scoffed, then paused their fighting to help Brown find the head hole in all that cozy, maroon wool. He looked grateful for her help, then highly confused by it, and wound up hopscotching away from her to straighten the hem of his shirt. Lina stood at a distance, watching as the now crisply dressed Brown moved her pillows to the foot of the bed to pull the top sheet straight and smooth. His silence and the pout marring his brow made her worry she'd yelled too hard.

Cripes. Her own figurative sweater was unraveling.

"I'm hardly the Mafia," she finally said in response to his comment. "I'm just saying, we could have gotten ahead of this. You could have told the others that I was being lazy, sleeping in, and we wouldn't have had to tell Freddie about us."

"You're just upset we got caught," he said as he fluffed one of the pillows.

"No, I'm not."

Yes, you are, her mind immediately shot back on Brown's behalf. She hated when her brain conspired with him, especially when their conversation with Freddie left her with unseemly reservations, so she reached for the pillowcase closest to her and thwacked him with it.

"Fifty days," she grumbled. She plumped up the pillow, pulled the duvet cover over it, and put a little more power than was necessary into karate-chopping a crease into the blankets. "You once went fifty days straight getting up later than I did but not making up the bed. Sure, you can make up the bed from some mattress firm made out of avocados or recycled cola bottles or whatever, that you didn't even sleep on, but not when we were married and actively living together!"

Brown stood back, crossing his arms and slouching against the coolness of the apartment's exposed brick. "Fifty days?"

Lina was self-assured, righteous. "Yep. I kept count."

"And," he said, trying to find the most respectful way to put his confusion into words, "you don't see anything pathological about that? Or about getting huffy about it now?" He spread his arms in a conciliatory gesture. "I mean, it suggests to me that you're upset about something else."

"I'm not."

The look he leveled at her said, *Lina. Come on. Yes, you are.*

"Look, the divorce isn't about us not having a baby, okay?" she said. "Why would you assume that?"

His arms dropped to his sides. "Well, we had that talk, you said not right now, and then before I knew it, some service processor was handing me a manila envelope. Why *wouldn't* I assume it was about that?"

"Okay," she conceded, "it isn't about that for me, but it didn't help. I never said we couldn't start a family, but we certainly weren't ready to. You have to do a lot of planning before you have a kid, and we could barely decide where we were going to dinner without getting in a fight."

"Who says you have to plan for a kid?" Brown demanded. "We had the house, we have good jobs; at that point, don't you just get started and see what happens? My parents didn't plan for kids, and I turned out fine."

Lina kept her thoughts to herself.

Brown glared at her smug expression. "What I'm saying is I would've adapted to fatherhood like I do all my goals—if you'd just given me the chance. That's what I did when I started bartending, when I've achieved anything in my life. Sure, there's a learning curve, but soon I've got it mastered. You know I'm a big-picture guy. I set my sights on something and figure out how to get there along the way. I mean, that's how I got you."

Lina scoffed. "No, it's not."

He nodded, insistent. "I did too. The night of the first PDP, the first time we met, I fell in love with you. Of course, I couldn't tell you that right away. You would've freaked out. I just had to hope you would fall in love with me too."

His honesty set Lina back on her heels. She had melted for Brown, too, from the minute she laid eyes on him, but she had never assumed he would feel the same way. Instead, she had spent months of careful planning, asking his friends how he felt, laying a conversational groundwork before that one lucky night, the night of the scorched risotto, felt effortless enough to take the leap.

As she tuned back into the bedroom, she noticed Brown looking at her with some concern. "Are you all right?" he asked.

She didn't want to continue down this conversational path. "I'm fine," she lied, shrugging deeper into the warmth of her anger sweater. "We're going to be late."

She grabbed her phone and marched her way down the hall to Sophie's selected unit, #301. If Brown had his head so far up his nether region that he couldn't understand how frustrating it was to see him only now, after it was too late, kissing her in ways that made her feel something, performing a postmortem of their relationship, asking her if everything was all right, then he was beyond her help. And in sore need of a proctologist.

She heard his footsteps behind her.

"Wait," he murmured, keeping his voice down in the echoing hallway. "It isn't because you didn't want a baby? I brought it up one last time, we fought, and then, well, the D-word. Isn't that a classic case of correlation leading to causation?"

Lina squinted back at him, wondering why there was a hint of hope to his tone. "No. Correlation does *not* imply causation. Ever. Especially not in this instance."

"Oh." Brown frowned. "I can never get that one right." He looked up at her. "So, what was it about then?"

Lina huffed. "We'll talk about this later. Tabling it for now." She tossed her hair over her shoulder and smoothed a hand over her features, in a bid to make her racing heart calm down. "Ready?"

Brown exhaled and squared his shoulders. "Ready."

Lina nodded and flung open the door to Sophie's apartment.

Sophie was in her kitchen, accompanied by a very reluctant Mara.

The social media influencer stood in front of one of the apartment's original oak support beams, grinning like a flight attendant and pointing at random spots in the air around her —Lina assumed where text might appear in an edited video later—in time to some pop song that was playing out of her phone.

It was too early to guess what the hell was going on, so Lina strode over to the burbling coffee pot and poured a roast that smelled soothingly of hazelnut into a waiting mug. She sipped, peering over the rim at whatever Sophie was doing.

Brown wasn't far behind her. His eyes bugged as he walked into the apartment and edged toward the coffee bar. "Am I the only one seeing this?" he asked Freddie, who was now sitting on the sofa in the living area.

"Nope, we're all having the same collective drug dream," they said.

Brown snorted. When he turned to Lina, his face held none of the flummoxed frustration it had during their fight in the hall. While that was a relief, the smolder that had replaced it was equal parts intriguing and disconcerting.

"Any coffee left?" he asked her with a sideways smile.

She hooked a thumb at the pot. "Tons. Help yourself."

Smile still in place, he stepped toward her, effectively pinning her between his body and the countertop. His hand was low on her hip, thumb hooked treacherously near her thigh, as he murmured, "Let me reach around you," in her ear.

"Um...?" she asked in a panic.

Lina heard Freddie make a strangled noise from the couch. They typed something frantically on their phone, and then her own phone buzzed.

Brown's smile had compressed into a self-assured smirk. He moved even closer to her, one arm aloft, the other hand still possessively on her hip, then pulled back, now holding a mug.

"Here we are. Thanks, babe."

He hesitated a moment, capturing her eyes with his. Lina's lips parted of their own accord. Somehow, she'd forgotten how to breathe. Between the eye contact and the, well, *actual* contact, the evolved parts of her brain had shut down. If this was a new offensive tactic from Brown, she hated to say it, but it was working. If only he were far less frustrating to be around, they might have had a shot.

Her ex tilted his head mischievously to one side. "Problem?" he asked.

The problem, she thought, *is that I expressly said no embellishments.*

When she snapped her mouth shut and shook her head

wordlessly, he spread his fingers over her flesh and squeezed the outside of her thigh for good measure before moving over to the carafe.

Lina moved her own mug down the counter and picked up her phone. It was suddenly way too hot to think about drinking coffee.

"Don't mind me, guys," Sophie said out of the corner of her smile, throwing a twerking move into her pointing song-and-dance.

"Really hard not to," Lina muttered, eyes firmly fixed on her phone. In reality, she couldn't have been less focused on Sophie. The world had tunnel-visioned down to her body, which was flushed and bothered by Brown's physical contact.

Sure enough, there was a text from Freddie: *Why do I feel like I'm not getting the whole story here?* There was a tea emoji followed by the word *SPILL!* in all caps.

Lina sighed and texted them back. *It's complicated. Find an excuse for us to be alone and I'll tell you?*

Freddie shot back a quick thumbs-up.

Sophie, oblivious to all that was happening on the phones in her apartment, continued explaining herself. "Just batching some content for next week. You know, five steps ahead or five zillion behind."

"Please, can someone change the subject?" Lina croaked.

Mara had beelined it away from Sophie once filming was done. "Well, speaking of five steps ahead, I've looked at the National Hurricane Center's storm tracker." She wiggled her own phone in the air. "We're still good staying put. Shouldn't be more than a Cat 1 when it passes through Jacksonville tomorrow."

While the rest of America couldn't fathom responding to a hurricane with anything other than clearing supermarket shelves of bread and distilled water, the state that was home to Florida Man had other feelings. Hurricanes are ranked by weather scientists in categories from 1 to 5, with lower numbers being less intense. If a storm was a Cat 2 or lower when it made landfall, some Floridians were just as likely to set up a beer pong table or inject a watermelon with vodka as they were to make for higher ground.

Lina and Brown's old building was sturdy—constructed of brick, at the top of a hill, with below-ground power lines. They'd never been flooded once when they lived there, and given how long the lines at gas stations would be, not to mention the parking lot 95 North was about to become, it was a lot safer to stay put.

As Lina's hot flash ended, she looked around at her friends' faces. The faint smiles suggested they were reliving similar memories: how Memorial Park's bronze statue had swum in the Saint John's River, how the basement parking garage in the Wells Fargo Building was flooded four blocks down the hill, but they had been dry as a bone, building up their 'sit at home and do nothing' muscles for the pandemic four years later.

Brown had mercifully ended his flirting offensive and was rattling around in the cabinets. "Hey, Soph. What's for breakfast?" he asked.

"Oh, you shouldn't eat breakfast," she said brightly. "Gwyneth says it's the leading killer of Americans today."

"Yeah, totally more than guns or heart disease or cancer," Mara said.

Without a shred of irony, Sophie nodded once up, once down.

Mara groaned and massaged her temples.

Lina's phone vibrated with a new message from Freddie: *On it.*

"Hey, I have an idea," they piped up, pocketing their phone. "I'll go out and grab something. Who's up for bagels from Chamblin's? Knowing Florida in hurricane season, they've got to be open at least for a few more hours."

"Ooh! Me! Me!" Mara said as she chose a spot on the couch.

Freddie turned and gave Lina a knowing wink. Here was her opportunity to tell them everything.

"That *does* sound great," she emphasized. "Need help carrying it all back?"

"Sure thing. Thanks, Lina!" Freddie said. "Everybody who wants breakfast, text me your orders. We'll be back in a jiff."

CHAPTER
SIXTEEN

One four-person bagel order later

Before anyone could question them, Freddie had grabbed Lina's hand and slipped out the front door.

Lina took a moment out on the sidewalk to breathe. She was *not* reeling after a bit of handsy flirtation from her ex. She couldn't be.

"May I say," Freddie declared, "that that is the most action I've ever seen two people in the middle of a divorce get? Sophie's kitchen was about to need an R rating and a scrub-down! What is going on, Leen?"

The confusing feelings weren't going away, certainly not given how Brown had squeezed her waist to move past her to Sophie's coffee station. And given that Freddie had promised her their friendship—no judgments made, no sides taken, for which she was exceedingly grateful—she might as well confide in them. If she didn't, she might explode.

"Okay, Freddie, I'll spill," she said as they turned the corner. "You know how Brown and I kissed last night? That wasn't fake. At least not for me. We kissed in the basement during a séance like a couple of teenagers, and I liked it. It was a onetime thing, I thought, but then, well, Sophie's kitchen just now? What *is* happening? We are quite literally in the process of"—she lowered her voice as they entered the café—"of ending our marriage! I don't need to feel feelings right now, but I am." She gripped her own elbows to steady herself. "Freddie, am I doing the right thing?"

Freddie held up a finger to Lina and read off the order from their phone to the cashier. They ordered some extra bagels to stock up, just in case the storm was worse than anticipated.

"And a cup of ice," Lina added.

Freddie and the cashier stared at her.

"What? It's warm in here. Isn't it warm in here?" she asked.

After they paid, Freddie turned to brace her shoulders with both hands. "Okay, first of all, breathe. Then tell me exactly how far into the divorce you are. Like, is it final?"

With the help of Freddie's hands, Lina forced her shoulders back down below her ears. "Hardly. The preliminary papers are filed, but Brown's dragging his feet over some minor line items. It's ridiculous."

Freddie hummed in the key of Doubtful Major. "I'm not an expert, but maybe you should use the Live-In to explore how you're feeling. Sounds like you clamped down on divorce as an option really quickly, am I right?"

She nodded.

"Yep, that's the Lina I know. Dollars to donuts—or, I guess, bagels—Brown is dragging his feet because he's not sure about this yet." Freddie eyed her up and down, clocking the way her heart palpitations were written all over her face. "Maybe you aren't either?"

"Maybe?" she allowed. "Or maybe I'm worrying about this too much? I see this happen with so many clients at the firm."

"Really?" they asked.

"Really really," Lina said. "It's like, as things are finalized, as your decision becomes more definite, you start panic-yearning for what might have been. Human nature, I guess?"

Lina tried to take her own empty comfort as gospel truth. Like her anger, she now had a term and a definition for what she was feeling, a box she could put it in, and she felt more confident to handle it.

"I've seen this whole song and dance before, Fred," she said, trying to convince them both that she knew what she was doing. "In the past, we'd realize we weren't doing well and take a getaway to 'work on us.' On the getaway, Brown would promise to do better, I'd promise to be more forgiving, but then when we got back to real life, nothing changed." She watched the café staff load up their bag with assorted bagels and cream cheese. "He's listening attentively now, but would that happen if we actually got back together? I don't think anything would change."

"All I'm saying," Freddie concluded, "is that you don't have to decide whether you've made the right or wrong choice yet. It's not like your suit can move forward until after this storm anyway, right? Spend this downtime gathering information about how you're both feeling and then figure out your next step."

Lina sighed. "I hate it when you make sense."

Freddie checked their nails. "Hmm. You must be angry a lot then."

She snorted appreciatively until the next thought hit her. "You're rooting for us to get back together, aren't you?"

"Hey, Miss Putting Words in My Mouth!" They feigned annoyance. "I never said that. But Brown *is* a sweet guy. The sweetest one I know. And would he have gone along with this whole charade if he didn't still care about you?"

Lina opened her mouth to agree, then decided that was sharing too much. "He's probably trying to gaslight me," she said instead. "You know, trick me into questioning my feelings and giving things with him another go. Which I've done, time and time again."

Freddie shrugged as if to say, *I've given my two cents; take 'em or leave 'em.* "Look, I'm not going to push back on that, Lina; just please be careful. Two people's lives are on the line here. Listen to your head, which I know you already do, like, *way too much*, and, more importantly, to your heart. Remember, it's better to admit you've made a mistake and try to fix it than to try to be perfect and miserable."

They accepted a large paper bag from the cashier. Grease spots from an asiago bagel were already staining its fibers.

Lina ignored the queasy feeling in her gut. She popped the lid off her cup and selected an ice cube. The burst of cold against the roof of her mouth helped a little.

"Right," she mumbled around it.

As they left the bookshop, they saw a woman in dirty clothes lying on the sidewalk.

"Ma'am, are you hungry?" Freddie asked. When she didn't reply, they pulled out a plain bagel and a sauce cup of jelly. "We have extra, so if you change your mind, I'm going to leave this here."

They handed the sack to Lina, and, after rummaging around in their fanny pack, they pulled out a business card to hand to the woman as well. "I'm also leaving this," they said. "I don't know if you have somewhere to ride out the storm, but here are the numbers and addresses of some places you can try."

"Thank you," the woman mumbled.

"Stay safe out here, darling," Freddie advised, and they were on their way.

Lina caught up with their long-legged stride and gave them a genuine smile. "You're a good person, Freddie Morales."

Freddie shook their head. "I'm just doing what I'd want somebody to do if it were me."

As Lina opened the door and they took Otis up to the third

floor, she felt warmed by her outing with her friend. Her head was still spinning, but this conversation had helped.

Maybe her weird feelings were nothing more than regret by another name. Or maybe, and she was a tiny bit mad at Freddie for incepting the idea into her brain, but maybe they were something more.

CHAPTER
SEVENTEEN
MARCH 6, 2021

A year ago

The thing about temaki, or sushi hand rolls, is that they're pretty fun to put together. Once the individual ingredients are chopped and laid out in a beautiful fashion, the assembly process is so easy that this is one of the few types of sushi regularly served in Japanese homes instead of just restaurants.

The thing about *prepping* sushi hand rolls, though, is that they take a great deal of patience and attention to detail.

Lina was running pretty low on both.

Since she and Brown had moved out of the apartment, they had tried on several occasions to organize a house-hopping PDP. They had failed to throw one before Sophie made her great exodus to Los Angeles. Now, with Mara's impending move to Georgia, the four participants still living in Jacksonville had picked a date for what Freddie was wickedly calling 'Mara's Last Supper.' Lina had laughed at the bon mot, though it was hard to wave farewell as her very best friend moved out of state. They'd decided house-hopping wasn't a great idea, not with Mara's moving boxes or all the tools Freddie was keeping in their space during the building's renovation, so they'd convened in Lina and Brown's Avondale kitchen.

Three of the friends were now gathered around the granite-topped island. Two were swirling sake cocktails and gossiping excitedly. One was trying to slice ahi tuna into perfect rectangles just like she'd practiced earlier in the week.

Brown was nowhere to be found.

"I promise my new Lucky Cat tattoo is *not* in honor of tonight," Mara said, turning over her forearm to reveal the fresh ink. "I didn't know Lina was making sushi."

Freddie leaned closer to take it in. "It would be a little bit of overkill if you were starting to get tattoos for special occasions. Remind me what the triangle above it means?"

"The divine feminine, I think," Lina supplied. "Her first one. *Very* symbolic."

Mara rolled her eyes. "You can't imagine how many times I get asked about it. At this point, I just say, 'I like triangles.'"

Lina laughed. Her hands were cramping and a bit sticky from checking the sushi rice. She rubbed her itchy forehead with the back of one and checked her Apple Watch on the other wrist. *7:08 p.m.* Brown had said he'd be home over half an hour ago with the seaweed salad and veggie gyoza she'd asked him to pick up from the store.

Temaki is kicking my butt!! she'd texted.

She sniffed back her hurt and disappointment. Brown's MIA status had become a pretty common occurrence in the nine months they'd been homeowners. She knew he'd come through that door, handsome and charming as ever, probably an hour late, begging for clemency owing to the fact that work had been a nightmare. She, in turn, would keep her mouth shut about what a trusting and understanding wife she was, not to be making this a thing.

Temaki, according to the research she had done last week, was an easy party food. You prepped the nigiri, or sushi rice, and other fillings; cut the seaweed, or nori; and hand-rolled it all together, with dry hands, into the shape of a cone. "Lots of prep work," one recipe site advised, "but then you can sit back and enjoy!"

Of course, the site assumed that she would have a couple of hours to slice in precise and even lines the raw tuna, to julienne the cucumbers. That she would have time the day before to make seasoned sushi rice, which should be, all websites advised her, at least a day old. That she wouldn't be busy taking on one of her first cases as the client's primary counsel and that the fact she pulled into the driveway fifteen minutes before her guests was nothing short of a miracle.

But yeah, no, Brown's work had been a total nightmare.

Lina suppressed her bitterness and laughed again as Mara fed her a sip of her sake cocktail, tipping the rim of the glass up to Lina's lips, since it would be too much effort to wash and dry her hands before making them sticky all over again. The cocktail flowed over her tongue, tangy and sweet with yuzu. She declined their offers of help. They were her guests, weren't they? They were supposed to relax while she prepared their meal.

She loved Brown, she reminded herself as she turned her attention to the hothouse cucumbers; really she did. She was just genuinely confused as to why he wasn't pulling his weight. They'd both wanted this dinner party, hadn't they? They both had demanding jobs, didn't they? But more often than not, she found herself the only one responsible for getting things done, and the wear was beginning to show.

The other morning, she'd been getting ready for work. Brown was graciously up with her at six o'clock, though he'd just gotten in from closing the bar a few hours prior. She inhaled his perfect musk, the smell of a hard night's work rinsed off by a steaming hot shower, as he wrapped his arms around her waist from behind. They were standing in the corner of their bedroom, in front of the chevalier mirror they had fallen in love with at an antique store. She watched his mirrored reflection bend and nestle his nose into the hollow of her neck, inhaling her own scent before planting a kiss there, as though she were some rare and living flower.

He stood behind her, nude except for a pair of navy briefs, and ran his big, beautiful hand, with all its cuts and nicks from life behind the bar, over the blue, pinstriped cotton of her blouse. It rested just below her navel, heavy with meaning.

"We should have a baby," he murmured into her shoulder. "We would make such a beautiful kid."

Lina was at a loss for words. She slowly burrowed out of his grasp and looked him in the eyes. "Brown, you can't be serious. Now?"

"Why not now?" he asked with an easy-going smile.

How about the fact that we argue constantly?

"Why not now?" she spluttered. "I'm barely holding on with all my responsibilities at home and work, and I barely have any time left for myself at the end of a week. If we threw a baby into the mix…"

She saw the moment his eyes deadened and his lips clamped together. Brown had officially checked out of the conversation.

"If this is about splitting chores," he muttered sheepishly, "I'm working on it…"

She shook her head. "Working on it is fine under our current circumstances, but it wouldn't be if we had a kid, Brown. If we had a kid, it would in no way cut the mustard."

She couldn't tell him what she wanted to: that as the primary earner she couldn't take a year or two off work to nurture a baby while keeping a roof over their heads, and that, without his genuine half-and-half support and ownership of parenting responsibilities, she would soon become one of those frazzled, nagging mothers who lived perpetually on the cul-de-sac of Wits' End.

He stayed quiet, hands crossed over his chest as though to fend off her next verbal attack.

"Look," she said, trying to soften the edges of her rejection. "I didn't mean for this to become a heated discussion first thing in the morning. But I can't—"

"Okay!" Brown muttered. "Okay, fine, I get it. No kids."

He looked down at the floor, and her heart broke. His laissez-faire approach to starting a family had irked her, but she hadn't wanted to hurt him. She caught a glimpse of them in the mirror, hating how severe she looked in her corporate skirt suit and high pony; how bare and vulnerable he did in his night-clothes.

She tilted her head back and sighed. "Look, I'm not saying forever to 'no kids.' Just not yet, okay?"

"Okay," he had repeated, a little more resigned this time.

"Okay?" she said again, and forced her features into a silly expression to make him laugh; to help him realize that, despite this rough patch, she was still his Lina.

"Okay!" he chuckled. He gave her shoulder one last pat before returning to his rumpled side of the bed. "For the record, I would make such a good dad."

"Hello? Earth to Lina." Mara was waving her hand in front of Lina's face.

"Oh! Sorry. What's up?" She finished plating the julienned cucumber and placed it in the refrigerator while she tackled her final task of the evening, rinsing radish sprouts for garnish.

"We were wondering if you had heard much from Sophie?" Freddie said. "It's like she moved out west and forgot about us."

"Like we're not good enough for her anymore," Mara added a bit sullenly.

Lina toweled off her hands, relieved to no longer have the smell of fish or the texture of sticky rice on them. "I haven't, but I'm sure she's busy, just like we all are. You can't fault her for making new friends out there; remember, we'll always be her OGs." To lighten the mood she said, "You're not going off to Savannah to forget about us, are you, Mara?"

Mara simpered in a fake Southern drawl, "Forget about you? I would never!"

Lina tenderly patted her hand. "Glad we have that settled."

The three friends turned to the sound of the front door unlocking, the rustle of plastic bags announcing Brown's presence.

Thank God he's home, Lina thought, straightening up and smoothing her hair. *I can pop the gyoza in the bamboo steamer, and we'll be good to go in ten minutes.*

Only the plastic bags weren't from the grocery store. Brown rounded the corner into the kitchen, looking gorgeous and bedraggled and perfect, his shirt a little rumpled, his curls frizzed with the spring humidity, smelling of the bar's ineffable blend of whiskey, citrus, and brick walls.

He carried two bags from Taco Bell.

"Oh my God! Brownie!" Mara shrieked, embracing him as though she hadn't seen him in years.

"And you brought tacos, bless you!" Freddie said. "I'm *starving.*"

Brown came around the kitchen island and, despite their recent struggles, gave Lina a genuinely happy 'honey, I'm home' kiss.

"Sorry I'm late," he said. "Work was insane. I totally spaced on the dumplings, but I brought home tacos, which are pretty much the same thing, right?" He grinned as he looked into her eyes, as infuriatingly handsome and charming as ever.

CHAPTER
EIGHTEEN
SEPTEMBER 24, 2022

Three Saturdays ago, after one much-needed heart-to-heart with Freddie

Food remained the universal peace bringer as everyone tucked into breakfast.

Lina hunkered down in her mental foxhole, savoring her everything bagel with lox and capers. The longer she took to eat, the longer she had to figure out how she was feeling about the morning's many developments. Freddie now knew about the divorce, including that Lina was second-guessing her decision. That was happening thanks to last night's kiss, her earlier fight with Brown, and some hot-blooded canoodling. Lina had decided she wasn't mad at Brown's coffeetime performance, but while she still wasn't confident what she wanted—divorce or working it out—and had *no clue* what he really wanted, she knew it would be wrong to take advantage of him physically.

Freddie had given her good advice, she thought, as she bundled up the trash. She'd do what they suggested—get more intel before she made any more snap judgments.

"So we're trying to campaign for petition signatures," Mara

was explaining when Lina tuned back in. "It's tough because so many people in town are focused on the incoming storm, but we're basically making a chain of friends and acquaintances we can send the petition link to, then following up with a phone call or a text encouraging them to sign and to think of up to nine friends they can forward it to."

"What's she doing?" Freddie pointed over at Sophie, who was decidedly not making phone calls or sending out links. She had made a temporary war room on the couch and coffee table. She lay with one hand on her heart, the other on her abdomen, taking deep belly breaths while Brown, who clearly had *I got roped into this* etched on his face, rattled a single-serve smoothie shaker.

"Her green smoothie," he explained, hating that he knew this. "Apparently, one of these at 11 a.m. doesn't count as breakfast."

Sophie sat up. "It's more to ground my energy to keep making calls for you guys," she said. "I'm doing everything I can to help, but there's only so much you can make an A-list influencer do on short notice and a tight budget. Gwynnie was, um, incommunicado." Her eyes were downcast for a moment before she said, "On the bright side, I have two of the five *Queer Eye* folks ready to come out here at a moment's notice. They're so great, and they're used to visiting the armpits of America."

"Sophie's... different," Mara finally said to Lina. "But for all the celebrities currently snubbing her, she's raising a ton of donations through her social media followers. The fund is going to be split fifty-fifty between the campaign itself and a fund that offsets Freddie's future tenants' rent."

Sophie overheard this on her way to grab a mineral water from the refrigerator. "Well, not exactly," she said after taking a sip. "There is, of course, my finder's fee for helping with all the fundraising."

"What finder's fee?" This was news to Lina.

"Oh, you know, just a little cut to say thanks for my help." Sophie waved a vague hand in the air. "Five percent, fifteen percent, whatever. We'll figure it out later."

Mara looked at Freddie and raised an eyebrow. "Red flag?" she mouthed.

They shrugged. "That's probably just how they do it out in LA."

When the first drops of rain splattered the windows several hours later, Mara seemed pleased with their efforts. She and Lina had called almost a hundred people, following up on the petition link either Brown or Freddie had emailed them.

Brown seemed as relieved as Lina felt that Sophie didn't ask for more than some candid shots while they were volunteering. Mostly, he worked by himself on a spreadsheet, cold-emailing residents while he listened to the New Romantics in his earbuds.

At one point, Lina had tapped him on the shoulder.

"Hey," she whispered, looking around. "What the heck was that about? Earlier. You know, with the hands and the hips and the coffee? I'm not mad, but... what the hell?"

"Oh, my bad," he said with a wink. "'No embellishments.' I'll do my best to keep that in mind."

She had done her best to live up to her lie—*I'm not mad. Not flustered either*—and make her next phone call.

It was now late afternoon, and the rain was falling steadily. There was no thunder yet, so they had opened the windows to let the refreshingly stormy breeze play over Sophie's gauzy curtains. It was a relief after hours of stuffy, quiet phone banking. When Brown disconnected his Air Pods and suggested a dance break, everyone was on board.

He chose "Don't Stop" for their first song, and soon,

Lindsey Buckingham's voice was belting out of Sophie's speakers.

"I haven't heard this song in ages!" Mara said.

"Yeah, the last time for me was on a car commercial," Freddie teased her.

Ignoring their banter, Brown walked over to Lina, held out his hand, and asked, "May I have this dance?"

She was wary of getting anywhere near him after the events of that morning, but with Sophie already livestreaming again, she couldn't say no. She forced herself to laugh as she accepted his hand. "Of course you may."

"Brown, what's up with you and that album?" Sophie asked from behind her phone. "I remember you playing it a lot when we all lived here."

His cheeks colored subtly as he looked toward her camera. "Well, it's really special to me. It's kind of Lina's and my album. It's what we listened to the first time we... you know." He spun her out, then pulled her back in.

"Oh," Mara chimed in knowingly, doing her own little Twist next to the phone banking table. "The first time you... *cooked risotto*."

Really? Lina wondered. Had they listened to *Rumours* that night? It was so long ago that she had forgotten. She looked up at Brown, who had released her so they could dance freestyle. She couldn't help feeling charmed that he'd remembered such a detail.

For now, though, the pressure was off them both as Sophie pressed her cheek to Freddie's and turned her phone to face them. "Hi, lovely followers! We just phone-banked, like, *all day*, and we're blowing off some steam with a dance party. We're still accepting your donations, though, so Freddie, why don't you tell all the lovely people at home why they should chip in, why you want to save the building?"

They smiled serenely as they two-stepped. "Security. Peace. Because everyone deserves a warm, dry shelter!"

"A place to be yourself," Mara added.

"Bellini, what about you guys?"

Brown didn't look into the camera this time. He stared down at Lina and gave her a rather self-satisfied wink. "It's where I learned to cook risotto."

Lina's jaw dropped open, and she gave him a light smack. She still couldn't tell if he was hamming it up for their cause or if he was using the cause to tell her the truth about how he felt, so when Sophie nudged her for an answer, she deflected with a smile. "You've had plenty of me on camera." Before Sophie could stop her, Lina had wrangled the phone into her own grip and was pointing it at the influencer herself. "Sophie van der Wahl, interior design goddess, you've been in so many gorgeous homes. Why do you want to save *this* old building?"

Put on the spot, Sophie shyly tucked her hair behind her ears. "It's where I've felt safe and loved," she said, quieter than Lina had ever heard her. "It's where I've made good friends. I never could have gone to LA without this building, and I'm grateful for everything it continues to give me."

The song faded out and the room was quiet for a second before Mara started drawing out a big, cheesy *Aww* in response.

"Wow, Miss America," Freddie added. "When will tapes of your speech be available for purchase?"

They all dissolved into giggles.

Lina soaked in the mirth of the moment, happy to be around her closest friends. Who knew the next time they'd all be together? And—she cut her eyes at Brown, who was figuring out which song to play next—Lina wondered when any of them, save Freddie, would want to see her again if they learned the truth. She swallowed the thought like a stone.

After the dance break, the apartment was sweltering.

Neither Mara nor Lina could resist the temptation to crawl out the window and enjoy a beer on the small, flimsy fire escape.

"It's weird being back in my old unit," Mara said. "Remember how we used to sit out there every weekend?" She pointed to the unused balcony ten feet away from them. It looked sad and small in the rain.

"How could I forget?" Lina nodded. "We'd split a bottle of Two-Buck Chuck out there back in the day."

"Ugh, pretty much every Friday night before going down to wreak havoc at the bar." Mara took a sip of her beer. "We must have been insufferable."

"And have had iron livers," Lina supplied. "But I don't think we were annoying! And if we were, who cares? I had never really had a friend like you, not one that I was that close to. If other people were bothered by the way we became joined at the hip, I say that's their problem, not ours."

Mara squinted at her, like she was actively changing her mind. "You know what? You're right. Screw those hypothetical people for being annoyed by our friendship."

Lina clinked her bottle against Mara's and enjoyed the silent, empty street.

"I'm glad we're doing this," Mara said, her face upturned to the rain. It hit her wide, smooth forehead and dimpled cheeks, made her glitter like neon. "This building was so important to us, and it feels good to try to fight for it."

"Yeah," Lina said, still in phone-script mode. "It helped me pay down my law school loans, and being so close to the seat of city government helped you attend all the meetings and events you wanted to. Which is how you ended up getting in good with the nonprofit up in Savannah, right?"

"Well, yeah." Mara fiddled with the beer label. "But I meant if I hadn't lived here, I would have never met you. I would never have found such a wonderful group of friends like the one I have now." She looked up at Lina with her big, brown eyes. "I love you, lady. Miss you a lot too. I feel like we don't talk as much as we used to." She cast her eyes down and worried her lip before saying, "You know you can tell me anything, right?"

"Aw. Babe, of course I know that!" Lina gathered her up into a great, big, wet hug, hoping it distracted from the fear and doubt etched across her face. "I love and miss you too."

"Hey!" a voice called from inside the apartment. Sophie's white-blonde head popped out of the window. "Any chance I can get in on this love fest?"

"Of course!" Lina cheered. "I think the fire escape's total capacity is one person at a time, but hey, who's counting?"

Sophie perched on the windowsill with a satisfied sigh, then turned to the other two women. "We did good work today, didn't we?"

"Yeah," Mara said. "It felt really great."

"Great job, too, with the apartment redecoration," Lina added. "They're so luxurious. You're an incredible designer."

"Ugh, thanks," Sophie said. She jokingly stuck her tongue out, but it didn't deflect what she seemed to be feeling.

Mara sensed it as she sat up straighter. "What's up, Soph?" she asked.

The rain was beading in Sophie's hair. "Don't get me wrong. I love design, but it's only one part of who I am. When I think back to how I approached success six years ago, when I think of playing my different Instagram verticals against each other instead of picking one, I..." She shook her head and slicked back her damp hair. "I just wish I hadn't let other people dictate who I was supposed to be in front of them, you know?"

Lina lay a sympathetic hand on hers, all the while thinking, *You have no idea.*

Later that night, Lina lay wide awake on thousand-thread-count sheets. Their silkiness was cool against her skin, and the quiet hum of the city out the open window was relaxing. Even so, she couldn't sleep. Thanks to the previous night's witch hazel spill, she was flat on her back in her backup pajamas—an oversize T-shirt she'd once stolen from Brown—a conscientious distance away from him, where he was lying just as stiffly on his side of the bed.

"You awake?" she asked.

He shifted for what felt like the fifth time in a minute. "What gave me away?"

Lina sat up on her elbow in the dark. "I can't sleep either," she said. "I keep thinking about this couple Mara knows up in Savannah. They're getting divorced too. She can't stand the woman anymore even though they used to be close." She turned to her right, took in the clean lines of his body under the sheet. "When we're divorced, who do you think will get our friends in the breakup?"

"Like who gets custody of them?"

She wrinkled her lips. "Kind of. I mean, there's always someone who wins the friends in the breakup. Who would get ours?"

"Me. Easily," he said. "I'm the fun one."

She could hear the teasing smile in his voice, and she remembered how it felt to press her cheek to his chest, to hear it vibrate there.

"Sorry if that hurt," he said. When she stayed silent for a while, gnawing on her thumbnail, he sighed. "You probably want to go back to communicating through our lawyers now."

"I try to be fun," she said. "I feel like I *used* to be fun. I know I'm acting tightly wound this week, though, and it's because I'm worried about the others being your friends first. I met them around the time I met you, so I'm scared that they see us as a package deal. If you're not with me anymore, will they even want to spend time with me? I've spent so much of my life working so hard that these are the only adult friends I have—the only fun I have."

Brown sat up and switched on the light. Its beam blinded Lina for a second before she adjusted to the warm, yellow glow it cast on his bare shoulders, the reddish birthmark nestled in his collarbone.

"Mara loves you," he said, comfort in his voice. "More than she loves me, I promise. She would never abandon you, you know that."

"Easy for you to say," Lina started, but for some reason, all her fight from the night before was gone. Maybe it was the fact that this was the most she'd seen Brown, much less talked to him—not just cursorily or in the logistical parlance of divorce proceedings and not just in two weeks but in a few months.

Brown looked like he was finding the best way to say something important. "If you didn't file for divorce because of the baby fight, which you have to admit was a regular point of contention," he ventured, "what was it?"

Lina stared up at the smoke detector studded into the ceiling. "It's not like it was one thing," she admitted. "It was more like an avalanche of little things."

The sheets on his side of the bed rustled, and he frowned. "How do you mean?"

"Well, um"—there wasn't a nice way to say it—"a lot of little disappointments, I guess? Like, when we were here in the apartment, early in our relationship, I felt so supported by you. So safe. You may not know this, but I'd never felt safe enough with a romantic partner to lean on them. I had prided myself on being self-sufficient... until I found you."

She snuck a peek at him before turning to pick at her cuticles. "But then around the time we moved out, I was majorly stressed. Work was rough, I wasn't seeing Mara as much as I had when we lived here, and though I'd gotten used to having you as a shoulder to cry on, I felt like you were suddenly dismissive of my needs.

"You were hardly ever home because you were working hard, too, but when you were there physically, you weren't there emotionally. Or it was like my work stress was in a competition with your work stress. I think one time, after I'd vented about a case over dinner, you even said something like you didn't want to hear about my job anymore.

"You probably didn't think anything of it, but it really hurt —like not just the rug was being pulled out from under me, but the floor I'd come to rely on was giving way beneath me." She tried and failed to meet his eyes. "So, over time, without realizing it at first, I think I closed myself off to you, walled myself up to prevent more hurt and disappointment."

Brown was silent for a moment. "I had no idea any of that was going on for you."

Lina nodded. "I know you didn't, and that's what made it even worse. I felt like shit, expecting you to fix things that you couldn't even see were wrong. It's like that dinner party we had before Mara moved away. I'd had just as long a week at work as you; I had *told* you how long it was. I'd come home to sweat over a beautiful meal for her and you and Freddie, and then you waltzed in an hour late and won them over with cheap tacos." She threw up her free hand in frustration. "You're right," she said as an aside. "You probably will get our friends in the divorce. They're mercenary when it comes to a fun time."

Brown squinted into the inky blackness beyond the circle of light. "Wait, tacos?"

She turned toward him fully. "You don't even remember? You're kidding me! I had made sushi hand rolls. *By hand!*"

"Oh." He hummed. "Now I remember. Those were delicious." He met her gaze, blue to deep brown. "Lina, hon, I didn't realize you were even upset that night. I got your text that the hand rolls were kicking your butt. I knew you had been struggling a lot with work that week, and feeling sad that Mara was moving away, so I thought I was doing a nice thing, surprising you with a backup option." He scratched his nose in thought. "How was I supposed to know you needed more support? I'm not a mind reader. You could've asked, and I would've done anything I could to help. I was busy and distracted by work; I was barely able to be there for myself, let alone read between your lines."

Lina meditated on that. How many times had she heard colleagues at the firm talk about how communication break-down was a leading cause of divorce? *It must happen to the best of us*, she decided, *because we assume we're special, we're too strong; that it'll never happen to us.*

"Well, mind reader or not," she said, "I pushed you away when that happened. Remember when we started fighting a lot? About little things, nitpicks I perceived as flaws? I think that happened because anger felt easier for me than sadness. And then the night when you didn't fight back, when you walked out —well, I figured if you'd given up, I should too."

Brown had turned away from her so that his face was half in light, half in shadow. His lips were downturned, his brow furrowed.

"I just needed some air," he croaked. "Nothing I was saying was getting through to you, so I went back to the bar, and when we closed, I slept in the office. I planned to come back the next night and make it all up to you, but then, well—"

"The process server," Lina finished for him. She sighed and kneaded her temples, where a headache was forming. "I really wish you'd told me that. If I'd known where you were, what was going on in your head, maybe things would have worked out differently."

"I guess there really are two sides to every conversation," he mused.

She laughed bitterly and threw an arm over her eyes. "Oh, Brown. If we're getting divorced because we were bad at communicating, I'll remarry you just so I can divorce you again."

"Honestly? I'm feeling relieved," he said. "All this time, I haven't known what I did wrong, whether I should feel guilty or hurt, and frankly, I've been feeling both. My life was better with you in it. I know you don't want to hear this, but if I could do anything to have you back, I would."

Lina wasn't sure what surprised her more: his statement or her reactive tenderness toward it.

Brown was silent and stared straight ahead for a long moment. Then he moistened his lips and said, "When we were good, it was effortless. I know it takes work to get back to good, once you fall out of it, but I think I resented that we would even have to make that effort. We were brilliant, dazzling. We were supposed to be better than that."

Lina felt hot tears pricking her eyes and hated herself for them. She found his hand, clutched his long, tapered fingers, and wondered how many more times she'd get to do this before it was all over. "We were, weren't we? We were really, really good."

He slowly nodded. "The best." Not letting go of her hand, he gingerly reached over and turned out the light. "Man," he said, just before drifting off, "couch sleeping over the age of thirty ain't for the faint of heart."

Lina hummed in solidarity, even if her thoughts were screeching to a halt in front of a great, big neon sign.

What had she thought earlier that day? Oh yeah. That if Brown were less frustrating to be around, they might have had a shot.

Crap.

Lina was blinded by it, the sign blaring there in the darkness.

She was catching feelings for her husband all over again.

CHAPTER
NINETEEN
SEPTEMBER 25

One ex(?)-lovers' quarrel later

The next day dawned with light gray skies. Strong winds raced down the brick-lined courtyard behind the building, rattling the old sash windows in their frames. When Lina opened one, the morning air smelled like petrichor.

"Hurricane weather," she told Brown, who was already up and pouring himself a cup of coffee.

She had a vague memory of him lying close to her in the middle of the night—perhaps she had pulled his arm over her shoulders or he had kissed her neck. She couldn't recall the particulars. Maybe she had dreamed some of it...

Whether the canoodling was imagined or not, she knew with mounting clarity that she no longer wanted to split up. From their kiss in the basement to the groundbreaking heart-to-heart they'd had last night, she was realizing that she and Brown weren't done. Not yet. Sure, they may have been miles from safe harbor, navigating the tiny boat of their marriage between twenty-foot swells, but they hadn't capsized yet.

It was like Brown had said in the escape room. Lina over-complicated things by zooming in on insignificant details, and in doing so, she often got in her own way. He had played his part in complicating their relationship, but by and large, this was how she'd landed here, on Divorce Island—by reading so many situations incorrectly, refusing to ask for clarification, and then unilaterally deciding that she and Brown were through.

She watched him scrolling through his phone, admired the handsome double lines that appeared between his brows as he focused on the screen. She hated that her choices had caused him pain; she wished she could walk over to him, wrap her arms around him, and kiss his lips good morning, but the cold light of day seemed to negate that possibility. If she could figure out how to reverse this snafu, she'd never get in her own way again.

He moved aside so she could grab her own mug. "The National Hurricane Center says we'll be seeing bands of it by this afternoon. Stores will probably shut down soon, so I'll make a last-minute Publix run here shortly. Message the others and see if they need anything."

Almost immediately Sophie demurred. *Brown doesn't need to go out in this weather. I've got us covered!* she told the group chat. *Hurricane party downstairs in two hours.*

Mara responded with a GIF of Judd Nelson fist-pumping at the end of *The Breakfast Club*, which Freddie reacted to with a heart emoji.

Lina read their messages to Brown, and when she looked up, he was quirking an eyebrow and pouring himself more coffee. "Gird your loins, hon. A full day of pretending to still be my wife."

"God help us," she lightly snarked. Then she surreptitiously texted Jill—*SOS! Need appt. after hurricane. Stay safe!*—and got ready to start the day.

. . .

A sign on the door of The Blind Pig greeted them when Lina and Brown made their way there about an hour later. "Bar closed for private hurricane party. Stay safe!" it read in Sophie's perfect cursive. As Lina looked up, she noticed that Mara had hauled her #SaveTheBuilding banner back inside to save it from blowing away.

They hurried across the narrow, rainy gap between the two buildings' awnings. Lina surveyed the ghost town their street had become. Besides her and Brown, there was no one else in sight as the wind drove the rain down in sheets. It was as though the world had left them behind. Even so, the air felt charged with electricity, and Lina hoped she wasn't the only one who felt it.

Last night, after Brown turned out the light, Lina lay there, still sleepless, still holding his hand in the dark. If she let go, she had the feeling she would rocket, untethered, through space. She felt it all: her anger and sadness at herself; Jill's cautious questions; Freddie's reasoning for why she might be feeling such confusing, conflicted feelings.

In the heavy humidity before the storm, she decided she shouldn't censor her emotions. She *should* let herself feel it all. She had set a plan in motion to end a relationship she had once thought timeless, and now she was trying to reverse it. If she failed, or, rather, succeeded in her original goal, wouldn't that be cause to grieve? Instead of glossing it over, pretending it was all fine, shouldn't she spend at least a little time reconsidering her choices? Shouldn't she say things she'd been scared to before, things that were beautiful and terrible all at once? She knew she should do these things, *needed* to do these things, especially because, as Freddie had said, two people's lives were on the line.

She had smoothed her thumb over the inside of Brown's palm, and he hummed sweetly in his sleep. Yes, she decided;

she would treat this remaining time with him, however long they had, as a gift.

Inside the bar, the others had pushed club chairs and low tables out of the way. Four air mattresses were in the process of being inflated on the poured-concrete floor.

"Look!" Mara enthused. "It's like a big sleepover!"

A big sleepover was certainly the vibe Sophie and her sponsors had curated. Sophie must have hinted at the impending storm earlier in the week because a loungewear sponsor had sent over the softest jersey-knit pajamas in navy and purple, as well as a high-fiber, gourmet brand of popcorn and a case of probiotic seltzer Lina had once seen at Whole Foods for five bucks a can. Sophie was taking a flat-lay picture of all these props before they hunkered down for the storm.

Freddie held one of the pajama sets up to their chest. "I can't tell you how much I hate that we're going to match," they groused.

"We'll just wait till Sophie's done with her phone to put them on." Mara winked. "Less evidence that way. But, come on, get in the spirit! It's a hurricane party!"

They say if life gives you lemons, make lemonade. In Florida, if life gives you a hurricane—well, a *minor* one, Lina amended—you throw a hurricane party.

Sophie joined them a moment later and waved her hand over the meager, if very expensive, spread. "Well, what do you think?"

"You're like our own fairy godmother," Lina joked. "I've never been to a branded hurricane party before."

"So cool, right?" Sophie said. "These snacks should tide us over for a movie marathon later." She held up a few DVD cases, all prominently featuring Molly Ringwald. "I figured after our séance the other night, we should probably stay away from horror movies."

"Good idea," Lina said.

She looked up at the others, and from Brown's dubious shake of his head to Mara's widened eyes, she knew that if this was all the food they had to ride out the storm, things might get soccer-team-in-the-Andes pretty fast.

Luckily, they wouldn't have to live off popcorn and probiotic seltzer alone. Sensing correctly that when Sophie said she had things covered she meant light and snacky at best, Freddie and Mara had made plans to actively cook all afternoon. Freddie had a lamb shank from one of the more decadent meal kits braising upstairs, and they and Mara brought down heartier fare like mozzarella-and-pesto grilled cheese throughout the day. They ate the lamb with a bruised kale salad around dinnertime. Freddie finally stopped bringing down food when the wind tried to knock a platter of caramel brownies out of their hands.

"How are y'all doing with all this?" Freddie asked Lina, when she helped them tote down the lamb shanks. She had readily volunteered for the task not only to update Freddie on her late-night epiphany, but also because Sophie's threats to make her and Brown play a round of *The Newlywed Game* live on camera were getting wildly specific.

Freddie pushed the elevator button and turned back to Lina. "I mean, I'm really grateful for what you're doing for me and the building, but sleeping in the same bed as your soon-to-be ex? That can't be easy. Let alone on an air mattress."

Thunder rumbled to the east.

"It would be," Lina said, "but Freddie, I realized something last night: I don't want to get divorced."

Freddie paused under the bar's overhang and shot her a look.

Lina shifted the dinner platter to one hand and tucked a hank of wet hair behind her ear. "When I fell in love with Brown, it was effortless, the way we puzzle-pieced together. So the instant we needed some work, the instant our honeymoon phase faded and we gained an edge, I got scared. I think he did too. Neither of us had assumed we'd ever have to work at it like other couples do. When it looked like we had to, it felt bad. *Wrong*."

She adjusted the dish in her hands. The tempting fragrance of braised meat spilled out from under its cover. "But now I want to work at it. More than we have in the past. Brown and I talked a little before we fell asleep last night. I don't think we've fought hard enough for us yet—not to the point where we should be giving in. I don't know how he feels, but I know I want to work at it as much and as long as it takes."

"Well, I'm proud of you," Freddie said, sotto voce, as Lina opened the door for them. "Truly. It's not easy to admit to such a big mistake. Let's just hope Brown sees it that way too."

Lina nodded tightly as they walked back into the bar. She planned to talk to Brown later that night, whenever they could find a moment, but she didn't want to think about that yet. She wanted to enjoy the night, and she did for a time, as Brown pronounced that Sophie's sponsors had no taste in alcohol and opened a bar tab for his friends; as Mara's infectious laughter rolled through her belly when Freddie lost to her, for the fifth time, at a game of quarters.

Around nine o'clock, the gang was a movie and a half into their Brat Pack marathon, cozy and snug on made-up air mattresses. Filtering through the projector's warm light and onto a screen against one wall, a young James Spader snuffed out a cigarette in a school stairwell.

Brown had snuggled up against Lina during St. *Elmo's Fire*. It had been longer than the divorce filing since she had had his strong, safe arms wrapped around her waist, and though it may have only been since the previous weekend that his hips had been pressed against hers, that had been in a panicked moment of convincing Mara they were still together. Tonight, in the dark, with Brown's hand laying tantalizing inches beneath her breasts and his breath feathering over the tender spot on her neck, Lina needed no convincing.

Now she turned over to smile at him, so that they lay nose to nose.

"What?" he said with an uncharacteristic giggle, as though she was making him nervous.

She kissed the tip of his nose. "Nothing," she said. "Come with me."

"Where?" he whispered.

"I want to talk to you." She squeezed his hand but didn't let go. "Come on."

As they stood and headed toward the back of the bar, Brown's warm palm against hers, a chorus of knowing oohs and catcalls accompanied them.

"Where are you lovebirds going?" Freddie asked.

"Don't do anything I wouldn't do," Sophie advised.

"Yeah! But use protection," Mara snorted before yelping at the pillow Sophie had chucked at her head.

Brown followed Lina into the bar's single-stall bathroom, chuckling at their friends as he did. She could feel his pulse pick up in his wrist when her fingers gently traced over it, and her heart beat more quickly in a matching rhythm.

She used her free hand to flip the light switch, and a low glow filtered over the Art Deco wallpaper. Fitting with the bar's old-timey décor, a vintage, wood-topped Victrola sat in one corner of the room, and a cinnamon-and-sandalwood candle smoldered on a cabinet near the sink, setting as good of a mood as Lina could have asked for from a public bathroom. She'd take what she could get. Who knew when she'd have another chance to make her feelings physically known to her husband?

But once the door closed behind them, Brown immediately let go of her hand and pulled his phone out of the pocket of his sponsored pajama pants. As he scrolled through hurricane updates, the blue light reflected onto his face.

"Um. Brown?" Lina asked, determined not to let his disinterest kill the mood.

His head whipped up, and he put his phone on the edge of the sink. "Oh, sorry. Did you actually need to talk about something? I figured if we want them to think we're doing stuff, we'd hang out in here for ten, maybe make the occasional animal noise, and then go back out there looking all bedraggled and happy." He frowned. "That is what you were thinking, right?"

Lina leaned against the Victrola. "Kind of, but... there really is something I need to talk to you about."

She had Brown's full attention.

She scratched the nape of her neck, unsure how to tell the man she'd loved, then hated, that she loved him again. "You know, um, you made some really good points last night," she started. "About there being two sides to every conversation. And if I could go back in time, I would tell myself to consider your point of view more often."

The look on Brown's face was both suspicious and hopeful. "Lina, what are you saying?"

But when presented with such a direct question, Lina clammed up. Suddenly, this didn't seem like the right time or place to come clean, not with Sophie and her ever-present smartphone out there, ready to document anything it could. Beyond the importance of set and setting, she realized she didn't know how Brown would react. What if they had to get through some yelling, but their friends barged in to see what the commotion was all about before they could reach understanding?

So instead of coming out with, *Screw getting divorced; I love you, Brown Mitchell*, she went with the much safer, "I'm saying that I wish I'd appreciated you more. When I had the chance."

His smile was as benign as her words. "Yeah, I get that. Me too." He gave her an *If that's everything?* look, tousled his blond curls into sex hair with the help of the mirror, and started to reach for the door. As he did, Lina saw what might have been her last chance at closeness slipping away from her, like a leaf eddying down a storm drain.

"You know," she blurted out. When he froze, she said more slowly, more seductively, "You know... if we want them to think we're hooking up, we could also just... hook up, right?"

Brown turned away from the doorknob. He folded his arms against his chest, sized her up, and, after a long moment, whispered, "I thought you said no embellishments. Hooking up seems like it would be a world-class embellishment, doesn't it?"

Lina pushed off of the phonograph and stepped closer to him. He looked snuggly, sexy, so damn good in the pajama set, and she made a mental note to buy him another, until she remembered it wasn't her place to do that kind of thing anymore.

"Don't listen to me," she said, running her hands up his firm chest. "I'm the idiot who doesn't know what she wants."

Brown looked down at her, perplexed. "So the kiss the other night..."

She licked her lips, feeling a throb build below her waist even as his body responded to her closeness. "Okay, fine, I admit it. I lied. I liked how that kiss felt. Didn't you? I needed it." She dropped her hands to her sides. "I... I needed *you*," she croaked, hoping he took her meaning.

They could hear the rain hammering through the exterior wall of the building. It created the effect of a warm, dry cavern, one where no other souls remained, where there was no sound except their mingled breathing; a safe haven where it could just be Lina and just be Brown, where maybe there was a spark of hope to what came next.

The electricity of the storm was impossible to ignore. Brown closed the gap between them and held Lina's waist in his strong hands, like he had never snatched up his keys and left. Like the old *them* had never left.

His lips closed over hers, and she welcomed their softness,

their firm pressure, the way they made her crave him with a maddening need. She pressed her hips into his and bunched her hands into the fabric near the hem of his shirt when he bucked against her. He squeezed her closer, and in an instant, she had hopped into his arms, and he'd swept the knickknacks off the Victrola to make room.

"I love you," he whispered huskily, a confession against the base of her neck, and she pulled his chin up to kiss him again.

Their sponsored pajamas hit the floor soon after that. She held him as close as she could, like she had his hand the night before. She kissed the birthmark over his clavicle, he kissed his moan into her mouth, and Lina did her best not to cry at this particular reunion, this possible goodbye.

When she did, she lied to herself and called it sweet release.

Lina was floating in the middle of the Saint John's River. It was a balmy summer afternoon, and she was sunbathing on the deck of a sailboat. Brown was at the helm, and their friends were chatting and laughing between them. She lowered her sunglasses and caught his wink at her cherry-red bikini before he turned back to steering the ship.

She had just turned over to get some sun on her back when her fingers grazed something cold. Something wet. She looked down to see river water seeping onto the deck. It wasn't your usual spray from over the bow, but the creeping terror of a hole somewhere in the keel making itself known. Lina sat up in a panic. They had to call the Coast Guard, had to find the life jackets they'd all, like idiots, decided not to wear, but she couldn't stand. She was paralyzed by the fear of sharks and drowning and—

"What kind of *Bedknobs and Broomsticks* crap is this?!"

A voice from outside invaded the walls of her dream. Freddie's voice.

Lina jumped back to consciousness, and, as she opened her eyes, she caught the reference immediately. Whereas in that old movie the bed had floated out over a city, their air mattresses were sopping wet and floating in cold, brackish water.

Which her hand was submerged in.

"Whoa, my God!" She jerked it back and suppressed her gag reflex. The water smelled putrid, like the river at its lowest point. Whenever she jogged the River Walk at low tide, it always made her run faster, and boy, did she wish she had somewhere to run now.

At this point, Mara, Sophie, and Brown were also awake.

"What's happening? Did the river flood? What is happening?!" Sophie kept saying.

Lina had inched to the center of her mattress, where she felt safest and could smell the water the least. She could feel Brown's soothing voice rumble through her back as he said, "I don't think so. I think the heavy rain got the sump pump backed up. It must have flooded the bar."

"Sump pump?" Mara squeaked, fear etched into her brow line.

"You don't want to know."

Lina bit back another urge to hurl.

"We've got to get out of here!" Freddie said. "What can we paddle with? Are there bar spoons? Are bar spoons even big enough to steer an air mattress?!"

Brown took a fortifying breath, then plunged his legs into the standing water. "Guys?" he said, looking a little green. "It's not deep. We can stand."

"Oh, no," Sophie stated with a manicured finger pointed at the ceiling. "I am *not* going in that stuff."

"It's not ideal, but it's the fastest way out of here."

In their silence, more brackish water hissed in from the back patio.

"Then I'll take my time," she insisted with a sniff.

From the way Brown was glaring daggers at Sophie, it seemed clear to Lina that she had two choices. She could be difficult and face the consequences, or she could get dirty for five seconds and get the heck out of here.

"Okay, guys?" she said, trying to get Mara and Freddie's attention. "Guys?" She snapped her fingers till they were looking woozily in her direction. "Who knows how long these mattresses are gonna hold us up. The front door is maybe ten yards that way. We can get there in a minute, tops, but we *have* to get in."

"But Sophie—" Freddie protested.

Lina held up her hand. "We'll come back for her. Now, on the count of three, let's get off our mattresses and into the water." She hoped she sounded more confident than she felt. "Ready?" Mara's head was wobbling in a constant nod while Freddie was paralyzed in fear. "Okay. One, two—"

"Wait!" Mara shrieked. "Are we going on three or are we going on 'go'?"

"Oh my God, why does it matter?" snarled Brown, who remained in the water up to his shins, ready to support Lina when she got off their mattress.

Lina sighed. "We're going on three. Okay, ready? One, two—"

"Oh God, I'm not ready!" Mara moaned.

"—three!"

They took the plunge.

Lina stood up to her knees in the murky, foul-smelling water, clutching onto Brown for dear life. Freddie, who was closest to the exit, was frozen in place, making a hacking noise, which Lina imagined a moose might make if a moose could get hairballs.

Mara's face looked like Lina's felt. "Hold it in till we get outside, Mara, hold it in!"

Brown tossed Sophie, who was still determinedly sitting

cross-legged in the very middle of her mattress, an eight-quart container and a bar menu. As Sophie wrenched the lid off the container and attempted to use its flimsy, green plastic as an oar, Lina and the rest trudged, in their matching, ruined pajamas, to the front door as quickly as they could.

"Have a hurricane party, they said," Sophie glowered, as she continued to paddle. "It'll be fun, they said..."

Lina could feel the water's current pulling around her legs, weighing down her pajama bottoms as she joined Brown at the front door.

"What a mess," he muttered. "You get the others to safety... and a working shower. I'm going to have to go back in and deal with that sump pump."

He pushed open the front door, and they watched as the mess gushed over the sidewalk and joined the much less dramatic hurricane waters in their rush to the drain.

"Jeez," Lina said, the penny finally dropping. She looked up at Brown. "You have to deal with things like this at work all the time, don't you?"

He nodded matter-of-factly. "Not usually this bad, though. Anyway, it's a living."

There was nothing Lina could say to excuse the years of comparison-itis they'd given each other for their respective careers. Ultimately, the stress of a law firm and the stress of a bar were apples and oranges. Instead, she reached up, kissed him firmly in appreciation for all he did, and then rested her head against his chin, fingers stroking through the curls at the nape of his neck.

"Join us soon, okay?" she murmured. "You deserve a hot shower and a dry bed just as much as the rest of us."

CHAPTER
TWENTY
SEPTEMBER 27

After the storm

"This is a total disaster," Lina said.

They were standing in the middle of the Main Street Bridge —Lina, Mara, Brown, and Freddie anyway—peering down at the swollen river rushing past them. Though their building had survived the hurricane relatively unscathed, the Saint John's had flooded its banks by a city block. The tidal waters had since receded, and as the friends walked to the bridge, they'd skirted clean-up crews sawing down wind-bent palm trees and mopping mud out of bank lobbies. The green space down by the river looked as though it would need to be resodded after it dried.

Lina pulled her hooded jean jacket more tightly around her, against the first real chill of fall, and surveyed her friends, trying to get a sense of how they were all coping in light of their shared hurricane trauma.

She had no grounds to feel as optimistic as she did—that was, apart from what had happened to her the night of the flood. After the bar bathroom, close as breath to Brown on their air mattress, she'd considered adding a new entry to her trigger journal. But her phone was upstairs, and besides, he'd tightened his grip around her waist and sighed contentedly against her ear, so she'd decided to do it later. She did reflect on her entry from the day before, though, the one in which she'd wondered if people could ever have one last horizontal hurrah without feelings attached. Lina now knew that she could never be intimate with another person without feelings. Especially not with Brown.

Given their talks over the past two days, their relationship couldn't be as over as she'd originally thought. It would be quite the hill to climb, including figuring out how to tell her lawyer she wanted to reverse the divorce proceedings and how to stop feeling giddy and foolish for this emotional U-turn, but she wanted to find a way back into Brown's heart. Based on his eagerness to kiss her, to love her body, to go along with her—as he had called it—harebrained scheme, she thought she might have a shot at making this work.

It was now the day after they'd woken up to murky water floating their mattresses, and she had soaped and rinsed and soaped and rinsed the icky feeling off her skin. (The drive back to Avondale had been mildly to moderately treacherous, as the amputated limbs of oak trees clotted some of the one-way streets through Riverside, but she was grateful to arrive at her colonial-style two-story to find the backup generator had done its job. She finally could scrape and loofah and exfoliate the sulfuric smell from her skin with scalding-hot water.)

She'd heard that, thanks to the bar flooding, Nickerson and Associates were taking a beat before the October 11 hearing. Mr. Nickerson wanted to get an assessment of the sump pump to make sure his new property wouldn't flood as easily as the bar next door. At first, the friends chalked that up as a win, said it might even mean that Nickerson wouldn't want to keep, much less gentrify, the building, but Brown reminded them that the sump pump was a minor issue at best. Once Nickerson figured that out, he'd be back on the warpath.

They weren't back to square one, though, but rather some pre-starting point beyond that. As the four of them stood on the bridge, Sophie was on her way to the airport, taking her social media following with her.

"Did she actually say she thinks she's 'allergic to Florida water'?" Freddie asked.

"Indeed she did," Brown confirmed. "I don't know if she meant from the tap or the incident in the bar, but that's what she said when I helped load her rental car."

"I mean, I didn't love trudging through that mess either, but I'm still here," Mara griped, adding, "Probably has something to do with us getting her sponsors' pajamas ruined."

"She actually wanted those back?" Freddie said. "I thought sponsors were supposed to give you free stuff, not just on loan."

"Yeah, that seemed a little weird to me too," Lina agreed. "Do we even know the results of her whole #Bellini4Ever campaign?"

"I looked on my laptop earlier," Freddie said. "We're still not hitting the mark on donations *or* petition signatures." They put on a faux cheery grin. "But not to worry. Sophie has plenty of new followers! Six hundred thousand and counting!"

"Why do I feel like we've just been had by one of our old friends?" Brown asked.

"I bet we don't even know the half of it," Mara said darkly, frowning.

"We already knew Soph was a little mercenary when it comes to social clout," Lina said in their missing friend's defense. "We can't fault her for that. Face it: we were hoping we could use her for her campaign as much as she was doing the same to us in reverse."

"So much for symbiosis," Freddie murmured. They leaned

their head against their hands on the bridge's bright blue railing. Lina nudged them to straighten up so a pair of joggers could cross behind.

"Hey." One of the joggers popped out their earbud, running in place as they looked Lina up and down. "Are you part of that couple that's trying to save their old apartment building?"

"Yep. Well, we *have* been trying." Lina pointed down the row to Brown, but he seemed to calculatedly ignore her. "Dunno how well we're doing," she added, trying to cover up the unease his non-reaction prompted.

"Well, hey, I thought that was you!" the jogger said. "I recognized you from Instagram. Keep up the good work! I think you're doing something really important for our community." Then they ran to catch up with their friend.

Lina shared a sad smile with Freddie and Mara before staring down into the roiling waters of the Saint John's. She had a feeling before too long they'd be saying, *Oh well, at least we tried*, and grabbing a drink to soothe their souls after Nickerson's wrecking ball smashed into the brick and glass and memories of their old building.

"I'm sorry, but no."

Lina looked up. Mara was standing to her left, the light breeze lifting her short, brown hair and giving a sense of determination to her gaze. "'No' what?" she asked.

"We can't let the building go just because Sophie went home," Mara said. "I know Soph and I haven't always seen eye to eye, especially not with this campaign. I know she has a lot of clout, and I know she was trying to do something nice for us here, but I don't think, just because she's gone, we can act like we're beat." She spluttered. "I mean, we didn't even try."

She turned to the rest of them. "I came from out of town to help out too. I don't care if that goes unacknowledged, but guys? *I'm still here.* I'm here not for the added benefits this is giving me because, frankly, there aren't any. I'm having to squeeze in time for work, I'm sleep-deprived, I had to put my phone on rice thanks to the bar flood, but I'm here because I love you three. And I love our building. It was cool to be back in my old apartment for a little while, but taking to social media isn't going to achieve much more than an awareness campaign. You know how many armchair advocates tweet on different sides of every issue each day but then don't go to the ballot box? Don't go out and march? We need to make an actual effort at this with tangible results before we call it quits."

Brown shook his head. "And when Nickerson still wins the vote?"

Mara gave a jerky shrug. "Then he wins the vote! But at least we'll have shown the city council that they're doing something they can't rest easy about.

"I say we take this at a more measured pace, but we still get it done," she said. "This is what I was trying to say the day Sophie came into town. If each of us commits to attending one event or pitching one reporter or making one important phone call per day, that's four things getting accomplished every day. More if we get volunteers! If we team up with the organizations already working toward affordable housing in North Florida, if we let them know they can use our building as an example of what's going wrong, we can flood those council chambers with supporters a couple Tuesdays from now. We'll go to that hearing better prepared, with strength in numbers, and they'll think twice before the next condo developer approaches the bench."

A seagull swooped by as they all reflected on Mara's speech.

"We did have some volunteers check in today to see how they could help," Lina ventured.

"We did?" Mara asked, then seemed ashamed of her own eagerness. "That's, um, that's great. Also, I've fielded a few emails from local nonprofits—not to mention the council member for downtown's district—who want to help."

Her grin grew wider as they all turned to her in shock.

"You were just going to sit on that piece of information?" Freddie leveled at her. "Get a load of Ms. Mara Jilcott, sitting on a council member being on our side like it was no big deal." They playfully shoved her. "I'm done with you."

Mara winked. "Gotta keep some aces up my sleeve. Guys, I love you so much. Lina and Brown, Freddie, your friendship means so much to me. It's been a nice bonus that this effort lets me spend extra time with you."

"So, what?" Lina asked, surveying their little huddle. "Are we all still in?"

"I'm still in if you are," Freddie said.

"Brown?" Lina prompted. She wanted to reach out for him —doing so had been brainlessly easy the night before—but something held her back this time.

He rolled his eyes and said, "Yeah, sure, fine," using his patented Grumpy Old Man shtick as a cover for whatever was going on beneath the surface.

"Cool," Mara said. "Then, guys, let's save that damn building!"

On their way back to their cars, Lina gently tapped Brown's hand and encouraged him to hang back from the other two. They came to a stop at the foot of the bridge, the concrete barriers on either side of the pavement hemming them in.

"Are we okay?" she asked him. "You were quiet back there."

He tugged his hand back at the first opportunity. "I don't know about *us*, but yeah. I'm fine."

His terse answer clashed with the affable, willing-to-talk-it-out Brown of the past week. It was so much more like the dispassionate, over-it-all Brown that she had wanted to break up with in the first place that Lina got a little nervous to continue.

Finally, he prompted her with an impatient head tilt. "Well? I'm waiting."

She fought the impulse to cross her arms, and put on a slow, hopefully winning smile instead. "So, the other night was fun..."

Realization dawned before his eyes flickered back to numbness. "Yeah. Fun." He kept them fixed on the workers clearing the green space. "You know, I'm glad the pressure is off our shoulders, though. Now that the Live-In's over, we'll only have to keep our pretend relationship alive in public, around town. We won't have to fake living together or anything crazy like that. No more reality show–style interviews or rounds of *The Newlywed Game.*"

Lina's smile vanished. "Where's all this coming from?" she demanded, feeling her forehead wrinkle into concern. "I thought we were getting back to a good place."

"Don't worry about it," Brown said with false bravado. "In fact, Lina, you don't have to worry anymore. Look, the other night? You're right. It was great." He dropped his hands to his sides. "I'm so glad we could do that *without feelings attached.*"

The familiar phrase stopped her cold. "I don't understand..."

"You don't? Hm. I guess you could always look it up on your phone."

He marched off ahead of her, into the quiet, storm-battered downtown.

Lina, on the other hand, couldn't move. Her mind was flashing back to the group leaving the building, Operation Live-In over. She had asked Brown to hand her her phone. He had been smiling when he said sure, then tight-lipped when he handed it over. He must have unlocked it, she realized in retrospect. Unlocked it and seen her open Notes app, which was full of unpleasant observations about him, including the one he'd just quoted, which, as she recalled, ended with, *Can't believe I'm still lusting after a messy, sarcastic, know-it-all jerk who will never amount to anything.*

Heart heavy, she looked up at the sky, which was maddeningly peaceful after the havoc of the night before.

"Stupid trigger journal," she muttered, then headed for her car.

CHAPTER
TWENTY-ONE
SEPTEMBER 28 TO OCTOBER 6

In which Lina eats crow

The main difference between Sophie's social media campaign and Mara's community organizing was that Lina was meeting so many people face to face.

Mara would have smugly added that her effort was actually working, and in the face of so many donation checks and petition signatures, Lina couldn't say she was wrong. She was just stuck on the 'people' of it all.

In the week after the storm, Brown grudgingly handed out flyers and collected signatures with Lina. As the city's maintenance crews roamed the streets, clearing tree branches and restoring power lines, Freddie and Mara were snagging volunteers and taking over coffee shops for phone banking. They were meeting with thought leaders in the community who had been advocating for affordable housing and other civil equities far longer than the four friends had been able to vote. They were hosting town halls at libraries and event spaces, bars and restaurants like The Blind Pig.

The best part? These hundreds of people Lina was talking

to every day, they all believed in what she and her friends were trying to do.

Well, almost everyone.

At one particular town hall, Freddie's speech had just gotten a rousing ovation, and Mara had thrown it to the standing-room-only audience for questions.

After a couple of softballs, a redhead in the third row stood up. "I've heard this campaign wants the city to de-privatize all housing and make us go into a lottery system for where we'll live," she stated. "Is that true? Are the socialists going to make me give up my house?"

A woman two rows behind her—who had proudly shown Lina her tattoo of the Jacksonville skyline before the meeting got started—gave the question-asker a weird look. Funny, it was the same look Lina was desperately trying not to give her from atop the makeshift stage.

Freddie, to their credit, answered the crackpot as politely as possible. "Our campaign is not affiliated with any party, ma'am. You will get to keep your house. Our only missions are to save our building from gentrification and to open a dialogue with the city to provide more housing subsidies for those who need them. Thank you." They turned to a scraggly, bearded man on the same row as the woman, who now had his hand raised. "Yes, sir, how about you?"

The man hadn't even finished standing when he blurted out, "Is it true that this campaign is backed by lizard people?"

Freddie sighed into the microphone. "No," they said.

"How can you tell?" he demanded. "What if they're in disguise?"

"Sir, I assure you, it's not."

Though Freddie was being gracious, Brown was getting to the bottom of things. He hopped off the stage and marched up to the man and the woman. "What the hell is going on here? What's with the cockamamy conspiracy theories?"

Instead of standing up for their albeit kooky convictions, his questionees crumbled like a sack of potatoes. "Sorry," the woman said with a nervous wince. "I know that was a dumb question. That guy over there paid me fifty bucks to do it."

"What guy?" Brown snarled. He looked over in time to see Nickerson's staffer trying to sneak out, camera phone in hand.

"This isn't over," the staffer announced, only his eyes and comb-over visible as he edged his way through the disgruntled crowd.

"Sure, buddy, keep telling yourself that," Brown said, then turned to the throng. "Anyway, folks, that's all the time we have for questions. Thank you for coming!" He told them where they could sign the petition if interested, and after an awkward pause, the audience got up and mingled.

"Audience plants?" Lina murmured.

"Bob Nickerson strikes again," Mara replied.

"That was so weird," Freddie said when Brown rejoined them on the stage.

"Yeah," he agreed. "I've got a bad feeling about it. Nickerson's up to something, but I don't know what."

Freddie nodded, sucking in their cheeks. "Do you think he's trying to dig up some dirt on us? One of my tenants said a man with a comb-over and what she thought was a New York accent came sniffing around her new place. She slammed the door in his face when he started asking questions."

"But what dirt would they even dig up?" Mara rebutted. "We're running a clean campaign."

Freddie, Lina, and Brown kept their lips zipped, but when Lina tried to commiserate with Brown, he rushed off to glad-hand some donors. She took a sip of water to calm herself. If she'd thought Freddie telling the others their secret would be bad, she had no idea how much it would hurt if Nickerson found out. She didn't have much time to dwell on this newfound fear, though, as a crowd of supporters came over to express an interest in phone banking.

So, regardless of the occasional Nickerson-planted nutjob, the feeling of connecting with her fellow citizens on something so important was exhilarating to Lina.

The plan was to host a final pledge and petition drive, as well as an evening of talks from community leaders, the Thursday before the city council meeting. Then, even if not everyone could show up for the hearing the following Tuesday, they would have enough support in hand to be taken seriously.

In a rare moment of downtime, Lina checked out the... *fifteen, sixteen...* eighteen pages of signatures they'd collected that week. Surely this would count for something in the eyes of their local government.

And, surely, her continued, positive presence would count for something with Brown. Despite what he had said to her on the bridge, Lina was doing everything she could to spend more time with him. She didn't want to split up anymore, but Brown very suddenly, very vehemently, wanted the opposite. Luckily, he seemed too busy to focus on the divorce papers, but who knew how much longer she'd have to convince him that she'd changed her mind?

She choked down her frustration every time he grunted in response to her hello; each time his eyes lit up for a supporter, then deadened by the time he turned back to her. She found herself offering him rides from campaign events—and hey, if he hadn't eaten, would he like to stop for dinner on the way home? As she stole covert glimpses of him at stop lights, she wondered if, under his fresh hurt, he still felt the same way about her.

Doubtful, she thought. He had been frosty toward her since their non-conversation on the bridge. Permafrost, more like, after what he'd read on her phone.

Before he'd seen her trigger journal, they had been on the same page again for the first time in maybe a year. In hindsight,

Lina had to admit that some of her entries sounded pretty mean, but hadn't she needed to work through those ugly emotions to get to this point of reconciliation? Wasn't the journal supposed to be a personal, private safe space for her to vent what she was thinking, unfiltered? She wished he would listen long enough for her to explain that, although she had thought those things once upon a time, she didn't anymore; that she hadn't had time to write all the lovely things she'd rediscovered about him—his kindness, his fierce loyalty to his friends, his quick wit. The fact that he'd seen the journal at all drove her nuts. Why couldn't she have grabbed her phone instead of being lazy and asking him to do it? Whatever the case, she now had a *Mean Girls* Burn Book situation on her hands. If it ended up being the last nail in their relationship's coffin, dammit, Lina was finding a new therapist.

One night Brown did cave and accept her invitation to grab dinner on the way back to his apartment. Earlier in the day Nickerson had put out an actual, bona fide attack ad, and Lina guessed Brown's resulting feelings of vulnerability might have played into him saying yes. The video, which had leaked on Twitter, was composed of footage of him bum-rushing the audience plants at the town hall meeting. The grainy, black-and-white replay froze on the angry face he'd made as Nickerson's staffer made a quick escape.

"BULLIED INTO PAYING FOR FREE HOUSING SUBSIDIES?" an aggressive, red font bled onto Brown's snarl. "NO! DON'T LET HOTHEADS RAISE YOUR TAXES."

Lina wanted him to feel like he could confide in and trust her again, so she reached across the table to affectionately run her thumb over his knuckles as they waited for their pho. The weather was crisping up, and spicy broth sounded particularly good to both of them that night.

"I guess you were right that they were up to no good, huh?" she asked.

He grunted noncommittally in response.

"Well, I wouldn't worry too much about it. Sure, the ad shows Nickerson has teeth, but at the end of the day, it's not up to a public referendum. It's fourteen public officials voting on it, and when all our supporters show up, along with our impressive petition signatures, I'm sure that'll make the case we need."

Lina smiled gently. Brown stared at her smile, then down at her hand for a moment. Then, with a disgusted sigh, he shrugged her off and flagged down the waitress.

"We'll be getting our soup to go," he told her, his voice tense.

Which was how Lina wound up driving home, steering extra carefully over potholes, with a plastic quart of lava-hot soup between her legs.

She vented about it to Jill the day before the city council hearing.

"How is everything?" her therapist finally asked when, instead of sitting down, Lina elected to pace the length of the room.

"Not great, Jill!" Lina spluttered. "Brown saw my trigger journal, and now he's pissed."

"I didn't mean for you to let him read it," Jill explained on Lina's next lap around the office, as though her client didn't understand the concept of a confidential diary.

"Yeah, no, I got that," Lina sniped. She walked to the end table where her chamomile tea had gone cold. As she swished its tannic bitterness around her mouth, she tried to think calming thoughts. "He saw it by accident," she explained before groaning into the mug. "I think at one point in it I said I hated that I was still physically attracted to a guy who would never amount to anything."

"I understand your concern," Jill hedged, as though she realized Lina might be blaming this whole situation on her, "but maybe him seeing your journal is a blessing in disguise. Perhaps this gives you both a good opportunity to come clean to your friends?"

Lina laughed. "I don't know. All I know is now I've got a fraught situation with my ex-husband on my hands. Just when everything was going so well. Ugh, maybe I should have talked to him about reversing the divorce before I slept with him."

Jill blinked rapidly, trying to process this news. "I think you might need to fill in some blanks for me."

Lina arrested her forward motion and came to sit on the couch. "Look, I don't know if divorce is the right answer anymore. I went from pretending to still be with Brown to realizing I *did* still want to be with him. I just don't know if we're on the same page on that front. We've done a lot of talking lately, and I'm starting to see things from his side. We kissed, for real, and then hooked up in a public bathroom. But then he saw the journal and that all went to hell. All in the span of a weekend." Lina flopped back, realizing just how much had happened since she'd last seen her therapist. "Come on, Jill," she teased the older woman. "Keep up."

"Um..." Jill said.

But Lina was already voicing her next question. "Do you think people can change? Before the hurricane, I wondered if Brown was changing, the way I was changing my mind about the divorce. But now that he's reacted so poorly to the trigger journal, I'm worried there might be something dynamically flawed about our relationship. Like, even if we don't get divorced right now, would we down the road?"

Jill held up a finger as though to interject, but Lina dropped her hands and looked out the window, where a city bus was whooshing by. "You're right, I'm probably spiraling. Maybe I'm just now realizing what I could lose if we go through with this. Maybe I still want to split up and this is all part of my grieving process? All I know is that I'm trying to focus on the campaign for the time being. In a weird way, it's what I have left of Brown, so even if the divorce goes through, I'll have had these last two weeks. Right?"

"Well—" Jill said, clearly wanting to go back to the bombshell Lina had dropped on her, but then her watch alarm beeped.

Saved by the bell, Lina thought. Her therapist was sure to have some sage, safe, stable advice about why sleeping with one's ex-partner in the middle of a divorce was a horrible thing to do. Lina already knew that, especially from a legal angle, and she was trying her best not to think about it, much less examine her feelings about Brown or about lying to their friends about the divorce. If she was honest with herself, she wasn't even sure where to begin. It was nice to have the affordable housing initiative to focus on.

"Oh my God, look at me monologuing at you all session!" Lina said. "Even so, this has really helped. Thank you for listening." She took a campaign button from her satchel and put it on the end table, next to her cold mug of tea. "I need to run, but I'll leave this with you. See you again next week! Hopefully I'll have good news to share!"

With that, she couldn't get down her therapist's stairs and away from her voice of reason fast enough.

On Thursday, they marched downtown, starting at the old building and moving past the bars and theaters and restaurants, heading for a rallying point at The Jessie, a former library that had been repurposed into a coworking space for nonprofits. One of the leaders of the existing affordable housing movement in Jacksonville was going to give a keynote after Lina introduced them, a role for which she was very excited.

"Do you love my sign, or do you *love* my sign?" Freddie asked, as they greeted their friends outside of the apartment building.

In white and pink glitter and puffy paint across a light blue posterboard, they'd written, "He came in with a wrecking ball!" An impressive cutout of Mr. Nickerson posing atop a wrecking ball à la Miley Cyrus was tearing across the lower righthand corner.

"I more than love it!" Lina cheered, turning to the others and locking fingers with Brown, who, possibly due to nerves, squeezed her hand in return. "All right! Let's get this show on the road."

Regular citizens came out into the streets as they passed, lured by calls of "Hey, hey! Ho, ho! Investment properties have got to go!" Some joined the march while others turned up their noses at the demonstration.

The crowd at The Jessie was marvelous, the culmination of all the smaller events they'd had in the past week. Lina took to the podium with her notecards in hand and adjusted the mic to her short height.

"Can you all see me?" she joked.

The crowd rumbled appreciatively.

"I'm glad that you're here with us tonight," she said. "Not only for my friends' and my cause, but for the greater movement that's happening here in Jacksonville. That's why I'm so glad to be intr—"

She stutter-stepped then. She had looked out into the crowd and caught sight of a familiar, ugly comb-over grinning at her from the back of the room. Right beside him was none other than Bob Nickerson himself.

"Sorry," she said, looking down at her cue cards. "Lost my place. Ahem. That's why I'm so glad to be introducing the evening's keynote speaker…"

Though her heart was racing, Lina got through the rest of her introduction and hurried off the stage, under a hail of applause, to her friends on one side of the platform.

Mara looked at her with some concern, so Lina shook her head and pointedly took out her phone.

Guys. Nickerson is here, she typed into the group chat.

From the way the other three stiffened around her, it was clear they were all trying to focus on the keynote, though they were apprehensive of what was to come.

The big boss?! Freddie replied. *Guess there's gonna be a rumble.*

Mara sent an anxious emoji. *Do you think he'll try to poison the crowd against us?*

Nope, Brown texted. *No Q&A tonight. I think he's here to talk to us. One on one.*

That was what Lina was thinking too. She flashed back to Freddie wondering if Nickerson was digging up dirt on them, and it made her feel nervous as hell to consider what the real estate developer and his staffer might reveal to her friends.

She gulped, opened a separate text thread, and rapped out a message to Brown: *SOS! What if he tells them about us?!*

She looked up, saw the moment he thumbed over to and read her text, but was perplexed by his response. He gave a sort of *So what if they do?* shrug and pocketed the phone, effectively shutting her out.

Lina was not able to enjoy any of the keynote after that. When it was finished, she saw a few familiar faces in the crowd, and though she figured they'd tapped out their home team, collecting more petition signatures than they needed was the icing on the cake. She made sure to share her appreciation with those who had helped them already, like the producer of a radio show who had gotten them a last-minute guest spot to promote this rally.

"Thanks for everything, Katherine," Lina said, trying to keep the grimness out of her voice.

Katherine, a bright young woman with long, brown hair,

glasses, and an enamel penguin pin on her lapel, gave a firm smile. "Any time."

Lina forced herself to look around, to appreciate the crowd. It was incredible to see how the building she loved, the one hardly anyone had known about a month ago, was now a rallying cry for housing equity. It was moving to see people she adored serving as the firebrands that had started a whole city burning for justice.

The fly in the ointment, of course, was Nickerson. There was the brief relief that neither he nor his staffer had made waves by interrupting the evening's speeches, but he was still here. Which meant Brown was right: the developer wasn't done with them yet.

Lina clocked Nickerson staring directly at her. She did her best not to show fear or defeat, and instead stared back until he vanished into the crowd.

CHAPTER
TWENTY-TWO
OCTOBER 6

Last Thursday—on the proverbial edge of a knife

After the crowds had dissipated, Lina, Brown, Mara, and Freddie were left standing in the grand hall.

"Where is he? Where's Nickerson? Was it all a bluff?" Freddie asked.

"I somehow doubt that," Lina murmured. She nodded in the direction of a white-haired man, outfitted in a tailored puffer vest and a blue, button-down shirt, who was headed their way, accompanied by his jerk of a staffer. They took their time approaching, stopping to appreciate the art on the walls and even read the placards beside them.

Eventually, Nickerson clasped his staffer's shoulder and declared, "It's all right, Kenneth. I've got this one." Then he approached them, strolling right up to their circle and stopping between Lina and Brown.

A thick silence smeared itself over the group.

"I'm impressed," Nickerson began. "I know it's a cliché to say that of one's opponent, but I am truly impressed with all you were able to put together in such a short time. The march, the petition, all that. You've been a worthy adversary. I tremble to think what you might have done if you'd had my war chest or more time to plan."

He shoved a hand in his vest pocket and gestured the other one open-palmed toward the center of the circle. "Here's the deal. I'm willing to agree to a certain version of your demands. I'll provide a lower rent for one of the twelve units in the redeveloped condo, and I'll even consider converting the basement of the building into a free clinic or community aid office of sorts."

He extracted his hand from his pocket and proffered the business card in it to Freddie. "I realize your friend here thinks I took advantage of them in our original contract, so I could even offer a bigger sale price, if that's what they need. A seat on the condo board, maybe."

Freddie flinched, though they reluctantly took the card.

"I'm sensing a but," Lina said slowly.

Nickerson stuck his tongue in his cheek and smiled as though he were enjoying this. From the quick look Lina took around the group, everyone's hackles were raised. "But," he conceded, "you can't oppose me at the city council meeting on Tuesday."

The reaction to this insulting request was immediate. Though Mara stiffened and Freddie clenched, Brown's anger was explosive.

"How can you even say that?" he blurted. "That was clearly the whole point of tonight. Of, of everything! How can you have us step back just to do that?"

Lina laid a calming hand on his shoulder, though she felt him tense beneath it. "And if we don't?" she asked Nickerson in the calmest voice she could muster.

The developer grinned, his even, white teeth terrifying in the light. "If you don't? My goodness, Ms. Thompson-*Mitchell*, just listen to your vim and vigor. You have to understand, I'm really not a bad guy. I have big plans for this property, and I'm looking forward to investing in this city. Didn't it used to be called the bold new city of the South? What if we could make it great like that again, together?"

Lina stuck to her guns. "You haven't answered my question, Mr. Nickerson. What if we don't want to do that? Why would we even entertain your compromise? We've got the signatures we need. We've got the momentum to change the conversation about affordable housing in this city. That's bigger than this one building. We've worked too hard to back down now." She folded her arms across her chest, sizing him up. "I think you're only offering this eleventh-hour olive branch because you're scared."

Nickerson made quick and sudden eye contact with her, and Lina had the mental image of a butterfly pinned alive to a shadow box. "I think you know very well what will happen if you don't," he said.

"What?" Mara asked. "What will happen? Lina, what's he talking about?"

"I'm talking, Ms. Jilcott," he said, "about making life very complicated for your friends if you persist. Thanks to some tips I received from my silent partner, I thought something was fishy about your campaign. I asked Kenneth to follow all of you this last week, to see if there was anything underhanded going on with signatures or donations. I haven't found anything there —*yet*—but I did learn that Lina Thompson-Mitchell and Brown Mitchell, the couple at the heart of your social media campaign, are in the middle of divorce proceedings."

Lina did her best to keep matching Nickerson's gaze instead of giving in to the pull of Mara's.

The developer tutted. "Well now, Ms. Thompson, Mr. Mitchell! It seems I'm not the only one for whom this was news. I don't know how much your followers will trust you with every-thing else, like their financial donations, when they learn you've been lying to them about this. Who knows what you might do with their money if you lie about something as sacred as marriage?"

"Wait," Brown said. "Silent partner? Who the hell do we have in common that would go into business with you?"

Nickerson looked at Brown's faded baseball cap; his scuffed sneakers, grimed with months of bar work. He took out a handkerchief, wiped his hands in disgust, and said, "I think you'll find that your Ms. van der Wahl drives a hard bargain." He checked his timepiece and said to their collectively dropped jaws, "I have to go. There's a phone call I can't keep waiting. Take care; it's been a pleasure."

Lina watched Nickerson for as long as she could. Then, when there was no further pretense to looking out the automatic, sliding doors of The Jessie, she turned to face the music.

After Nickerson left, taking all the air in the room with him, Lina and her friends stood around in a foggy state of shock, holding their jackets on hooked fingers and waiting for someone else to have the first word.

"Sophie?" Mara said, flabbergasted. "How could she do this to us?"

"For sale to the highest bidder," Freddie murmured. "Somehow, even though Sophie keeps telling us who she is, she never fails to surprise me."

"We don't know that she *did* do this," Brown countered, sticking up for their friend. "Nickerson's silent partner could be anyone. He could be bluffing about this to rile us up and distract us into thinking there's no point in going to the meeting next week."

"Remember how she said she knew him at the zoning hearing? She probably was always coming into town to meet with Nickerson," Mara thought out loud, ignoring Brown's counterpoint. "She could pretend to be a good friend to us while schmoozing him into bringing her on, giving her a cut of the profits." She rubbed her temples as another wave of realization washed over her. "The redecorated apartments were probably to convince him to hire her for interior design work."

"We were squatting in a living portfolio," Freddie said.

Lina wiggled her head noncommittally. She mostly agreed with Brown; Sophie was certainly ambitious when it came to her influencer career, but mercenary? That didn't sound right. Even so, Lina wanted to keep the attention off herself and Brown for as long as possible. That would give her time to formulate what she was going to say to Mara when the floodlights finally pivoted her way and blinded her. It wasn't like she could excuse Mr. Nickerson's claims about their divorce as readily as she could his claims about Sophie.

Rarely had Lina felt more wrung out than she did in that moment. It was remarkable that the same physical sensation, one of being bone weary, could go from the feeling of a hard day's work well done to the world being on the end of its yo-yo string in no more than five minutes. But she needed to pull it together for the night's last morale boost.

"Guys," she said into the silence, "we have to get back on track. We did a great job tonight. We got people fired up for the council meeting on Tuesday. We have to ignore Nickerson's blatant provocation tactics and focus on that. He clearly said all that stuff to rile us up and forget his promises, which, by the way, we don't even have in writing. A verbal agreement in Florida is legally binding, but he's precisely the kind of snake that would say one thing to us and then tell city council he 'doesn't recall' it when we're in chambers next Tuesday."

It was then that Mara turned on her. "Fair point, but beyond the Sophie of it all, I keep getting stuck on what Nickerson said about you guys. Is it true? I mean, I'm not surprised, but—"

"What do you mean you're not surprised?" Lina asked.

Mara scoffed. "It was pretty obvious, Leen. I didn't know it was this bad, but something has felt off between you two, at least since last month. I wish you'd trusted us enough to say something."

"Trusted you?" Lina spluttered defensively. "I tried to tell you. Way back the night of the escape room. I tried, and you as good as told me I'd be dead to you if I did. Is it any wonder I didn't feel comfortable confiding in you?"

Mara crossed her arms. "Once," she stated. "You tried to tell me exactly *once*."

Lina flashed back to sitting with Mara on the apartment's balcony. *You can tell me anything*, she'd said. Lina had said something dismissive in response, and they had laughed and hugged in the glistening rain. Lina hated herself for not admitting it then, but maybe, she thought, she could smooth things over now, given how well this week had been going with Brown.

"Look, it's not a divorce yet," she offered up. "We're just separated for now."

"So, is it a trial separation?" Mara asked. "Like, you're trying to figure some stuff out and then you'll get back together?"

After Nickerson left, Brown had moved a little ways away from the group, leaning against a pillar as though its smooth, plaster surface could camouflage him, keep him away from their pointing fingers. He now stepped forward and stood next to Lina.

"Well," he began, "it isn't that simple, Mara. It might have been at one point"—his jaw clenched—"but I don't think we can get it back anymore. This time together, campaigning with all of you, has been a wonderful memorial to what we had." He looked down at his hands, then back up at them. "All the papers should be finalized by the first of the year, and then we'll be over."

If this news was hurting Mara, it was apple-coring a new

hole into Lina's heart. She had really thought they were doing better, were pulling back from the cliff's edge of her own devising. She had fooled herself into thinking that a few dinners out after the misunderstanding with her trigger journal would fix everything.

She tried to meet Brown's eyes, but he refused to give her that small satisfaction. When Brown Mitchell made up his mind, he really made up his mind. She cursed herself for marrying—and then separating from—someone as stubborn as herself.

"Can you believe this?" Mara asked Freddie. When Freddie did a lackluster job of pretending to be surprised, her jaw dropped. "Wait—did you already know?"

She turned her ire onto Lina. "I can't believe I'm the last one you told about this," she said, her eyes shining.

Lina scrambled for a rebuttal but could only come up with: "It's not like Brown told you either."

"Real classy, Leen," Brown muttered.

"It hurts more coming from you." Mara's eyes were filling with tears. "We used to be best friends. I was one of three people there for your actual wedding day. I can't believe I had to find out from a Scooby-Doo villain like Nickerson that you're getting divorced! We used to be close, closer than sisters; why didn't you feel like you could tell me?"

"Mara," Lina begged, "it wasn't like that. I—"

Mara had unhooked her gray leather jacket from her white-knuckled fingers and was shrugging it over her shoulders. "I think I need to head back to Georgia, get my head on right, get some space from all of this." She looked at Freddie, then at Lina and Brown. "I sincerely wish you all the best next week, but I need some time to myself."

"Mara—" Lina called, though she had no idea what she could say to make any of this better.

Mara looked rumpled and entirely defeated as she walked

out into the October night. As Lina stared after her retreating back, her reflection—and Freddie's, and Brown's—stared at her from the building's glass wall, blending in with the dark city outside.

She turned to the flesh-and-blood Freddie, not ready to deal with Brown and the fresh hurt he'd doled out.

Freddie seemed to anticipate her look and shook their head. "Sorry, Leen. I hate to say this, but... I need to take the deal." They shifted their Wrecking Ball poster to one hand and scratched the back of their neck with the other. "It's—it's the best I'm going to get. It can help me finance my other building in a way where I can make it affordable for a wider range of people. I'm not saying this campaign isn't important. Even if Nickerson wins the battle, there's still the war. Our little building has helped bigger organizations get this conversation out to more citizens who hadn't heard of it before."

"Freddie, please listen to me." Lina was clutching at straws at this point. "Nickerson is a very public individual. I did a little bit of my own digging with some friends who practice law in New York. He has a history of paying lip service to people he does business with and then doing nothing to follow up on it. He may not even honor his deal with you, Fred."

Freddie closed their eyes and breathed through their nose. "This is the best deal I'm going to get," they reiterated. When they opened their eyes, they smiled wearily at Lina and Brown. "Good luck, you guys. With, um, everything." They, too, left the building, dragging the poster they'd been so proud of not an hour ago behind them.

This left Lina and Brown alone.

In the silence, Brown wavered on his feet. He looked a little woozy after the hairpin curves of the evening, but firm in his conviction. Not too firm, Lina hoped.

She swallowed a wave of nausea, then choked out, "Can we talk about this? About us?"

He gave a hollow laugh. "You've made tons of decisions without talking to me first. What's there to talk about now?"

"I'm so sorry," she said automatically.

"Good. I'm glad you're sorry," he said. "It's the least I deserve after everything you've put me through lately. Didn't you realize that having the woman who filed for divorce against me parade me through what used to be my house, hang on my arm, pretend to still be madly in love with me would hurt so much?" When she remained silent, he smirked. "Of course you didn't. You were too focused on the project at hand to see the real human life right in front of you. Classic Lina."

She shook her head. "At first, I was pretending," she clarified, "but then I realized how much of an idiot I had been. I started to wonder if I was making a huge mistake."

Brown squeezed his eyes shut, the way he would have if he'd stubbed his toe on a doorframe. "I don't want to hear it." He licked his lips, retrieved his righteous anger. "If you want to talk about mistakes, why don't we talk about how you blurred the lines with stuff like the bathroom during the hurricane party? I mean, what was that, Lina? If one of your girlfriends told you a guy did that to them, you would be furious."

Lina bit back her reflex to defend herself. If she looked at this from Brown's point of view, only knowing what had happened in the bathroom and what he had read in her trigger journal, then she, too, would think she'd done a horrible, exploitative thing.

"You're right," she admitted, "but, Brown, you don't understand. Please look at me. I don't know what I can say other than I'm sorry. I know you saw the note on my phone—"

He shook his head. "I don't want to talk about that either."

"Then what?" she blurted out, unable to hold back anymore. "What do you want?"

"*You!*"

Lina blinked as the word pinballed through the empty atrium.

Brown ripped off his baseball cap and sighed in frustration.

"Well, I did," he muttered. "I wanted you, but then I realized it was a lost cause. You've changed the locks; you've kicked me out. It's clear we're moving on."

Lina ground her back molars and balled her hands into fists. To know Brown Mitchell was to love him and want to punch him at one and the same time. She wanted nothing more than to march up to him, grab his shoulder, and say, "Hey, you idiot, I still love you, goddammit," but he wasn't giving her the option.

He walked a few feet away, then turned back. "I want to be clear. I'm going to be there on Tuesday for the official vote, but I'm not doing this for you. I'm doing this because I finish what I start, and I'm doing it for all those under-served people who didn't go on to become lawyers. They deserve better than couch surfing or fifteen roommates in a flophouse."

He sized her up, and then he left, too, resurrecting the same horrible, aching feeling Lina had had when he'd finally stopped fighting, grabbed his keys, and walked out on her the first time.

CHAPTER
TWENTY-THREE
JUNE 2020

Two years ago—the happier past

"I feel like we've been waiting forever to get married," Brown said one morning three months into the pandemic.

He was standing near the apartment windows, enjoying the summer sunlight as it streamed in. The day hadn't burned over into sizzling yet, and the warmth was fresh with possibilities. Or, it had seemed that way until their wedding planner called and said that due to yet another spike in COVID cases, they would need to reschedule until at least the fall.

"Yeah," Lina commiserated. "Love how we all thought life would be back to normal after two weeks of lockdown."

He nodded. "If we keep waiting for this to blow over, we may never get married."

"Or we might change our minds," she teased.

Jacksonville—well, Florida, in general—was developing a complicated relationship with COVID. Lina was still working from home and arguing cases over secured Zoom channels, and Brown was on furlough from the bar—a phrase which here meant 'crawling the walls with boredom'—but folks were cautiously edging back out into some semblance of the real world.

Lina's first tentative trips out to pick up food instead of DoorDash-ing it were both thrilling and terrifying. Otherwise, there wasn't much to look forward to. She had personally been on so many walks downtown that she had some memorial bricks on the River Walk memorized, and there were only so many rewatches of *Tiger King* you could do before you started quoting Joe Exotic without thinking about it.

In short, they were close to, if not already in, cabin fever territory. Their original wedding date had been postponed from early April, right after the lockdown began, and if Brown was saying what she thought he was saying... well, she was on board.

She took a sip of her coffee, savoring how it tasted like rich, earthy chocolate; how the air conditioning felt cool as it streamed down from the ceiling vent; how the apartment smelled like sunlight baking on brick and the peaches growing ripe in their bowl on the counter. She wanted to remember every element of this moment, the one that came immediately before what she was going to say next: "Hey, do you want to just do it? Do you want to just get married?"

When he turned to her, the sun created a boyish halo around his blond curls. "Are you serious?"

"About this? Absolutely."

He set down his coffee mug and wrapped his arms around her, a giant smile on his face. "Good. Me too. I don't know how we're going to do it, though. Obviously, it's a lot to plan on such short notice."

Lina looked at an old Polaroid snap of the PDP gang they kept tacked to their fridge.

"What if I told you"—she slid her hands up his strong chest and clasped them behind his neck—"we don't have to have very much of a plan at all?"

· · ·

The evening was muggy when they cautiously convened on the building's front stoop for the first PDP they'd had in four months. The idea, renovated for COVID times, was to stay outside and have each person bring out their dish as it came instead of progressing from room to enclosed room.

To combat the heat, Sophie had made a batch of French 75 popsicles for cocktail hour, and they sat in lawn chairs arranged about six feet apart, in a circle on the sizzling sidewalk.

"It's hot as balls," Mara groaned from her chair.

"How would you know?" Freddie teased her.

She used her alcoholic ice pop to swat at the air close to them, the rosy coloring of the traditional American tattooed woman on her bicep, the one she'd gotten before lockdown commenced, peeking out from under her shirt sleeve as she did. "Freakin' six-foot rule," she grumbled. "You know what I mean!"

After everyone had had at least one ice pop, Lina and Brown announced to the others that they indeed had Wild Card and that the others should join them in the courtyard in—

"Ten minutes?" Brown conferred with Lina.

She frowned and waggled her hand. "Maybe make it fifteen?"

"Compromise?" When she nodded, he said, "Okay, yes, meet us in the courtyard in twelve and a half minutes."

"The courtyard?" they heard Mara say as they headed back inside and up the stairs to their apartment. "How mysterious."

They were laughing madly as they shucked off their casual clothes and pulled on something slightly finer: a blue summer suit and open-necked, white button-down for him; a clean, white shift dress for her. The buzz of the champagne popsicle thrilled through Lina's veins, chilling her lips and setting her heart racing. They felt elegant and daring and full of mirth; the moment felt fleeting and like it would last forever. Lina nearly twisted her ankle dashing around the apartment in the eight minutes and change she had left, so she hustled down the back stairwell barefoot and wedged her blue heels on just before opening the door and walking out into the sunset-dappled courtyard.

In the waning light, she doffed her matching white mask, tipped her head back, and inhaled deeply. The wind rustled through the leaves of the courtyard tree, and she felt warm hands wrap around her, just below her breasts.

Brown's lips kissed her forehead. "You're sure about this?" he murmured against her skin. "There's still time to say no, or not right now."

She stood upright again and turned around in his embrace. "Never. You're stuck with me, Brown Mitchell. From here on out."

His blue eyes danced. "From here on out," he echoed.

The door to the building pushed open and Mara and Sophie stumbled out into the courtyard, another round of champagne popsicles in tow.

"All right, we're here and ready for Wild Card," Sophie was saying from behind her mask. "I hope it's not a piñata again. I'm a horrible shot. Plus, it's way too hot to swing a bat."

"Having our choice of a Louisville Slugger or a hospital crutch was a nice touch, though," Mara added. With a laugh, she turned to Lina. "Hey, you changed outfits!"

Lina beamed at Mara as the realization hit. From what she could see above Mara's face covering, she beamed back, though her brow was rumpled with emotion.

"Can I hug you?" Lina asked, looping the straps of her own mask back over her ears.

"Really, really quick," Mara said, and the dear friends collapsed into a tearful hug. "Oh my God, is the Wild Card that you're getting married?!" she asked when they pulled away.

Lina was so overcome that she could only nod. She felt

Brown put a stabilizing hand on her shoulder, and she clasped her own over it.

Sophie had already whipped out her phone. "Best. Wild Card. Ever," she pronounced as she began recording. "And what amazing shoes!"

"Thank you! They're my something blue," Lina said as she modeled them. "I guess the building is our something old, though I don't have anything new or borrowed."

"Correction," Freddie said as they entered the courtyard, holding aloft a rhinestone tiara that caught and refracted the evening light. "I bought this right before the pandemic for a drag night that never happened." They presented it to Lina on bended knee. "For the lady."

"You were in on this?!" Mara gasped, as though she wished it had been her instead.

"Well, yeah," Freddie countered. "I can keep my mouth shut."

They all laughed at that.

Lina felt a little silly with a flashy tiara on her head—she hadn't planned on wearing a veil even when the more struc-tured version of her wedding was on—but the others pronounced her lovely.

Brown stood behind her, his hands lightly massaging her shoulders. "I, for one, think Lina and I have waited long enough for this day. Sophie, Mara, would you do us the honor of witnessing our wedding?"

Neither woman could speak. They nodded, tears streaming down their faces, and melted onto the bench against one wall of the courtyard. Sophie kept her phone out, documenting the ceremony from beginning to end.

"Let the record reflect that they answered in the affirma-tive," Freddie intoned. They tapped a button on their own phone, prompting Pachelbel's Canon in D to pipe tinnily from its speaker. After Brown and Lina got into position, they tapped the pause button, took off their mask, and, looking up with a smile, began to speak.

"Dearly beloved... it's hot out here, y'all." They gestured to the royal blue tuxedo jacket they were wearing over a black-and-white tank top and gray Bermuda shorts. "I don't know how Brown's doing this in a full suit, and I'm already roasting in my jacket, so I'll keep my bit short. I believe Lina and Brown have written their own vows. Babes, the floor is yours."

Their vows were full of all the hallmarks we have come to expect at weddings, all the things that, in retrospect, may one day be lost by the couple who vows them—mutual trust and admiration and respect. Brown promised to make Lina laugh each morning; Lina promised to keep an open mind and an eye out for adventure. They said that their being opposites had not only attracted them to each other but had helped them grow as people. They didn't dream of adding promises like, "I'll always talk to you first before getting angry," because when had they ever gotten angry at each other? When would they ever?

It could be said that neither Lina nor Brown really knew on that day all that went into a marriage, but that wouldn't be fair exactly. It's one of life's puzzles: you can never fully know what of yourself you'll gain or lose until you've already said I do.

Freddie said some magisterial things, rings were exchanged, and before Lina knew it, Freddie told Brown he could kiss his bride. Brown's lips were still cold from the popsicles, and as such, his kiss tasted of gin and lemon and sparkling new beginnings. Their friends cheered, and they turned to pose for Sophie's picture, impossibly big grins underneath the courtyard tree.

Life was warmth and honey, and should have forever been that way.

. . .

It was a Wild Card that lingered. That September, during a lull in the pandemic, Lina and Brown duped their families and all but their closest friends into thinking their second wedding ceremony was their one and only.

Their families would enjoy memories of the usual wedding stuff: their first dance, cutting the cake, tons of portraits featuring a revolving door of relatives. But every once in a while, Sophie or Mara or Freddie would pass Lina and Brown on the dance floor or walk by their dais on the way back from the open bar, and they would exchange a wink.

Because they would remember the raw and real wedding stuff: The door to the building clanging shut the moment Brown kissed his bride, locking them all out. The gaggle of them high-stepping it past the row of garbage cans, through the courtyard and a very smelly, damp alley, past the unlocked iron gate, before spilling out onto Laura Street, Lina whooping all the while, "We just got married! This is the best day of my life!"

Whether it was true or not, she believed it in that moment, as she basked in the fairy tale of it all.

CHAPTER
TWENTY-FOUR
OCTOBER 10, 2022

Yesterday

"So, how are you doing this week?"

Lina was sitting in Jill's sun-soaked office. It was the Monday after the rally, and it was Jill's very first appointment of the day, the earliest she could slot Lina in on short notice. Lina had thanked her therapist profusely for being available for so many emergency appointments lately. Jill had nodded, then sat down in her chair as though she was bracing herself for what fresh hell Lina Thompson-Mitchell would bring to her appointment today.

Lina couldn't blame her, given everything she'd shared last session, and she was silently grateful Jill hadn't pressed a button under her desk to signal the white-coat men to detain her in a padded room. She had decided to switch it up, moving from her usual upholstered club chair to the soft-looking, cream-colored couch. She regretted the decision immediately; it was still warm enough out for shorts and skirts, and the couch's nubby material was going to leave bumps all over the backs of her legs.

"Really great, actually," Lina replied to Jill's query. Couch bumps aside, this was true. She felt energized every time she thought about the conversations their movement had prompted in town. "Work's great, and the campaign's gathered momentum. City council is voting on the zoning decision tomorrow night. I'm feeling optimistic that they might even vote in our favor."

"Good," Jill said, observing Lina over the bridge of her tortoiseshell glasses. "I must confess that you seem calmer today. Your optimism feels like something you actually believe in. Last time you were in, you were..."

"Manic?" Lina supplied.

"Your word, not mine," Jill said drily. "I was going to say 'perplexingly forthright yet evasive,' but tomato, to-mah-toe. Even so, it must feel good to reap the fruit of your efforts. And to reconnect with old friends. I'd like to hear more about how that's going with Freddie and Sophie and Mara, not to mention this situation you and Brown currently have."

Lina went for the low-hanging fruit first. "Funny you should mention Sophie. Nickerson showed up the night of the rally, told us he'd been digging up dirt on us for the last week, told our friends that Brown and I are in the process of getting divorced, but—and here's the real kicker—he also said Sophie had been his silent investment partner this whole time. She might have even been where he dug up his dirt, to be honest." She sighed. "I don't know what to believe. Soph did some good for our campaign, but I don't know if she's turned coat against us or not. All we have is Nickerson's word. If he's telling the truth, she was really in town to undermine us, help our direct competitor, and eventually profit off the sale of Freddie's building. She as good as told us she knew Nickerson the first day she was in town. I don't know why we didn't listen to her."

Jill gave no reaction besides a widening of her eyes. "That's certainly a lot to process. How did everything on Thursday make you feel?"

Lina had to give it to therapists; they knew how to suppress their human need to respond to drama.

"Um, about as well as you'd expect," she said. She slipped her foot out of her blue suede ballet flat and tucked it under her. "I tried to reach out to Sophie on Thursday night to get her side of the story, but she'd blocked me on every mode of communication and taken herself out of our group chat. I'm not sure if it's because of the silent partner thing or because the divorce news made its way back to her, but..."

"...but it makes it pretty hard not to believe your opponent," Jill finished. "That kind of betrayal must have felt terrible. How do you think it has impacted you?"

Lina shrugged hesitantly. "I'm trying not to let it impact me? I kept busy over the weekend with a few last flyering runs, which is good because every time I check my phone and see that no one has said anything in our group chat, it does the opposite. It impacts me the most."

"Why hasn't anyone said anything in your group chat?" Jill pressed. "Are they all as angry as you are at Sophie? I would think they would use the chat, now that she's out of it, as a place to air their frustrations."

Oh, right. Jill didn't know. It wasn't like she'd been looking over Lina's shoulder on Thursday night, when the accusations and fingers started pointing her way. "Well, you see, it's not so much that they're mad at Sophie, but that our divorce is out in the open. Sorry, I said that earlier but kind of glossed over it. So they felt betrayed by Soph, but Mara especially felt betrayed by me not telling her sooner." She snicked her thumb over the lip of her teacup and whispered, "A double whammy."

If therapists suppressed the human urge for drama, then they at least also blessedly suppressed the urge to say, *I told you so.* Jill was silent for what felt like long enough to eat into their session before she said, "Even Brown? Is he still feeling betrayed by your trigger journal?"

"Seems that way." Lina stared at an earthenware vase on Jill's shelf, one that looked like it could have come from Sophie's home goods line. "After Nickerson dropped our news on Mara, I wanted to tell her that I was starting to change my mind about the divorce proceedings. But before I could, Brown essentially told her the opposite. That he had enjoyed this last bit of our time together, but he was seeing it as a nice goodbye before we officially split up. We hung back after the others had left. I tried to tell him he didn't have the whole story, but he insisted that he didn't want to hear it and that he felt strongly that I had used him. He told me he'd be showing up on Tuesday, but not for me, and then he left."

She forced herself to make eye contact with her therapist. "He got a little angry, which he'd never really done in our fights before. When we fought before, I was the angry one and he was kind of checked out, like he was waiting for me to be done being mad so he could move on with his life. This time it felt like he had something he wanted to fight for... I don't know."

"Interesting," Jill said. "And do you feel the same way?"

Lina could hear another therapy appointment concluding down the hall. She gathered her thoughts as she listened to footsteps clomping down the stairs outside Jill's room.

"It's weird," she finally said. "I just realized that I haven't heard from Brown for four days now. I think this is the longest we've gone without talking in a long time.

"It's weird, I think, because we've had to talk a lot more lately. Even if it was through our lawyers to coordinate the divorce, or now, talking and working together on this civic project, we're talking a lot more than we did when we were living together." She felt overwhelmed for a moment and lightly pummeled the knuckles of one fist into her other palm to regain control. "I am going to be so mad if we're ending things—if we failed at loving each other—just because we needed to talk more. If we drifted apart. That is the single most boring, sad-sack reason any two people can break up."

Jill rubbed her nose. "The divorce isn't final yet. Is there any way you can reach out to him to try to talk more? Or at least ask him if he's all right with putting it on hold until you both make up your minds?"

"I'm not sure," Lina said. "For one thing, there's the way he shut down my attempts to talk last Thursday night. Plus, my gut keeps telling me different, contradictory things. Unless one of those different, contradictory things shoves its way to the front of the pack and jumps up and down screaming, 'Look at me!,' I don't know how I'm going to make up my mind." She cleared her throat. "Anyway, that's all a morass I can't clamber out of right now, which is why I'm focusing for the time being on tomorrow's vote."

Jill's watch beeped. "Well, I, for one, wish you luck, Lina." She stood and opened her office door. "See you again next week."

Lina stood on the porch of her therapist's office, taking in the beauty of a Florida autumn. In the parking lot, trees were exploding into pink and yellow blossoms that bees dozily buzzed around. They looked a lot like the ones in the courtyard of her old building, the one she was working to save from a real, bona fide jerk.

She was trying her best to feel Zen, so she breathed in deeply and exhaled an affirmation: "I am ready for and capable of taking on whatever tomorrow will bring." She put on her sunglasses, unlocked her car, and headed home alone.

It was Tuesday afternoon, half an hour before the full city council meeting, when Lina learned just how much her thera-pist-porch affirmation was bullshit.

She was driving downtown, listening to the radio for a last-minute vibe check of how Jacksonville was feeling about the vote—or if the general populace was even thinking about it at all.

She didn't get to learn the answer to her question. Instead, a perky young anchor's voice came on to do the afternoon traffic report. "Yikes! There's a bad accident between a tractor trailer and a white Chevy SUV, turning eastbound I-10 into a parking lot," the anchor advised. "Jacksonville Fire and Rescue has medevacked someone from the scene, so serious injuries are suspected. JSO has cordoned off the eastbound lanes; alternate routes are recommended."

Lina knew Jacksonville was full of trucks and SUVs, but she couldn't help picturing one beat-up, white SUV in particular, picturing its driver lowering the brim of his baseball cap and winking out from under it before driving away. She bit her lip hard, so she wouldn't picture that Chevy Blazer turned into an accordion against an eighteen-wheeler. Things must be bad if JSO was recommending an alternate route for one of the city's major highways, so even though there were probably hundreds of owners of white Chevy SUVs in town, even though Brown was probably fine, at a stoplight, Lina tapped her Bluetooth and called him, just to make sure.

She immediately got his voicemail. "Hey, this is Brown Mitchell," the outgoing message greeted her. "I'm not here at the moment, but please leave your—"

She hung up and drove through the green light, trying to tamp down a creeping feeling of dread. She was close to the city hall parking garage. She'd probably missed him because he was in traffic too. She'd call him again when she parked.

She entered the garage, snagged a spot, put her ticket on her dash, and scrolled through her phone with the engine idling to get her mind on something, anything, else. But she couldn't escape it. The local news' Facebook page had already put out a bulletin about the crash. The aerial shot from a helicopter, accompanying the link to the article, did not look good.

She called Brown again. Again, the call went to voicemail. This time she let it play through to the beep, which prompted her to record a message.

"Brown, hey, it's me," she said, trying to keep her voice light, to push out the consonants and vowels around her heart, where it was lodged in her throat. "Sorry to bug you, especially if you're driving. I just got downtown for the hearing and wanted to check in with you. I'll probably see you before you get this. Um. Yeah. Yeah, I will. Okay. See you soon."

She hung up and put her phone in her center console, but her mind would not switch off. Instead, it was giving her a VIP, private showing of the most panicked, guilt-stricken montage of her life.

She pictured Brown's easy, beautiful smile blooming into its blinding fullness. She pictured the way his eyes danced over her entire person whenever she entered a room, like he didn't want to miss a single thing. She remembered him sullen and angry with her, him fighting for their relationship, his chin defiantly raised with pride for his post-separation apartment, how he'd made do with the horrible circumstances she'd given him. She felt Brown kissing her forehead, kissing her lips a thousand different times—on their couch, in their bed, on their wedding day. She felt his hands low on her stomach, his deep, even voice intoning in her ear that he would make a great dad.

She choked back a sob.

She thought of her living room, as it stood now: clean, picture-perfect. Austere. It might have been cluttered when Brown was there, but it had been lived-in. Literally full of life. It might never be that way again.

She snatched her phone out of the center console. She navigated to the group chat and watched her dark-purple manicure dance over the keyboard.

Hey, I'm sorry because I know y'all probably don't want to hear from me. Just wondering if anyone else could call Brown? There was a bad accident on I-10 fitting his vehicle's descript., and I can't reach him. @Brown Mitchell, if you get this, check in to let us know you're ok.

Outside the car, her panic got no better. The parking structure was dark and dingy, and something about its pavement made the tires of passing cars make a horrible screeching sound. There was an acrid smell of urine in the elevator vestibule, made only slightly better by the breeze blowing off the river.

Lina took a moment to ground herself by staring at the colors of the mural on the parking garage's exterior. Though bright, they were covered by a thin film of city dirt. It was a perfect reminder of the ways in which her town was trying to put lipstick on a pig. They would improve downtown cosmetically, with a few half-hearted attempts at affordable housing, but for the most part, low-income housing would be relegated to the borders of the city, two hours' bus ride away from anywhere anyone else lived, worked, or could buy groceries.

She took a deep breath and, reminded of her mission, hurtled forward. Jill would want her to think about what she knew and what she could do about it in the moment; it was the exercise she was always encouraging when Lina started catastrophizing. *Picture a big, red stop sign,* Jill would say. *Stop and think about what you know for certain.*

Well—Lina blew out her deep breath—all she knew was that there had been an accident on I-10, a bad one. All she knew was that Brown wasn't answering her calls. There was nothing she could do to help him in this moment, even if she dropped everything and drove westbound on I-10, hopped the freeway barricade and demanded the officer on the scene tell her, the crazy, disheveled lady, what was going on. But there was a ton she could do to try to help the cause they had all worked hard for. Lina would do her best to put her anxiety on the back burner and go crush this hearing—for Freddie and their tenants, for Brown, for Mara, for herself, and for the city they loved.

She marched toward the meeting and had managed to get her fear out of her mind for approximately two and a half minutes, but then she was greeted with cheers and whoops from the movement's supporters on the steps of city hall.

There was a fair number of dissenters, too, toting hateful signs that read, 'Want a home? Get a job!,' and, 'Read my lips: No new taxes!,' but the sheer tidal wave of people who had come out to try to save her little old building from gentrification was overwhelming.

"Lina! Lina!" they cried to her like she was some minor celebrity. When she looked over, she saw that they were trying to show her their signs, their shirts. One group of friends had even gotten theirs printed with Sophie's hashtag—*#Bellini4Ever* —across the chest.

Maybe it was the torrent of noise, the crowd of supporters and news crews, but she was suddenly, once again, panicked, dead sure that she would never have the chance to roll her eyes with Brown at that nickname ever again.

She braced herself against a column and checked her phone. Nothing from Brown in the group chat, though Mara had lifted her communication embargo to say she hated that she was back in Savannah, too far away to check in in person, but that she hoped he was all right.

4:48 p.m. The meeting started in twelve minutes. Lina needed to head in if she was going to do this thing. Right before she did, she forced herself to dial another number. Mercifully, Freddie picked up.

"Fred!" she cried, then broke into fresh tears.

"I know, babe, I saw your text and then I saw the news. Oh my God. It can't be him, right?" She could visualize her fear mirrored back to her in Freddie's warm eyes.

"But what if it *is*? He could be hurt or grievously injured or—"

"Don't you even say it," Freddie said firmly.

She heard rustling on their end of the line, maybe pants being buckled or a bag being thrown over a shoulder.

"Head on in, sweet girl," their comforting voice said. "I'm just across the park. I'll be with you in a minute."

Lina took one last ragged breath, then plunged in through the front door, unclear how she would keep her head on straight, much less get through an entire city council meeting, without knowing Brown was all right.

CHAPTER
TWENTY-FIVE
OCTOBER 11

Right now

"I can't believe it took me this long to realize it, you know?" Lina was saying. "I mean, everyone was screaming it at me—my therapist, my friend Freddie, kind of even my ex—screaming at me, 'Are you sure you're done with this? Are you sure you want to get divorced?' And I was like, 'Yeah, I am,' because that's something you have to know about me, once I fix my mind on something, I pursue it till I get it. Anyway, I was starting to wonder if they might be right, just starting to come around, but—but now there's this."

She pushed her hair off her forehead and tried unsuccessfully to breathe through her stuffy nose. "Divorce and death are *so* different. So different, you know? Even if you're divorced, the other person still exists out in the world. They're still breathing and speaking and walking around, and I guess there's even this weird part of you who thinks you might pull a mom-and-dad-from-*The-Parent-Trap* and get back together someday, you know?"

"Ma'am, I'm going to have to ask you again to put your bag

on the counter and go through the detector," the security guard said with a blank stare. "You're holding up the line."

Lina blinked soddenly and pivoted to take in the line waiting to get into city hall behind her. There were some concerned faces among the protesters, but mostly a bunch of *Somebody get this lady out of here* scowls. She turned back to the guard, wondering how exactly a simple question like "How are you, ma'am?" had gotten her monologuing like this.

"Oh... Sorry," she said.

Lina felt her lips wobble as she set her bag down and strode through the metal detector. ("That's one way to get her through, I guess," she heard the guard say to her coworker.)

Now that the security bottleneck had broken, people were flowing into city hall, and the atrium was growing increasingly emptier. Lina ushered herself into the council chambers, meekly waved hello to a few supporters, and picked a free aisle seat halfway up the left side of the room.

Once seated, Lina did her best to ground herself in her physical surroundings. There was a sense of overwhelm—good overwhelm—at how many people had come out tonight. The hearing started at an inconvenient time, just as the nine-to-five workday was ending, and yet hundreds of people were here, wearing shirts and toting signs in support of their little building and its big cause. So many people had shown up that there were news crews outside, awaiting the result of the council vote. The room was full of lively conversation, which the council chair had to combat with an extra pounding of his gavel before the meeting could begin. In the silence, Lina caught sight of Nickerson, sitting toward the front right side of the room. He glowered at her, no doubt puzzled by her red and puffy face, and turned back around as the meeting commenced.

There were some preliminary administrative matters for the council to get through. Lina checked her phone as they did. She checked it again as the time for public comment on their building came, but there was still nothing from Brown. She turned her phone off, put it in her bag, and forced herself to focus on all the wonderful, different arguments her fellow Jacksonvillians were making against tearing down their building and in favor of affordable housing.

She felt a gentle pressure on her shoulder and turned, hopeful that it was Brown. Instead, Freddie crouched in the aisle next to her, wearing a red-and-blue ascot over a striped sweater set. "Any word?" they asked.

Lina bit her lip and shook her head.

They frowned sympathetically. "I'm so sorry. Are you doing okay? Are you going to be able to give your speech?"

Lina tried to tell them she was taking it minute by minute, but the words wouldn't come out. Like Freddie was saying, she had prepared a statement to deliver to city council, but her notecards sat untouched, beside her phone, in her bag. There was no way she was going to be able to speak coherently in public. Not tonight.

Freddie squeezed her hand briefly before straightening. "Don't worry. I have enough to say to Bob Nickerson for the both of us." In response to her startled look, they wrenched their lips to one side in a wry smile. "Hey, if lying down and rolling over is what it takes to get his money, then I don't want it. I'll find another way."

They joined the line in front of the citizens' podium, and before long, it was their turn to address the council. Freddie gave Lina a quick thumbs-up before turning back to the dais.

"Hello, I'm Freddie Morales," they said into the microphone. "I had the pleasure of meeting some of the council a few weeks ago, back when we were less prepared." They spread a hand behind them to indicate the crowd and all their posters. "Well, we're here now, with all this support and twice the necessary number of signatures to be heard, and so we're grateful for this full council allowing us to share with them what this building means to us." There were a few whoops and cheers before they moved on.

"I am the child of Cuban immigrants. My grandparents came here, well, to Miami, fifty years ago. They were broke as hell and actively learning English, but as dishwashers and housekeepers and secretaries, they were determined to make a better life for themselves. And they could. Because there were programs back then to help them out, to make ends meet, you know?

"Fast-forward to ten or so years ago. I had come up to Jacksonville and graduated from UNF. I wasn't making a living wage yet, but I still had student loans. My family couldn't afford to help." They cleared their throat. "People say, 'Go to college, get a good job.' Well, after paying back my loan minimums each month, I could only afford food or housing. That doesn't leave you with much choice, so I lived out of my car."

Freddie's words were breaking through Lina's swirling thoughts, and she felt a fierce sense of pride in her friend. They didn't have to be in these chambers—it was putting the money Nickerson had promised them at stake—but they had shown up for her and for their city. They had been brave enough not only to stand up in front of all of Jacksonville and speak, but they'd shared a story they had once been ashamed of to drive their point home. Lina surreptitiously turned her phone back on and recorded the end of their speech. She had a feeling Mara would want to hear it.

After explaining how the building's low-income unit had put a roof over their head that wasn't the roof of their Camry, Freddie stared each council member in the face. "A lot of people want laissez-faire government, with no overreach. They say companies are people, too; that they are inherently good; that developers can choose to offer low-income units without being forced to. But guess what? I know firsthand they won't. I wouldn't have even entertained the idea of selling to Mr. Nickerson if I hadn't tried to pay it forward and offer my tenants an affordable rent. But I was losing money as Downtown gentrified, and I had no choice.

"No one in life pulls themselves up by their own bootstraps. It's physically impossible, right? So if you won't say no to rezoning this building, at least consider ways we can offer more residents affordable housing. Of course we want Jacksonville to be the best it can be, but we can't assume that having low-income residents is a stain on our city. They are part of what makes us great. We need to be there for everybody because we're all trying to have a better quality of life. Anyway, that's my two cents, and the two cents of the people I've been talking to for, like, half my life. Thank you."

The crowd of supporters burst into applause.

Lina couldn't help smiling as Freddie picked their way over to the back wall. They had said everything she wanted to say, but ten times better than she could have ever done.

"Freddie's an excellent public speaker, aren't they?" a voice behind her rumbled into her chest. "Maybe when all this is over, they should run for office."

It was too good to be true, but Lina whirled around—and there he was. Brown stood behind her, smiling down at her. For once, he had dressed up, and he looked remarkably unlike himself in a dark jacket and thin, black tie.

"Brown!" Lina gasped. She bobbled her phone before clutching it in both hands as she stared up at him. A few people around them turned and shushed her. She stood, feeling shaky and boneless with relief. "I, you—"

Brown took a look at the shushers. "Maybe we should step outside to talk," he whispered.

He led Lina out the chamber doors, back into the atrium. Apart from the security guard, whom Lina noticed giving her some side-eye, they were the only ones in the echoing marble hall.

"Hey," Brown started, though it was quickly followed by an "Oof!"

Lina had thrown herself into his arms, temporarily knocking the wind out of him. "You have no idea how happy I am to see you," she blurted. "Why didn't you answer your phone?! I called twice and messaged a couple more times, and you didn't say anything."

"Yeah," he said, kind of puzzled by her emotions as he pulled back. "There was a horrible accident on the interstate—because, of course, Jacksonville—and I was stuck in traffic behind it. I'm really sorry that I got here so late, but I came here... as fast as I... could." He surveyed her face. "Lina, are—why are you crying?"

"I thought you were in that crash!"

And then it hit her. In that moment, she realized how freaked out she had let herself get over a bunch of circumstantial evidence. Most people wouldn't have jumped immediately from, "That's the make of my ex's car," to "Clearly he's the one in that crash. Clearly he's dead." At least, most rational people wouldn't have. What's more, most rational people wouldn't have proceeded to throw a hissy fit, especially not over the person they were breaking up with. They might have been mildly concerned, but they wouldn't have sobbed their heart out to a random security guard or been so debilitated as to not be able to comment on an issue very important to them.

But Lina wasn't rational.

She'd said, *Um, excuse you. In this case, correlation* does *mean causation, you unfeeling jerks*, and why had she done that? Why had she not been rational? Because love wasn't rational. And she was still in love with Brown.

Brown wrinkled his nose at her. "No offense—I'm honored, truly I am—but why are you making such a big deal about me potentially being in that accident?" He spread his arms as though to demonstrate his physical presence in city hall. "Which, again, I wasn't."

"Well, beyond thinking it would be a horrible way for anyone to go, it was a big deal to me because..." Lina stared down at the patterned marble floor. "Because I'm not over you yet," she admitted. "I still love you."

She looked up at Brown, whose face was knit with concern —concern that she was okay, perhaps, or maybe concern that he hadn't heard her correctly.

He shook his head in disbelief. "No, you don't. I read that stupid note on your phone. I know exactly how you feel."

To know Brown Mitchell, Lina reminded herself as she tried to keep her cool, was to love him and to want to punch him at one and the same time.

"No, you don't know how I feel," she ground out. "You only read, like, two entries and then jumped to a whole bunch of conclusions! God, do you have to be so frustrating right now?" She took a deep breath. "If you'd let me explain myself to you, you'd know I realized I was being an idiot. I didn't have sex with you in the bar bathroom for a no-strings-attached farewell tour. I did it because I still love you, you dork"—she emphasized her point by lightly slapping his chest—"and I didn't want to lose you."

She looked up and realized the security guard was listening in on their conversation and was apparently very invested in any forthcoming details about their bathroom rendezvous.

Brown clocked her gaze and turned to the guard. "Do you mind?" he demanded, and the guard turned back to the front of the atrium.

Lina regained her train of thought. "Brown, if this whole farcical charade for our friends has done anything, it's helped me realize I still care about you. I think—no, I *know*—I still love you. I would be devastated if I could never, ever talk to you again, even if it was to argue with you. That became more than clear today." She took both of his hands and squeezed her eyes shut as she felt their solidness, their comforting warmth. "Brown, I've been a total, miserable idiot, and I'm sorry I've put you through so much. I can't say goodbye to you. I don't think I'll ever be able to do that. We're both a bunch of jerks, and sometimes I don't think we know what we want. Sometimes, I think we make stupid decisions without the other person in mind. But there are also times when we are really, really good together. That's when we make time to talk, to cuddle on the couch, to listen. I miss those times. I don't want to be done fighting for us yet."

She opened her eyes and looked at him, trying and failing to keep the mood light. "So, to sum up, I love you. I miss you. I don't want to get divorced."

"You love me?" Brown said hesitantly. "Even if I'm a messy, sarcastic jerk who will never amount to anything?"

Lina squinted. "Oh *God*, I hate that you had to read that. I hope you can forgive me and give this arrogant, detail-oriented, anal-retentive slime ball another chance."

Brown had such a gorgeous smile. It started small and hesitant, but once you coaxed it into the sunshine, it bloomed into something thousands of megawatts bright. It was doing that right now, as cautious relief spilled across his face.

"You're so cute when you're mad," he said.

She rolled her eyes and began to give him one of her patented rejoinders, then gasped as his lips met hers. It felt like everything had led up to this moment, this particular kiss. Her lashes were wet with freshly pricked tears, but she exhaled through her nose and held tight to him like she'd never held tight to anything before. Here was a person she had once confided everything in. Here was her best friend. They may have slipped apart, but maybe, if they fought their way to the surface, they could find a way back to shore together.

"I love you, too, Leen," he said, when they broke apart. "I

miss you like you wouldn't believe. But... what do you want to do instead?"

"I—" She let go of him to wring her hands. "For once in my life, I have no idea."

"It's okay that you don't." He closed the gap between them and tilted her chin up so that he could look fully into her hazel eyes. "Why don't we figure it out together?" He grinned at her eager nod and gave her another, softer kiss. "Ready to go back in?"

They walked back to the chamber door to catch the close of the hearing.

"Nine for, five against." The city council chair banged his gavel. "Let the record show that, whereas on November 1, 2022, Nickerson and Associates will be the sole owner of parcel 505B, Bob Nickerson is to undertake, with this council's approval, the redevelopment of said parcel into a condominium."

There was a rising murmur of disagreement from the assembled protesters, though Lina could still hear a cheered 'yes!' from Nickerson's staffer that she thought was in poor taste. She felt Brown's hand wrap around her own, and she squeezed it as she searched the crowd for Freddie.

There they were, in a far corner, their patriotic ascot popping against the drab walls of the council chamber. Some of their supporters were comforting them with fist bumps and pats on the back, and when there was a gap in the crowd, Freddie met Lina's eyes. They obviously weren't thrilled with the outcome, and yet they offered Lina and Brown a defeated smile.

I feel low in this moment, the smile seemed to say, *but for what it's worth, I'm glad we're all down low together.*

Together, Lina thought, feeling Brown's comforting sturdiness by her side. That part, more than anything, was important.

CHAPTER
TWENTY-SIX
OCTOBER 29

Two and a half weeks from this moment

The thing about hosting one last PDP is that you have to do it before they tear down your building.

Two weeks after city council voted in favor of Mr. Nickerson and three days before parcel 505B was officially his, Freddie unlocked the front door of the old building one last time and ushered in their friends. Downtown was busy that evening, given that it was the weekend of Halloween *and* the Gator Bowl, a major football game between rival universities. Brown liked to call it 'the perfect storm,' and it was a testament to the renewed effort he was making in his relationship with Lina that he'd asked off of work, essentially edging himself out from earning a metric ton of tips, so he could attend this dinner.

"Hey, welcome to the PDP to end all PDPs!" Freddie said.

"We came prepared," Brown replied, holding up two reusable grocery bags full of pre-prepped food. "I'm going up to our old space to get the main course warming in the oven."

When Freddie had suggested in the group chat that they

take these proverbial lemons and make fresh-squeezed lemonade with one last PDP, they hadn't had to draw new course assignments. First Mara, then Freddie, then Lina and Brown revealed to the others that they had sentimentally kept their scraps of paper from the last dinner drawing two Augusts ago—Mara in a lockbox, Freddie on their vanity mirror, and Brown in his fraying wallet.

"Oh my God, we're a bunch of saps and hoarders," Freddie had messaged.

Lina sided with Mara, though, who had replied, "Hey, I never knew when or if we'd have another dinner! I wanted to be prepared." She had been easily moved to tears lately, and the image files, featuring Freddie's even, block-lettered handwriting on two-year-old scraps of notebook paper, made her well up all over again.

While Brown took the main course up to their apartment, Lina and Mara accompanied Freddie into theirs, which was the sparsest Lina had ever seen it. She was given the choice between a Last Word and an Old-Fashioned, picked the Last Word, and stood where Freddie's living room rug had been, where the floorboards were now bare, nursing her gin drink.

Nickerson thankfully hadn't aired her dirty laundry in public. He could have turned her supporters against her, invalidated Freddie's campaign out of spite, but he hadn't needed to, not with the majority of city council's support. He had even gone on the record, saying he would at least consider having some low-income housing units in the new space, an idea he would never have considered without the help of his worthy opponent.

Freddie was jazzed by the response their speech had gotten after the hearing. In a stroke of social clout that would have made Sophie jealous, their Twitter account ramped up by five hundred followers, mostly in North Florida, overnight. To her credit, Sophie stuck to one part of her promise. A week after the hearing, Freddie received a check in the mail, half of the funds raised by Sophie's Instagram campaign. They were considering donating the funds to an existing housing nonprofit or else using them to run for city council the next time a seat in their district opened up.

"Which district will that be, now that the building is closing?" Brown asked. He grabbed an Old-Fashioned—"Typical Lina, always has to have the Last Word," he joked to Freddie— and stood next to her, hand resting low on her hip.

"I'll be up in Springfield, near my other property," Freddie said, "getting involved and doing a little community organizing on the side."

Mara toasted them. "Proud of you, Fred-o." She polished off her Old-Fashioned and looked at the others. "Should we move on to the main course?"

One last time, Lina and Brown led the way up to their old apartment.

"I hope you like Southern comfort food," Brown said as he opened the door. On the kitchen island were three steaming dishes—one of potato casserole, one of dressed green beans, and one of macaroni and cheese dotted with generous pats of butter.

Lina pulled the chicken Brown had hand-breaded and double-fried out of the oven. "We figured this old place deserved a proper sendoff," she explained, "and what says 'my condolences' better in the South than far more cheese than is medically responsible?"

"Man, when you said 'Southern comfort,' I thought you were going in a different direction," Mara teased as she entered the room, bringing up the rear.

Brown reached into the refrigerator and pulled out a premixed batch of Alabama Slammers. "Gotcha covered."

Lina caught his eye over the pitcher and broke out in an

infectious grin. She and her almost-ex-husband had realized they had a lot of work to do, a lot of problems they had to untangle, but they were determined to do it.

"I don't think we're starting from square one," Brown had said when they got back home the night of the hearing.

They were lying upstairs, sated and limp under the covers. Neither of them had been able to think straight, much less hash out their feelings, before Lina had taken Brown by the hand and led him back upstairs for some physical reconciliation.

"*Shyeah*." She rolled onto her back, thinking of the uphill climb before them. "More like square zero."

"No, I didn't mean that." Brown traced lazy circles on her inner arm. "I meant that we've come a long way. It takes maturity to realize a rough patch isn't grounds for ending it all. We have to find our way forward, not back. I think when we get back to normal, our *new* normal, it'll actually be at a place higher up the mountain."

"Higher up the mountain," Lina echoed. She smiled warmly, then kissed Brown's lips. "I really like that."

"Me too." He grinned back. "So, what do we do exactly? How do you reverse divorce proceedings? Do we just, like, cancel it?"

Lina figured her attorney would know their particular case better than she, so the following morning, they had called up their lawyers together and told them collectively, "It's not you; it's us."

Now in their old apartment, Lina looked over at Brown, who was using tongs to hold out a chicken thigh and a leg to Freddie. Freddie made a quip in return, and Brown roared with laughter. Though she and Brown were so different in so many ways, Lina was grateful they were the same in this: they were not assuming that because they wanted to stay together, everything would be fine. They were slowly picking up the pieces, crouching to look under chairs and near baseboards to find any shards they'd overlooked the first time, and then patching them back together as best they could, not with burnished gold but with much more honest, accessible superglue filling in the gaps.

"Leen, do you want light or dark meat?" Brown asked, as he started fixing her a plate.

"Light, with tons of mac and cheese on the side." She gave Mara a hug and a Slammer. "Saying goodbye to this place needs a whole lot of comfort."

The thing about hosting one last PDP is that you aren't in denial it's the last one. Instead of wasting your time in that way, you accept it for what it is and enjoy it to the fullest. You tell your favorite stories from PDPs past, you enjoy the warmth of track lighting reflecting off wooden surfaces, and, sure, you may make plans to get together for brunch or drinks, but you don't do the cruel thing and assume that this time with these people will ever come around again.

Mara was regaling them all with her version of the time Freddie rigged up a meat hook and aged an entire side of beef in their apartment just because they'd pulled Main Course when there was a low buzz and the apartment was plunged into darkness.

The pitch-black was completely silent, save for the cheers and laughter coming from the still-lit back patio of The Blind Pig next door.

"Is this the Wild Card?" Brown joked, switching on his phone's flashlight.

"Unfortunately, no. I think they cut the power," Freddie said.

"Early?!" Lina protested. "Can they do that?"

"I stopped paying for electricity a week ago. If Nickerson doesn't want to keep it going before they tear it all down, he's well within his rights."

"This is actually a fantastic development," Mara admitted, "because I had nothing planned for dessert."

They all laughed. Mara made the executive decision to phone the high-end steakhouse a few blocks away, hoping to get their crème brûlée to go. When the restaurant was too busy with tourists in town for the football game to accommodate such a small order, she said, "Grab your coats, kids. We're going trick-or-treating," and led them in the opposite direction, to grab three boxes of snack cakes from one of downtown's few remaining corner stores.

They re-entered the building by phone light, and Freddie braved the basement to find some candles. Even so, the dimness was really cramping their style.

"Hey, I know! There's one view of the building not all of you have gotten to see," Freddie said. "I figure our last time here is as good as any to enjoy the roof." They unlocked the caged ladder to the top of the building, and, handing their drinks, treats, and candles from one to the other, they took it in turns to clamber up.

"Have you been on the roof before?" Lina asked Mara. She held her drink and a box of snack cakes so her best friend could climb the ladder.

"Never," Mara replied over her shoulder. "You?"

She shook her head. "Nope."

"I have." Brown's voice came to them from the rooftop. "Once or twice, at the end of a shift, when I was too wired to go to bed," he said, his head popping into view. "Freddie let me come up and we shot the breeze. You were already asleep, Lina, or we would have invited you."

Excited, she accepted the hand that pulled her onto the roof.

"Not as breathtaking as I had thought," she admitted once she'd had time to catch her breath. She leaned into Brown's side, resting her head against his chest as they surveyed the industrial rooftop's tarred shingles, covered in tiny, biting gravel and peeling gray paint.

"At least the view is nice," Brown said, winking at her, then indicating the treetops of the park one block north. They all chose to ignore city hall beyond that, if only for the night.

"And to think this is going to be a hydroponic garden soon," Mara said.

"Ugh, don't remind me," Freddie replied.

They all picked spots along an inner wall, one where they couldn't, as Freddie warned, "plummet to their deaths," and listened to a playlist on Brown's phone. They chatted and laughed and used a corkscrew to etch their initials into the brick. "No one else will know," Mara intoned, "but we will. That's what matters." Down below, people dressed as vampires and sexy nurses and superheroes screeched in delight as they roamed the streets, not a clue of the farewell that was taking place above them.

Lina nibbled on a Swiss roll and considered the rooftop in the low light. She could see some cracks in its surface and thought of the long-ago leak in her apartment's brick wall. She thought of the way the windows tonight had looked grimy and a little uneven in their frames. Tired.

Someday soon, this building, which had stood, solid and eternal, for a hundred years, would be gone. She was bummed that they couldn't save it, but at the end of the day, it was just bricks and beams, drywall and insulation and glass. She looked up at Brown's handsome profile, his strong jaw and sparkling eyes. The things she truly loved about the building would never be gone. Not if she didn't let them slip away.

There was a cheer whipping up from the football stadium, followed by the whistle and pop of fireworks. Taller buildings around them crowded out their sightline, but Lina could see the pinks and blues, golds and greens reflected and fizzling in their glass. It sounded as though the game would be letting out within the hour.

"We better leave soon if we want to beat stadium traffic," Mara said.

Before that statement, the evening had seemed like it would never end. But with a short, practical phrase, it was all rushing to a close, hermetically sealing them out of this era of their lives with the quiet *snick* of a well-oiled door.

Lina brushed her hands off on her jeans and reached for Mara and Freddie. "I love you guys," she said. "I need you to know that. I was so scared, when I thought Brown and I were over, that all of us were over too. I'm glad I don't have to worry about any of that anymore, but..."

When it became clear her emotions wouldn't let her go on, Brown saved her with a well-timed joke. "I've been meaning to talk to you about that, Leen. It's kind of a lot of pressure on them to be your *only* friends."

"Yeah, consider this an intervention. Join a kickball league or something," Mara added with a wink.

But Freddie nodded, their chin lifted proudly into the air as they yanked Brown into the fold. "Lina's right. I love you all too. This place might be gone, but that doesn't change anything else. We are still friends, and you can call me for anything. Any time."

"Any time," Mara echoed, clearing her throat to keep the emotion out of her own voice.

As her friends collected their garbage—"Oh, just leave it! It's not like they aren't wrecking this place next week," Freddie said—Lina turned to her husband, where he sat next to her on the low inner wall of the roof.

"I love you too," she said. "You know that, right?"

"I do now!" Brown teased her. "Though I'm glad this old place could remind you."

"Yeah?" She quirked her head to one side. "Me too."

She swung one leg over the wall, cradled his head in her hands, and she kissed him. His mouth was warm against the cool, late October evening. The boom of the fireworks vibrated in her throat.

When she pulled back, Brown grinned and nuzzled his cheek against the top of her head. "I love you, too, Lina. Let's go home."

EPILOGUE

In the beautiful after

Happily ever after. The concept had always seemed impossible to Lina. Fairy tales ended with true love's first kiss, when Prince Charming and Sleeping Beauty were still in the honeymoon phase. The rest of their hopefully long lives lay before them, unwritten. So, how could they know if they would be happy forever?

But maybe someone should have told her to adjust her sarcastic expectations. Happily ever after didn't have to mean castles and horse-drawn carriages—usually those came with land wars and obscene stable fees. Lazing on the couch in their sweatpants, stroking her fingers through Brown's thick curls a day before New Year's, a few months after they'd nearly called it quits, felt like something she could happily do forever.

Brown laughed as his playlist skipped to "Dreams" and Stevie Nicks's voice floated, ethereal, out of their stereo system. "I can't believe you don't remember listening to *Rumours* our first night together." When she pursed her lips, he sat up and said, "Seriously? The fire alarm started shrieking after the first chorus of 'Go Your Own Way.'"

He stared at her as though he expected this detail to give her a bolt from the blue, that she would suddenly recall streaking out to the kitchen, naked as the day she was born, only to see her Dutch oven engulfed in flames to one of the greatest pop rock albums of all time.

She shook her head. "Still nothing. Though trust us to make 'our album' the one that came out of the entirety of Fleetwood Mac breaking up with each other."

I'm just glad we *didn't.*

Brown seemed to share her thought.

"I'm glad we both found that building," he said. "Even now, every time I walk past where it stood, I say a mental thank you." He tucked a strand of her dark hair behind her ear and gave her a sweet kiss on the cheek. "It brought us together time and time again."

Lina was grateful for the building, too, especially for its role in their lives a few months ago. She had never expected her foray into civic responsibility to turn out the way it had, but boy, was she glad it did.

"Why did you go along with it?" she asked him, twining her fingers with his. "My plan, I mean. You could have so easily said, 'Hell no, go away,' or come out with the truth to Mara, but you didn't. You made the insane effort, and somehow, it paid off."

"You want the truth?"

Lina goggled her eyes at him as though to say, *Well, yeah?*

"I..." He stared across the room, his tongue caught between his teeth in thought. He turned back to her once his mind was organized. "If I'm being honest, I had this hunch, this notion that I had the world's tiniest chance of getting you back, if only I could have time with you to talk things through. Away from our lawyers. Away from our fights. Just us, on our own, with one last chance. And then there I was, presented with the perfect opportunity, and so all that subterfuge and you sniping at me and our friends clearly seeing through it was worth the risk."

Lina smiled softly. "I'm sorry I almost foiled your diabolical plan," she said.

"Oh, with Jill's trigger journal?" Brown asked. "Nah, I'm glad even for that. I mean, not for the misunderstanding, but I'm glad that when I pumped the brakes on my all-out offensive, it showed me you were back to all-in too."

Lina nodded. She was indeed back to all-in. They both were. They had covered a lot of ground since October, since their near divorce, their near loss of all this had served as the wake-up call they'd needed. A big surprise was that the ground they'd covered since then mostly consisted of communicating with each other, even when the words weren't pretty; even if it felt more comfortable, less risky in the moment to keep a feeling bottled up inside. Letting it out was bringing them closer, like Brown was doing with Lina now.

He settled his free hand in the right spot on her thigh. (Lina had come to cheekily think of it as 'Old Reliable.') His warmth burned into the skin just below her hip crease; his lips parted in desire, but she teasingly moved hers away.

"Hey now," she murmured, waving a hand around the living room. "None of that until after we've cleaned. This place is a mess, and Mara will be here at three."

They weren't the only ones the building had brought back together. Their old PDP gang, minus Sophie, was spending New Year's weekend together. Mara was driving down that afternoon, and Freddie was throwing a party the following night in their new digs, which they had renovated with some of the exorbitant cash offer Nickerson had finally forked over. Freddie said that as much as they loved property management, they were grateful for their own space away from their tenants; it helped create a better sense of work-life balance for them.

"Man, you really know how to set the mood, Leen." Brown checked his phone. "Why do we have to clean first? It's only one o'clock now!"

Lina pulled a faux skeptical face. Chocolate wrappers littered the coffee table, and some of their larger gifts remained under the tree, unboxed but not yet put away. In her post-holiday laziness, it had even been a week since she vacuumed.

Brown furrowed his brow. "Oh, come on. It takes all of fifteen minutes to mess this place up. Exactly how long does it take to clean it?"

"Longer than you think," Lina deadpanned. "I mean, look at the state of this living room!"

She stared at Brown.

Brown stared incredulously back.

Lina broke first. With a mischievous grin, she pulled out her own phone. "Siri, set an alarm for two o'clock."

"Two thirty?" Brown negotiated with an eyebrow waggle.

"Split the difference?" When he nodded, she said, "Siri, set an alarm for two fifteen."

She wrapped her arms around Brown's strong back and kissed him deeply. By the time they came up for air, she had slid down to lay propped on a pillow while he rested on his forearm, hovering above her. She could smell his particular scent, as well as the musky aftershave she'd bought him for Christmas, and the combination made her toes curl.

He paused over her lips, seeming suddenly to have some doubt. "All my messy, sarcastic Brown-ness doesn't make you want to run again?"

"Not if all my overthinking, over-organized Lina-ness doesn't do the same to you."

"Nope," he said, popping the *p*. "It's part of who you are, and it's why I love you."

He dipped low to kiss her again, his lips mingling with hers, his hands in her hair, on her hips, trailing down her thigh.

"Face it, Brown Mitchell," she said, "you're stuck with me."

He beamed down at her. "From here on out."

A LETTER FROM JESSICA

Dear Reader,

Thank you so much for reading *How to Keep a Husband for 10 Days*! If you enjoyed it, and want to keep up to date with all my latest releases, please sign up at the following link. Your email address will never be shared and you can unsubscribe at any time.

www.bookouture.com/jessica-hatch

If you've read *How to Keep a Husband* and/or *My Big Fake Wedding*, then you know I like to drop a little of the real world into my romcoms. Here, Lina and Brown's story is set against a rising housing equity crisis in their hometown. If not for their friends' mission to keep their recently sold building from gentrifying into luxury condos, there would be no reason for them to pretend to be together. If not for the 1980s teen movie of it all, they would not save their marriage.

So I hope, while it has entertained you, this novel has also helped open your eyes to the fact that housing inequity is an increasing issue in our world, one that grew worse during the COVID-19 pandemic. If you feel so motivated, I would encourage you to research nonprofits in your area that help people struggling with homelessness and housing insecurity. Volunteer if you can, and be kind always. Help us turn this around.

(Okay, hopping off my soapbox now. Thank you for indulging me.)

If you enjoyed *How to Keep a Husband for 10 Days*, would you do me a kindness? Leave a sweet review on Amazon or give my books to your friends to enjoy. After all, novels make wonderful presents for bookworms!

I hope to have more fun and funny titles to share with you soon. To be the first to hear about any and all new releases, subscribe to my newsletter and follow me on social media.

With love, gratitude, and more to come,

Jessica

www.JessicaHatch.com

leftright.substack.com

facebook.com/JessicaHatchWrites

twitter.com/JessicaNHatch

instagram.com/JessicaNHatch

ACKNOWLEDGMENTS

Every time you write a book is different.

Sure, your rites and rituals and process may look the same, but for every project, they're expanded or contracted along a timeline. You might wrestle with plot issues where characters were last time's hang-up. Whereas my first novel, *My Big Fake Wedding*, took nearly a decade to move from idea to publication, *How to Keep a Husband for 10 Days* took mere months! All this to say, my list of people to thank this time around is shorter but no less heartfelt.

To the editing, publicity, marketing, rights, and sales teams at Bookouture, I remain so grateful that you've got my back. Especial gratitude goes to my editor, Jess Whitlum-Cooper, who helped me through an acute bout of second-book-itis; you are the very definition of 'stalwart.' Thank you.

Thanks also to my beta readers, Michelle Lizet Flores, Alexandra Staeben, and Hurley Winkler, who pointed out a few forests I couldn't see for their trees.

To Dr. David Jaffee of the University of North Florida's JAX Rental Housing Project. Thank you, a serious academic, for spending a morning with a commercial novelist, discussing the many moving parts that have led to this moment's housing crisis. Your work and research are doing profound things for the Jacksonville community and beyond. Godspeed.

To Rachel, in Chester, Virginia, for her ability to find and recommend quiet writing spaces. To Kelly, Jamie, Leslie, and Mandy at Alewife Bottle Shop, for providing our community with a safe space that serves many functions, including, for me, a quiet editing space and a wonderful venue for my first ever book party. To Katherine Hobbs, for her help figuring out some 'life stuff' while I was actively writing a novel (i.e., the most inconvenient time to ever figure out 'life stuff').

To my family and friends, thank you for keeping me grounded and centered. I especially want to acknowledge my husband, Paul, who helps me laugh and loves me hard when my brain is telling me to doom-spiral. We aren't two halves of a whole, but two whole people who make each other better for being in orbit with each other. I love you more and more each day. (Thank you, also, for being *so* much easier to live with than Brown Mitchell! I hope you can say the same about me and Lina.)

Finally, to my readers, all the gratitude in the world goes to you for enjoying my books. I write in order to share my innate, campfire love of stories with others. Whether you hopped on board for my high-concept plots last August or just now, thank you for matching up your weird with my weird. Here's to much more quirkiness to come.